CHAPTER

ONE

GINA SEALY THOUGHT ABOUT DEATH as she walked along the beach. Would she see that blinding light at the end of her road? Would her parents guide her toward it? She looked out over the ocean. Weekend sailors glided their boats through the breakwater, heading for the downtown marina, their Sunday sail almost over. Kids splashed in the waves. Here and there mothers were packing up, getting ready to go, despite their protesting children. Death. She hugged the thought as she dodged a Frisbee.

"Sorry," a boy in a baggy swimsuit said as he dashed by, missing her by inches. The Frisbee had been overthrown.

"It's okay," Gina said.

The disc skimmed across the sand as he chased after it. He looked about sixteen. What a difference a couple of years made. The boy grabbed the Frisbee from the sand, spun around and let it fly. It soared into the sun. Not far down the beach a girl was running, hands waving. She made a diving catch and came up laughing. Young love, Gina thought. She'd never known it.

She walked over to the water. She was wearing a bright sun dress, yellow as summer corn. She was barefoot. Her long hair, blowing in the breeze, was the color of wheat. The water splashed around her legs as her feet sank into the wet sand when the wave ran out. A small crab scurried into its hole. A piece of driftwood and a soggy tennis ball floated past. She imagined them forever being pulled and pushed up and down the beach by the surf. But of course that wouldn't happen, eventually the tide would deposit them on the beach for the city caretakers to remove.

She took another wistful look at the sailboats before focusing her gaze on the twenty-two-story Sterling Hotel. One week till the grand opening. Sandy would be back from New Zealand by then. She could just see him, dressed to kill, handing out free booze to all comers. The Sterlings didn't discriminate when it came to inaugurating a hotel. The poor along with the well-to-do were invited, because today's pauper could very well be tomorrow's captain of industry.

Sandy had been to several Sterling inaugurations and from what he'd told her she was sorry she wouldn't be around for it. But she'd see the hotel anyway. If she could get in.

The Long Beach Sterling was on the sand,

TANGERINE DREAM

BY

KEN DOUGLAS & JACK STEWART

A BOOTLEG BOOK

A BOOTLEG BOOK
Published by
Bootleg Press
2431 NE Halsey, Suite A
Portland, Oregon 97232

Bootleg Books may be purchased for educational, business, or sales promotional use. For information please e-mail, Kelly Irish at: kellyirish@bootlegpress.com.

Second Bootleg Press Trade Paperback Edition.

September 2005

10 9 7 6 5 4 3 2

ISBN: 0974524689

Cover by Compass Graphics

Printed in the United States of America

For Charlotte Baker who passed away on 7 June 1838 at the tender age of 4 years and 10 months.

Life is a span, a fleeting hour
Homeward the vapour flies
Man is a tender transient flower
That even in the morning dies

I never knew Charlotte. I found the above words inscribed on her tombstone in Pahia, New Zealand ten years ago. Maybe somebody famous wrote them, or maybe they were made up by her grieving parents, I don't know. But I know this, those four simple lines have haunted me, made me think about Charlotte at the oddest times, reminded me often, that we are all just passing through.

Ken Douglas

Though it's been quite a few years since I've been to that hollowed ground where little Charlotte rests, I too have carried around the thought of her, the idea of what she might have become, what she may have accomplished. I've wondered how she went, did she suffer, is she happy now. I have a lot of questions. I suppose Charlotte has the answers and I suppose I'll have them too, one day. We all will.

Jack Stewart

TANGERINE
DREAM

overlooking both the sea and the marina. Gina looked at the hotel. Tall sliding glass doors behind large balconies reflected the late afternoon sun. The building glowed like a Godly creation. Gina studied the penthouse balconies. So high.

"Hey, can you take our picture?" He was about her ages, a tourist wearing shorts and a tee shirt. No shoes. "Please." He offered the camera. "Just point and shoot." His wife or girlfriend was wearing a summer dress, a lot like Gina's, only pink.

"Sure." She took the camera.

He wrapped his arms around his blonde sweetheart and they smiled at her. The girl made rabbit ears with her fingers behind his head. Gina laughed and snapped the picture. And she pictured Sandy in her mind's eye. Trusting brown eyes. Full smile. Light brown skin, almost white, but he still called himself black. She'd show him.

"Thanks," the girl said.

Gina handed the camera back. Then she took a cell phone out of her purse and punched in a number. She watched the young lovers walk down the beach as the phone rang.

"KYTV," a female voice squeaked.

"Can I speak with Nick Nesbitt?" she said.

"Hold and I'll ring through."

Gina waited.

"Newsroom." Another woman, another squeaky voice.

"Nick Nesbitt please."

"Who's calling?"

"Gina Sealy."

"Does he know you?"

"No."

"What are you, a fan? You can't just call the newsroom and expect to get him on the phone."

"It's about Dr. Sterling."

"I don't care who it's about, honey. Nick don't come to the phone unless he knows you."

"I thought he wanted news about Dr. Sterling. I guess I was wrong. I'll call someone else."

"Wait a minute." She recognized Nesbitt's voice. He'd been listening on another phone.

"Listen well, Mr. Nesbitt. I'm only going to say this once. If you want a story that can sink Dr. Sterling, get yourself and a camera crew to the new Long Beach Sterling. Set up in the marina parking lot next to the hotel. The action starts in an hour. That should give you plenty of time."

"Who is this?"

"I already told you. My name is Gina Sealy. Be sure to get it right."

"How do I know this is legit?"

"Sometimes you just have to take things on faith." She hung up, took another look at the young lovers, quite a distance away now, then tossed the phone into the sea.

* * *

Sanford Sterling thought fifteen dollars high for a movie. He'd been born rich, but he still counted his money. He was thirty-five years old and about as confident as a man who expected his fairy tale life to be snatched away at any second. As a psychiatrist he knew he was being delusional, but he couldn't help it.

"Are you gonna hand it over, or what?" The girl behind the glass had music in her voice. "It's a lot, I know, for old movies, but it's for a good cause." Her brown eyes were almost as wide as her smile.

"*Casablanca*, my favorite." He slid a twenty along the brushed stainless under the glass.

"It's everybody's fave," she said. "That's why we picked it." So she didn't work for the movie theater. She wasn't a ticket taker, cashier or candy counter girl. He looked at her again, even as he felt the eyes of the other people in line on his back. She had *café au lait* skin, more on the *au lait* side. Almost straight hair. She had to be in her early twenties. Old enough to drink.

"You work for the shelter?"

"This is my project." Her eyes twinkled. "A special presentation. An event." Everybody who was anybody in Long Beach had shown up, including the mayor and several television personalities. All dressed in the style of the '40s. All to help raise money for battered women.

"Really?" he said. "I'm impressed." He steeled himself. He wanted to ask her out, but what if she said no?

"That'll be five dollars back." She slid five ones toward him. He felt a vibration in his inside coat pocket. Maybe the message was nothing. But what were the odds. Only patients paged him, everybody else had his cell number. The girl flashed him another smile as his fingers touched the change.

For a second he thought about returning the call, but he was on vacation and besides, he'd left his cellphone in the car, because he was going to the movies and didn't want to be interrupted. He'd never seen *Casablanca* on the big screen and had been looking forward to it ever since he'd seen the ad in the *Press Telegram* last week. And it was for charity. He pocketed the money, but made no move to go into the theater.

The girl intrigued him.

"You gonna spend the rest of the afternoon staring at the lady?" a man from behind him in the line said. He heard a laugh. Then another. He decided to go for it.

"I'm not leaving this spot," he said without turning. "Not till she tells me her name and agrees to have dinner with me after the show." He clenched his fingers into fists and felt a slight shiver tingle up his spine.

"It's a double feature," she said, "with two cartoons, a long intermission and a fifteen minute plea for money. Doesn't let out till ten o'clock. A little late for dinner. Plus, I have to stay after. My job. I won't get off till eleven."

"I'm not moving," Sandy said. He'd gotten himself so worked up about asking her out that he'd forgotten about the second feature. *The Maltese Falcon.* Two great movies, in black and white, on the big screen. Life didn't get better than this. He tried to put the vibrating pager out of his mind.

"For crying out loud, he's a good looking man. If you're not married, tell him your name. Have dinner with him. Lots of people eat late," a woman in line said. There was laughter in her voice.

"Alright, alright." The girl smiled, showing the kind of teeth that belonged in a Crest commercial. She stirred him. It had been a long time since a woman had done that. "My name's Maggie," she said, "but there's no way we can get dinner so late."

"One of my favorite places is just down Atlantic. It's always open." He sounded eager. He knew it. He couldn't help it.

"What? I don't know any restaurant serving dinner that late."

"I do," the woman behind said. She was still laughing.

"I know it, too," the man behind said. "I've eaten there, food's good. Don't know if I'd take a date there, though."

"Where?" Maggie said.

"Denny's." Sandy pulled the five ones out of his pocket and slid the change back toward her. "For the shelter. See you at eleven." He was aware of the good natured laughter in the line and couldn't resist a quick turn and a smile. A young man gave him a thumbs up sign. Several people were smiling. Sandy winked, turned and kind of sashayed into the lobby.

Inside, to the right of the candy counter, adults with wide lapelled suits were working the joysticks usually used by grade school kids in baggy pants and jeans. From the screaming and laughing it didn't seem like they were doing very well. Next to the video games, on the wall, was a coin telephone. Damn, it was a sign. Sandy reached into his pocket for change. He couldn't not call, but whatever it was, he'd put it off. After all, it was after five on a Saturday night and he was on vacation.

He dropped the coins into the phone and punched the number in his pager.

"Homicide, Alvarez."

"This is Sanford Sterling. You paged me?" This wasn't going to be good.

"Sterling the shrink?" The voice was crisp, without a hint of the Chicano the name implied.

"I've been called worse." Sandy dreaded what was to come.

"Yeah, well I guess I have too," Alvarez said, no humor in his voice. "You're supposed to be on vacation in New Zealand, but I took a shot."

"I cancelled the trip at the last minute. What's this all

about?"

"Do you have a patient named Gina Sealey?"

"Yes." He felt his heart flutter. Gina was only eighteen. She couldn't have killed anyone.

"Then you better get on downtown. To the Sterling Hotel construction site."

"Why?" Sandy asked. His family owned the hotel chain. His brother, Simon, ran the business and although Sandy and his other brother, Stacy, each owned a third of the company, they'd always been content with the way Simon handled things. They never checked the books. Never questioned Simon's decisions. Never questioned Simon. They never felt they had to.

"Miss Sealey is up on the fifteenth floor, standing on the outside of the balcony of Room 1517. She looks like she's gonna jump. She says you're her shrink. You know how hard it was getting that out of her? We need professional help here."

"Where are you?" Sandy asked, all business now.

"Next room over, 1519. On the balcony. I'm talking on my cell. You'd best hurry. She's not looking too stable."

"I'm five minutes away."

"We might could get you here faster in one of our cars."

"Five, six blocks. I can get there faster myself." Sandy dropped the phone and started toward the doors.

A young man dressed like he'd been shopping at the Goodwill was blocking the doorway. "Watch it," he yelled as Sandy bolted past, knocking him into the door jamb. "Hey," he yelled after him, but Sandy barely heard.

He sprinted down Fourth like a thoroughbred in the stretch. People gaped at the runner in the outdated suit and tie, but they stepped aside. Atlantic Boulevard was coming up fast. The light was red, cars moving too fast to stop for a crazy runner. He turned right, pouring it on, the five eight minute miles he did every morning paying off.

Another red light as he approached Second Street. He ran it. Cars screeched, horns honked, but he made it across, charging toward First. He sucked in air. Quick breaths, like a steam engine. The light on First was red too. A bigger street, more cars. He was in it without thinking. More brakes. More horns. More rubber on the road.

A quick glance left. A small car. Red. Wheels smoking. The driver, California blonde, everybody's cheerleader fantasy. He stuck his left arm toward the car, palm toward the hood, like he was blocking for a pass receiver. Pain jolted up his arm when the car slammed into him and he went down, rolling through to the center of the intersection.

The adrenaline sparked as the pavement skinned the back of his right hand. He was up like a sprinter out of the starting block. The pain gone. He crossed Atlantic at Ocean, hard charging down the boulevard. Two blocks left and he saw the crowd in front of the new Sterling Hotel site. Pain stitched up his side. He was running flat out. He concentrated on his hands and arms, pumping them up and down, forcing his legs to match their chugging rhythm.

He saw the yellow tape and started his sprint, just like when he was in college dashing for the finish line. But he'd started the sprint too soon and the tape was too far. And there were people there, milling about and blocking his way. He slowed his run to a jog. Sweat dripped off his forehead. His chest, back, thighs and legs were bathed in it, causing his clothes to stick to his body.

Close now, moving toward the police tape, he mumbled out, "Dr. Sterling, let me through." People moved aside.

"This way, Dr. Sterling." The speaker was young, uniform crisp like new. Sandy read the name tag over his breast pocket.

"Right behind you, Officer Quinlan," he said.

"The elevators are working. That's how she got up there. Apparently she found a room unlocked and went out to the balcony. She's been out there a long time."

"Jesus," Sandy said.

"Yeah," Quinlan said. The elevator door was open and waiting. A plain clothes officer was holding it, ready to punch the button for the fifteenth floor as soon as they were inside.

"You any relation to the hotel?" Quinlan asked.

"My family," Sandy said.

"Any idea why she picked this hotel to jump from?" the plain clothes cop asked. His voice had a hard edge to it. He had paper-white skin, pale eyes. An albino.

The doors closed as Sandy was catching his breath. "I'm her psychiatrist. And you are?"

"Norton, Homicide. That mean you're not going to tell us? Confidential, like that?" The elevator started its trip upward.

"No. I'll do whatever I have to, to get her down. There is no confidence sacred enough to lose a life over. Not as far as I'm concerned."

"Then what's the deal here?" Norton asked.

"Homicide?" Sandy asked.

"We all do what we can in a case like this. Your hotel

was close to the cop shop. Alvarez and I got here first. He used to be a hostage negotiator. He's up there trying to keep her from taking a swan dive. Any info you give us would be useful."

"Her parents and younger brother were lost at sea. She blames herself. Her mother let her sleep in instead of standing her watch because it was her birthday. Mom fell asleep and a Korean freighter cut their sailboat in half. Mom was lost immediately, but Dad, Gina and seven year old brother Kevin held on to an overturned dinghy for hours. Sunup and poor Kevin couldn't hang on anymore. He let go and floundered. Dad let go and tried to save him. Neither was able to make it back to the dinghy. Gina watched them die. Twenty-four hours later she washed up on the coast of Mexico still hanging on to that dinghy."

"Poor kid," Quinlan said.

"She's been living with friends in Long Beach ever since."

"She can do that? Doesn't the court have a say? Isn't she supposed to be with relatives? Grandparents, something like that?" Norton said.

"She's eighteen."

"She don't look it."

"No, she doesn't," Sandy said.

The elevator stopped. The doors parted. Sandy followed Norton down the corridor. The carpets were beige, plush. The walls were eggshell white with orange and blue pastel patterns. It worked better than it sounded. Simon was right, Sandy thought. Hire the best designers. It makes a difference. He hadn't been in one of their hotels in over a year.

"One more thing," Norton said. "She's wearing a

mike. Everything she says is going out over the air."

"How'd that happen?"

"Some newsman beat us here. She wanted to make a splash big enough to get you wet in New Zealand. It probably wasn't too hard for him to get her to put it on. It's pinned to her dress, right shoulder. You might try to get her to take it off."

"Swell. How'd he get here before you? The police station's only a few blocks away."

"Who knows. He was here when we got here. We chased him off, but not before he'd given her that damned mike," Norton said as he opened a door. "She's in the next room over. Alvarez is out on the balcony trying to talk her in and not having too much success. Maybe you can do better."

"Why the room next door? Let's just go in her room."

"We tried that. She said if she even sees a head poke through those sliding glass doors, she jumps."

"She sound desperate?"

"Oh, yeah," Norton said.

"He looks done in," Sandy whispered as he stared through the sliding door at the man out on the balcony. He seemed a little shorter than Sandy's six feet, he was rail-thin with jet black hair graying at the sideburns. Sweat ringed the collar of his white shirt. Sandy only saw the right side of the man's face but it was enough to see the anguish there. It had to be Alvarez and to Sandy it looked like he thought Gina was going to jump.

"He'll be here any second, I promise," the man said, pleading.

"I'd get out there, Doc," Norton said.

"Yeah." Sandy stepped out on the balcony.

"Dr. Sterling," Gina Sealy said.

"I'm here, Gina. Now what's this all about?" Sandy said as Alvarez stepped back. Sandy took his place.

"I thought you were in New Zealand with your sister-in-law." Something about the way she said sister-in-law cut Sandy to the bone.

"No, I cancelled the trip," Sandy said. The sun was hanging low in the western sky. A bright yellow ball flaming through several shades of orange, red and pink. Nowhere in the world was a sunset as pretty as in the L.A. basin, or as deadly. Los Angeles, like smoking a pack a day.

"Won't she miss you?"

"Why should she?" Sandy shivered. What in the devil was she talking about? He'd told her he was going to New Zealand for two weeks with Gayle and Dylan, but why should she read anything into it? There was nothing there. Besides, it was none of her business.

"Don't know," she said. Then, "What happened to your hand?" She was standing on the outside of the outer railing, feet with a precarious toehold on the concrete floor of the balcony.

"What?"

"Your hand. It's all skinned up."

He studied the back of his hand. It looked like it should hurt, would hurt. But right now he didn't feel much. The stitch in his side was gone. He was breathing normally, his heartbeat slowing to its resting rate. He had to remain calm. Had to take charge. "I fell on the way over," he said.

"Looks like it hurts."

"It does, a little," he said. He was beginning to feel a slight pain, as if he'd spilled coffee on it and now it was soaking in cold water. "But I'm more worried about you."

"Are we on television?" she asked.

"I think so." He looked down into the parking lot below. There was a KYTV van down there. A cameraman standing next to it, camera on a tripod, pointing up at her. Like a sniper, the cameraman had her in his sights and like a sniper, nothing would deter him from his mission.

"It'll only take a few seconds," she said, looking down.

"Why, Gina?" He looked at her hands, bleached white as she clutched the rail. All she had to do was relax her grip on the top bar surrounding the structure and she'd go tumbling to the parking lot below. He wondered if they'd film her grizzly descent. Would they show it on the eleven o'clock news?

"Because nobody cares."

"I care."

"Only because I'm your patient and you get paid for caring."

"I don't charge you. They tried to get me to take money out of your father's estate, but I wouldn't do it. I take care of you because I want to. I've never turned you away and I never will."

"You took two weeks off to take a vacation with your sister-in-law and your niece." She was being petulant and it was none of her business, but this wasn't the time to call her on it. "And now I see you didn't go. How come you didn't call and tell me?"

"You had Dr. Madrigal's number in case of an emergency. But if I'd known you were this bad off, I wouldn't even have thought about a vacation."

"Really?"

"Really." Sandy tried to sound soothing.

"It's my fault they're dead." Tears streamed down her

cheeks. She liked to dress in bright colors, like the yellow dress she was wearing. She said they made her look happy even when she wasn't. She didn't want anyone to know how unhappy she was. She called it her private sorrow. Her bright dress didn't make her look so happy now. Her sorrow wasn't so private anymore.

"It's not your fault. You were asleep, she didn't wake you. There was nothing you could have done." He'd known from the time he'd met her three months ago that she was a suicide waiting to happen. He'd thought they'd made some progress. Obviously he was wrong.

"I know. I know. You keep telling me, but I can't get it out of my head. If only I had woken up, if only I had set the alarm. They'd be alive now." The wind picked up, whipping her hair around her face.

"Gina, I'm going to come over there and help you back in. We'll talk about it. We'll work it out, no matter how long it takes."

"No. They'll never let me. They'll take me to jail."

"No they won't. I won't let them."

"That's right, Gina," Alvarez said. "He's the doctor. We have to do what he says."

"Is that true?" she asked.

"Nobody's going to take you anywhere you don't want to go, Gina."

"Can you make the TV people go away?"

"Get them out of here," Alvarez said.

Norton said something into a handheld radio, but the cameraman was packing the camera away as two policemen started across the parking lot toward him.

"Odd," Alvarez whispered, so that only Sandy could hear. "I would have expected them to stay and claim their First Amendment rights."

"Yeah," Sandy said. He knew something about news people. More than he cared to. More than most.

"Now what?" Alvarez the former hostage negotiator asked, deferring to Sandy.

"Now we see if I have any balls," Sandy whispered back.

"Doc, you shouldn't," Alvarez said as Sandy stepped over the rail.

"What are you doing?" Gina said. Then, "I don't want you to do this. No, don't! Please, don't!"

"It'll be okay, Gina. I just want to get a little closer." A cool breeze chilled his sweat. Goosebumps peppered his arms. He was cold, so cold, like when he went ice fishing with his brothers in Wisconsin. He was out in the wind. There was no going back.

There was a gap of about two feet between the balconies and Gina had her eyes fixed on it. "You can't come over here," she said. "It isn't safe."

"I just want to talk," Sandy said. Sweat dripped off his lips and he shivered with the salty taste of it.

"Talk from there," she said.

He was at the edge of his balcony now. Nothing for it. They were watching from below. He didn't know where the camera had gone, but it was watching, too. If he didn't know anything else, he knew that. He was Senator Sterling's baby brother. Stacy wanted to be president. He deserved it and there was nothing Sandy would or could ever do to hurt his chances. He reached out over the space between them, fingers barely touching the other balcony.

"It'll be all right," he said, hoping he wasn't lying. One mistake, one misstep, and he'd be plunging to the earth below. He wondered how that would play in the media. Would it be good or bad for Stacy? Bad, he thought. Best not fall. Eyes ahead, not looking down. Surprisingly he thought about Gayle somewhere in New Zealand just before he pushed off.

"Don't!" she screamed as he grabbed onto the bar, feet scrabbling for the balcony. He snagged a toehold with his left foot.

CHAPTER TWO

GAYLE STERLING STOOD at the starboard rail and looked out over the sea toward New Zealand's North Island. She wished Sandy had come with them like they'd planned. It was supposed to be a sailing vacation, but more than that, she needed his expertise.

She suspected that her daughters, Dylan and Taylor, were sexually active, and it shouldn't have bothered her. After all she'd been pregnant with them when she was their age. It was only natural. But she suspected it was with the same boy. And she believed he didn't know. If it was true, it was wrong.

At first she thought she could talk to Dylan about it

while the two of them were on vacation together, then Taylor when they got back home. No way could she take them both on at once. They'd just laugh, giggle and tell her she was crazy. But she'd been putting it off and putting it off. Damn, Sandy should be here. He shouldn't have cancelled.

But maybe he was right. Stacy was getting more and more press. It wouldn't look right, him coming along. Even though they'd have separate rooms. Even though Dylan would have been with them at all times. Gayle knew what the press was like, after all she was a newswoman herself.

She glanced over at Dylan as the ferry rocked through the waves. Her golden hair was blowing in the wind. Gayle turned to see what she was staring at.

The shiny black sailboat cut through the waves like a hot razor through butter. She was heeled over, with all her sails out, and she was cooking.

"Isn't it beautiful, Mom?" Dylan said. Like her, Dylan was fascinated with the sea, unlike her father and her sister. Sailing in their family had been strictly a Mom, Dylan and Uncle Sandy thing.

"It's kinda windy," Gayle said. "I think he should reef up."

"Yeah, I was thinking the same thing. It's a fast boat."

"I'm sure he knows what he's doing," Gayle said.

"It looks like Uncle Sandy's Phoenix, but it's bigger."

"They built a couple of sixty footers. That could be one of them. Or it could be a one off." The boat tacked to the right and Gayle saw the giant phoenix bird painted on the bow. "It is. It's a Phoenix 60."

"Boy, I wish I was out there with them," Dylan said.

"It'd be more fun than this old tub, that's for sure,"

Gayle said. Then she decided to take the plunge. "Dylan what's the deal with Dougie Winters?"

"Huh?" Dylan turned toward her mother, face full of innocence, blue eyes looking shocked.

"Don't give me that expression. I've known you too long to be fooled by it." She knew she was right. The girls might be identical, but they'd never dressed the same. Dylan preferred bright colors while Taylor dressed mostly in pastels. Dylan wore skirts at home, Taylor wore faded Levi's. Dylan kept her long hair free and unfettered, Taylor kept hers in a ponytail. But no matter what they wore, Gayle had always been able to tell them apart. To her they'd always been unique.

"You were wearing Taylor's clothes on your birthday. At first I didn't think anything of it. But the next morning you two were smirking at each other over breakfast and I suddenly remembered that you were supposed to go to the movies with Haley while Taylor had a date with Dougie. Then it hit me. You'd switched. Of course Haley was in on it, but poor Dougie wasn't. Aren't you taking sharing a little too far? And to think he was Haley's boyfriend first. I'm surprised she has anything to do with you two."

"Haley didn't want him anymore."

"It was wrong," Gayle said.

"Nobody got hurt. Besides, Taylor broke up with him. So he'll never know."

"That's not the point."

"Look, I know it was wrong. And we won't do it again. Promise."

"Did you sleep with him?"

"Mom!"

"Come on, Dylan. Answer the question."

"There's some things you're not supposed to tell your mother."

"What in the hell for, Dylan? What ever possessed you? The three of you should be put on restriction for the entire summer." She was losing it and she couldn't help herself. The girls had everything and they were acting like sluts. She wouldn't have it.

"I didn't say I slept with him."

"But you did. You never could hide anything from me."

"It's no big deal. School's over. I'll never see him again. Neither will Taylor."

"I just want to know why." She felt the blood rushing to her face and she fought the storm she knew was coming. This should have been brought out in the open weeks ago. Then it would have been over and done with. Instead it had been at the back of her mind, festering.

"It was fun. It was like I was me, but I wasn't me."

"I always knew the day would come when you'd have sex with a boy, but I'd expected some feeling. It's not something you do just for fun."

"Why not?" she said.

"Jesus, Dylan."

"Oh, Mom!" Dylan screamed. "Look." She was pointing off to sea. Gayle turned.

"Oh, my God!" The sailboat looked as if it was going over.

"He's going to drop the mast into the water. I don't believe it," Dylan said. The boat went over, her port rail going into the water, then she was down, the mast buried in the choppy sea, the sails filling with water.

"If the mast breaks when they come back up, they're in real trouble," Gayle said. And even as she spoke the words the thousands of pounds of lead in the keel started to right her. Mother, daughter and several other passengers on the ferry gasped as water spilled out of the sails. Then the boat was upright and pointing into the wind.

"They made it," Dylan said, sighing. "Look, they're bringing down the main." A horn blasted. The ferry was nearing her berth. "Now they're rolling in the jib. Good idea, they don't belong on the sea."

"What makes you say that?" Gayle said, calmer now.

"How do you drop the mast in the water in this weather? It's blowing, sure. And they should have been reefed up, but it's not that bad. You really gotta be incompetent. If it'd been you and me on that big old boat, we couldn't have messed up that badly if we tried."

"You're trying to flatter me, Dylan and it won't work." The anger was back in her voice, but there was hurt, too. "I'm disappointed in you. I expected better."

"I'm sorry, Mom. It won't happen again."

Thirty minutes later Gayle was sitting in front of a smiling and apologizing Hertz agent. They'd ordered the car in advance, but there'd been a mixup of some kind. The Hertz guy said they must have rented it to someone else by mistake, he'd have another one in less than ten minutes.

They'd just gotten off the ferry from the South Island, where they'd had a wonderful time. They'd landed on top of a glacier in both a helicopter and a ski plane, parasailed off a mountain in Queenstown, jet boated on the Shotover River in the shadows of the Remarkable Mountains. They'd been to New Zealand's Marlborough wine country, seen all of the towns in the south, driven the length and breadth of the island, and now they were ready to go home, but there was no car to get them to Auckland to catch their flight.

It was annoying, but she had bigger problems on her mind. Her vacation was almost over, soon she was going to have to go back to the real world and face them. Nesbitt was after her job and the station sounded like they might give it to him. Her ratings were fine, but the network was skittish about having a senator's wife anchor the evening news. Never mind that she'd had the job before Stacy had the office. And then there was the presidency thing. If Stacy went for it, her life would never be the same.

When the replacement, a Nissan Sentra, arrived, Dylan tossed their bags into the trunk, put her PowerBook in the back seat, the map in front and smiled as Gayle slid behind the wheel. Nice day, nice car. They were going to spend a day in Wellington, then it was the long drive to Auckland.

She pulled out of the ferry terminal, looked both ways and entered into traffic, making sure that she pulled out onto the left side of the road, the opposite of what she was used to.

"Mom!" Dylan screamed.

Gayle looked up and saw the orange car speeding toward them, on her side of the street. She jerked the wheel to the right. There was a car there. The driver slammed on his brakes, trying to give her room. Time sped up, then screeched to a halt as she realized they were going to hit. "Jesus Christ," she said, calm now. The situation, her future, her life, out of her control.

A thud, like a wrecking ball, smashed into her chest. A thunder blast ripped through her body. Great pain shot up her right leg, like someone was driving a railroad spike through her foot. Crunching metal, shattering safety glass, tearing plastic, a whirling, spinning car. She was caught in a hurricane. Tires screeched. Burned rubber and brake lining smelled like death. Something hit her head. She bit through her lip, tasting blood. The car was going backwards. The world flashed by, a grotesque horror show. Sunlight flickered, reflecting off the windows of other cars, stabbing her eyes.

As fast as it happened, it was over. Cars stopped. From somewhere, everywhere, people appeared. Gayle's right foot was jammed under the clutch peddle, pain so intense she had to fight against screaming. Her right leg was twisted. She tried the door. It was jammed.

"Open the door!" she shouted, afraid of fire. She heard the sea off to the left, waves lapping against the shore, a familiar sound, like home. Like Newport Beach. "The door!" she shouted again. "Please, someone, open the door." She started to shake. She couldn't stop it.

"It's stuck." The voice belonged to a young man, maybe a college student.

"Then rip it off!" she said. Her vision blurred, the left side fading out. Her head hurt. A throbbing headache. She put a hand to her eye. Sticky. "Jesus," she said. "Blood."

More men running to the car. Concern on their faces. Big men. Strong men.

"Get the door off!" she shouted. She smelled gasoline. Any second the car was going to go up in flames. Three men ripped the door open and tore it off.

"Are you okay?" Dylan asked. Her voice sounded far away.

"No," Gayle answered, "you?" She'd forgotten about

her daughter, the pain had been so great. She clenched a fist against it. Dylan was all that mattered. "My daughter, can you get her out?"

"Best not to move her," someone said.

"My chest hurts," Dylan said. Gayle could see her. She was pinned in place, unable to move.

"Don't move till the ambulance gets here," the same cautious voice spoke.

"Smell gas," Gayle said.

"Yeah, we shouldn't move," Dylan echoed, voice fading.

"But the gas."

"There's no gas." Mr. Cautious again. "Help's on the way."

Gayle shivered from fear and shock. The pain came back, attacking her like a jackhammer pounding on her foot. "Can someone move my seat back," she pleaded. Someone did. It only moved a few inches and it offered no relief. Her foot and leg were scrunched. The pain was excruciating. She tried to move her foot out from under the pedal. No dice. More pain.

"Don't move. Don't even try." It was a command. "I'm a nurse. My name's Claire."

"Hi, Claire," Gayle said.

"Do you know your name?" she asked.

"Yeah, it's Gayle."

"On a scale of one to ten, how's the pain?"

"Eleven."

"You have a fractured femur. It looks worse than it is," Claire said. She held Gayle's hand and kept talking to her, telling her that Dylan was okay, that she was okay, that help was on the way. They were lucky. A taxi two cars back had radioed for help. Once Gayle saw the police and the firefighters she began to believe that they were going to make it.

"We're going to cover you while we break the window," a burly fireman said.

Gayle looked over at Dylan. A fireman was talking to her. She turned to Claire and squeezed her hand.

"Relax," Clare said, "I won't let go." And she leaned into the car as the firefighters covered them with a tarpaulin. She shivered, thinking of a shroud over a corpse. Then the tarpaulin was over her head and her world turned into a stuffy, fuzzy kind of place, like when she was a little girl and hid from imaginary monsters under the covers.

She heard the fireman tell Dylan not to worry about the sound. What sound, she thought as the firefighter's sledge holed the front widow. The crunching safety glass gave with a loud pop and she imagined an enraged elephant loose in a glass factory, snorting and stomping, crunching and smashing. It felt like the great beast was on her foot. God it hurt. Stab after stab of hurt. Stomp after stomp, that huge, leathered foot coming down. Thousands of pounds of pain.

"Okay, we're going to take the cloth off now," one of the firefighters said. They folded it back, bringing the daylight again. She squeezed her eyes shut against both it and the pain.

"Please hurry," she said.

"We're going to cut off the roof. Only a few minutes more," a fireman said. He sounded so earnest. So concerned.

"Hang in there," Claire said.

"Excuse me." A male voice.

"She won't let go of my hand," Claire said. Then,

"Give it to me. I'll do it."

"Ma'am?" the male voice.

"I'm a nurse, I've done it before." Irony and a smile in Claire's voice. Gayle felt a pin prick just below her right shoulder. She opened her eyes, Claire was there. "Just a small shot," she said.

It seemed like only seconds and they had the roof off.

"It's a convertible now," the fireman said. Gayle forced a laugh.

"They're going to take your daughter out." Claire gave Gayle's hand a squeeze. She watched as they put a neck brace, then a back brace on Dylan. They lifted her out, put her in an ambulance and whisked her away.

To get Gayle out they had to cut out the back seat, then cut the driver's seat from around her. Firemen and policemen lifted her out. Claire held her hand the whole time. They laid her on a stretcher.

"You have the kind of injury that has to be set immediately," a fireman said. "This is going to hurt more than anything you've ever felt before."

"It's okay to scream," Claire said, still squeezing her hand.

A man got behind her, put his hands under her arms and held tightly while someone else pulled on her leg, straightening it. The firemen was right. It hurt, but she didn't scream and she didn't pass out.

When it was over, they lifted her into an ambulance. Dylan was being taken care of. It was out of her control. Her life, whether she lived or died, was in the hands of others. The ambulance started to move. Two young men were in the back with her.

"My name's Bob." He had short cropped almost orange hair, sparkling green eyes, and a bushy orange mustache that set off the dimples in his cheeks when he smiled. "Oxygen," he said as he lowered the mask onto her face. "Just breathe normally."

"I'm Jimmy," the other medtech said. She supposed they called them medtechs or EMTs, she wasn't sure. He was Maori, with dark brown skin, a gleaming smile and a gentle touch. He took her hand. "It's our job to get you to the hospital safe and sound and we're very good at it." He couldn't be much older then eighteen or nineteen, about Dylan's age. Just a child. "I know what you're thinking," he said, "but not to worry, I'm older than I look. Not much." He laughed. "But I've done this a lot. So has Bob. You're in good hands."

"I wasn't worried," she said. Her voice sounded funny to her, like she'd been drinking. "Am I drugged? I don't remember."

"We gave you morphine at the scene." She must have looked startled, because he added. "Relax, you won't become addicted or anything." His smile wider than she'd thought possible. "You're tense," he said. "Relax." She felt a slight pressure as he squeezed her hand.

"You're not cooperating," Jimmy said, interrupting her thoughts with his soothing voice. "Just relax. Loosen up."

She sighed and let go. And just like that she was floating. It wasn't the drug. It was the complete absence of responsibility. Whatever was going to happen was going to happen. It was in God's hands. She sighed. Somebody else was in charge. She had no worries, no cares. It was like she was a child again, trusting these young men the way she'd trusted her parents.

The ambulance turned a corner, banking left. She felt the centrifugal force, like a wave of pleasure washing through her. She was at ease, at peace, at home with herself and who she was. The pain was still intense, but dulled by the drug, she supposed. Her life was still out there somewhere, waiting to reclaim her, but not now. Not today. She closed her eyes and sighed again.

* * *

"Possible pneumo," the Maori paramedic yelled out, busting through the door with a gurney. His face was a tattooed mosaic accented by swirling hair. The hair was supposed to be tied back, but it wasn't. It whipped around the blue and brown face as the young man jerked his head back and forth, looking for a doctor.

"Let's get moving," Dr. John Keith said. This was the last thing he wanted. Second day in the country, first day on the job, still suffering from jet lag. He flexed his fists trying to chase away the tension. He needed to be a hundred percent.

"Auto accident, head on collision," the paramedic said, pushing the gurney into place.

There was no blood. Thank God. "Get Dr. Roberts, stat."

"Can't do it, doctor. He just called from his mobile. Car won't start. He's still at home," Rachel Collins said. She was the youngest nurse on the ward, married to an orthopedic surgeon. The head nurse told him yesterday that she had a natural healing instinct.

"Shit," he muttered under his breath as he looked down at the girl. She was young. Her hair lay about her shoulders, long and light brown, almost blonde, but not. A rare color, like a palomino. Her eyes were kind of closed, fluttering. He didn't have to see them to know they were blue. "It's one of the Sterling twins."

"You know her?" Rachel said.

"Father's a United States Senator. Has a close shot at the Republican nomination."

"So?"

"Means he has a good chance of being the next president," Dr. Keith said as Rachel cut away the girl's sweatshirt. Tension pneumothorax, a collapsed lung. He knew how to handle it, of course, and he'd assisted on a couple during his internship in Chicago, but he'd never done one by himself. He was ready, but he'd feel a lot better if Dr. Roberts were looking over his shoulder.

"We better step it up or the senator's daughter is going to be in a lot of trouble," Rachel said, removing the sweatshirt. The girl wasn't wearing a bra.

"Okay, let's do it," John Keith said. The Maori paramedic helped Keith roll her onto her left side. The paramedic gently set her right arm aside, exposing the rib cage. Keith looked over at the wall mounted suction, then to Rachel. "Ready?"

"Will it hurt?" The girl's eyes were open now. Piercing blue, like a Kansas sky on a clear day. God, he wished he was back in America. Anyplace but here, now, about to do this.

"You're conscious," he said. Damn, he should have been paying better attention. Then to the nurse. "Better give her a local."

"You didn't answer my question, will it hurt?"

"No," Keith said.

"Here, doctor." Rachel slipped a syringe into his hand.

"Just a pin prick. You probably won't feel a thing." He gave her the shot.

"I felt it," she said, groggy. Then she closed her eyes.

"Think she's concussed?" Rachel asked.

"No, she seemed lucid," Keith said. "It's just a reaction to the local." A slow tingle moved up his spine, like a cold snake slithering up his back. He didn't want to fuck this up. He checked his hands, amazed that they weren't shaking. This was what it was all about, what he'd always wanted. Surgeon in charge. But he wasn't ready. She was so young. "Okay, once again, are we ready?"

"Yes, sir," Rachel looked every bit as efficient as he'd heard she was. For a second he envied her husband, but then he put his mind back to the task at hand. "You'll do fine, doctor," she said and she gave his arm a gentle squeeze.

"Thank you." He straightened his back, then slipped the middle and index finger of his right hand under her armpit and counted down five rib spaces. "Scalpel," he said. She'd anticipated him and the instrument was in his hand before he'd completed the command. Fingering the fifth rib, he made a one-and-a-half inch incision on top of it. A hemostat was in his hand without him having to ask for it and he blunt-dissected his way on into the chest cavity.

"Thirty-two French," he said and Rachel handed him a large-bore chest tube. He inserted it into the fifth intercostal space, pushing it on into the thoracic cavity. "We're ready for suction," he said. Rachel turned on the wall mounted unit and he sucked out the air trapped between the chest wall and the lung. He breathed a sigh of relief when the lung started to re-expand.

* * *

Gayle woke as she was being x-rayed. After the x-rays,

they gave her a shot of something. She dozed for what seemed only a few seconds, then she heard a voice with a Canadian accent.

"Do you know your name?" It was a caring voice, drifting into her consciousness like a smile sliding into a dream. The pain was gone now, not even an ache, no dull reminder of the horror she'd so recently suffered through. She started to smile, then a vision of Dylan being pulled out of the wreckage flashed through her.

"Dylan? My daughter?" she asked, running her eyes around the room. Huge. Concrete. Forbidding. Sunlight coming in from a pair of windows high up. She'd been asleep for longer than she'd thought. She was in a hospital.

"She's in surgery. She's going to be fine. Right now we're concerned about you. Do you know your name?"

"Yes."

"What is it?"

"Gayle." The word rasped out of her throat. She moved her tongue around the inside of her mouth in a vain attempt to find some saliva to swallow. She failed, waited a few seconds, then added, "Sterling."

"When were you born?"

"November Twenty-Second." Another pause. "Sixty-three."

"Famous date. Even in New Zealand."

"Yes," She said, weakly. She'd heard it all her life. She closed her eyes.

"Look at me," the voice soothed. She opened them back up. The man she saw didn't look like a doctor, more like a rugby player, close cropped hair, Irish green eyes, round face, rounder glasses, athletic build and a generous smile. "My name is Dave, Gayle, and you're going to be fine. Do you remember what happened?"

"Yes."

"All of it?"

"Yes."

"Tell me."

"Drunk — driver — head — on."

"How do you know he was drunk?"

"Car — slipping — sliding — my side."

"She's okay." Dave turned away, then said to someone she couldn't see, "Anna, we're gonna need some stitches here. Wanna look?"

"Can you see out of your left eye?" Anna, a young lady, pretty, late twenties, long flowing black hair, looked down at her.

Gayle tried closing her right.

"A little."

"Good." Anna smiled, using gentle fingers to probe the area around her eye. "Everything's going to be okay." She turned away. Gayle heard her say, "No problem." She couldn't see who Anna was talking to.

"How do you feel?" Dave was back.

"Fractured — femur — hurts."

"How do you know about the femur?" Dave asked and her mind flashed back to the accident and the girl with the angelic face.

"Nurse — at accident — helped me," Gayle said, back in the present.

"What nurse? From where?" Dave asked.

"Don't — know — where — her name — Claire."

"Well she's right. You have a fractured femur."

"What are you going — to — do?"

"I'm going to nail it."

"When?"

"In about five minutes." He raised his wrist and looked at a watch. It was a colorful Swatch, funny she could notice

that. Then he added, "Did your right foot used to look like the left one?"

"Mirror — image."

"Because it doesn't now."

She struggled to sit up and see.

"No, lie down. I'll show you the X-rays." He did. All five toes of her right foot were dislocated, popped out of their sockets and broken. It looked bad.

"Oh — Lord."

"I can fix it. You won't be running any marathons for awhile, but I'll make it right."

"Okay."

"A little shot," Dave said. "You won't feel it. Now some oxygen, breathe in, then count backwards from one hundred."

She didn't get past ninety-seven.

CHAPTER THREE

SANDY GRABBED ONTO THE BAR, left hand reaching first. Slick with sweat, it started to slip. Panic welled up. He was going to fall. He clawed out with his right. His heart was in his throat, thumping, thumping. His toes found the concrete under the bottom rail as he clamped onto the top with a tight fisted grip. He fought down the panic. Toes holding. Safe. The evening breeze chilled the sweat on the nape of his neck.

"Dr. Sterling!" For a crazy instant he thought she'd let go, that he'd failed. He pulled himself into the bar. It hit him between chest and stomach. She was shorter, the top rail was even with her breasts. He could only imagine how hard it had been for her to climb over the rail and get a toe hold without falling.

"It's okay. I made it. Don't let go." He was speaking in a loud whisper, fast, urgently. For a second the sweet taste of satisfaction filled him, but it was fleeting. He still had to get her down.

"I thought you were going to fall for sure."

"Pretty scary," he said.

"You could've been killed," Gina said. Her blue eyes pierced him. Her lower lip trembled. A slight shake quivered through her slender shoulders. How could he have failed her so badly?

"Not me, not today," Sandy said. "I had God on my side." He pulled himself in close to the bar. He felt the fist of fear wrap itself around his sphincter. He stiffened his back, tightened his grip, and tried to shrug it off, but it held on, like an old whore clinging to a young lover.

He turned his attention back to Gina and almost cried out when he saw the look of quiet desperation there. She was resigned. She was going to jump. All of a sudden he didn't care about the TV cameras. He put Stacy and his campaign out of his mind. They would take care of themselves. His own life didn't matter. Nothing mattered except this lost little girl with the desperation in her eyes.

"Why, Gina? Why here? Why this hotel?"

"I don't know."

"Is it because my family owns it? Is that why?"

"I didn't even think of that." She was lying. It was obvious, but this wasn't the time to call her on it. "Maybe God led me here." Not God, he thought. She wanted the newsmen here. She'd planned it all. He'd done something to turn her against him. What?

"So what now?" Sandy said. What else could he say.

He had to play it out. All he could do was wait for a chance and try and get close enough to grab her.

"You said God was on your side. How can you know that?" She stared at him as if he might disappear if she blinked. She was so small, so thin. His heart went out to her, but then that was nothing new, it had been going out to her since their first session.

"You know me," Sandy said, "the eternal doubter, but if there's a God in Heaven there's no way He would have let me down."

"Why not?"

"Because you're too valuable for us to lose, me and Him." Keep her talking, the thought ricocheted through him. She won't jump, not as long as she's talking.

"You and God?" She'd been holding on in the center of the balcony. She scooted toward the far side, away from him.

"Yeah, me and Him. We want you safe and out of harm's way."

"So you prayed, like you said a prayer before you jumped." Her voice was a whisper on the wind.

"Of course I prayed," Sandy said. "I'm an agnostic, but I'm not stupid."

"That's funny." She inched a little farther away, till she could go no further.

"That's me, a clown at heart," he said.

"I saw you on television this morning." She smiled. It was quick, then it was gone, but it was a smile nevertheless. Something to work with. "You were on with the newscaster who gave me this." She tapped the mike that was clipped to her dress. "Remember that interview you taped just before you went on vacation? You weren't so funny then." Another smile. Sandy was beginning to have hope.

"Yeah, well the guy was an asshole." Because of who he was and who Stacy was, Sandy knew this was going out live, probably nationally. And he'd just called Nick Nesbitt an asshole for all the world to hear. Stacy was going to be upset, but the girl was more important. He tried to force his brother from his mind, but Gina wouldn't let him.

"So do you think your color will cost your brother the nomination?" she said, imitating Nick Nesbitt's affected Kennedy accent. Sandy hadn't wanted to do the program. If he had to be interviewed, he'd asked Stacy, why couldn't it be Gayle? But he knew when he'd asked it that it wasn't possible, she was family.

"Like I said, Nesbitt's an asshole," he said as she looked down, settling her eyes on something. Sandy followed her gaze. The cameraman had moved to the far side of the parking lot, another news crew was setting up near him.

"I can say anything I want and everybody out there can hear me. That's true, isn't it?"

"I wouldn't swear," Sandy said.

"Yeah, they don't like that on television. But you said asshole, that's swearing."

"I guess it is." He couldn't believe it. She was acting as if they were in the office, not fifteen stories up holding on to the outside of a balcony in front of all the world.

She turned back toward the camera.

"You're an asshole, Nick Nesbitt," she yelled out.

"You swore."

"Oh yeah, sorry." She laughed and a quick glimmer of humor flashed from her eyes, but then she cast them downward and the despair was back.

Sandy started to inch toward her.

* * *

Stacy Sterling looked out over the sea from his penthouse view in the San Francisco Sterling. The Golden Gate spanned the bay in the distance. Beautiful. He never tired of the sight. He loosened his tie, then pulled it off. He looked down from the balcony. Cars no bigger than Hot Wheels toys moved on the streets below. He shrugged out of his coat, keeping the tie in hand. It was a hot San Francisco evening and there was a wet ring under both arms of his long sleeved white shirt.

Something told him to put his coat and tie back on and leave. It was a mistake meeting one of them in the hotel. He knew that. If he wasn't careful it could kill the campaign, or worse, his relationship with Jennifer. Maybe even his marriage. A twinge of guilt bit him when he realized that he cared more for his mistress than his wife. His twenty-year-old mistress, Jennifer Updike. Beautiful, brilliant, and totally satisfied as the other woman.

He slipped an arm back into the coat. It wasn't too late. He left the balcony and stepped into the plush two bedroom suite as he slid in the other arm. He was halfway through the room when he heard the knock. Too late. He took a calming breath and opened the door. She was stunning.

"Good evening." She stepped in and closed the door. She was wearing a floor length white gown that hugged her curves the way paint hugs a Ferrari. She was a tall, long limbed, green-eyed blond. And she was young. "I'm Randy."

It was insane, this thing he had for teenage women. Girls really, not women. But he'd only traded money for it that one time at the Surf Motel since Jennifer had come to work for him. Jennifer. Child genius. College freshman at fourteen. College graduate at sixteen. Senatorial aide at seventeen. Senator's mistress less than a month later. But she was pushing twenty-one now and the excitement was flowing out of the relationship.

"Do you have anything to drink?" Her voice had the melody of a Billie Holiday song and it unnerved him, made him feel like a high school kid in the backseat on a first date.

"I like the dress."

"Do you really? Like it I mean."

"Yes, I really like it."

"Then it seems such a shame that I have to take it off." She shrugged her shoulders and the straps fell as she put her hands to her breasts and cupped them. Then she curved her thumbs under the fabric and pulled the dress down, shedding it the way a snake does its skin.

"Holy shit," Stacy whispered. She faced him clad only in a lacy bra and skimpy panties that failed to hide the darker triangle between her legs.

"Tanqueray and tonic if you have it," she said, moving toward the sofa. She sat and crossed her legs, never taking her eyes off of his. "Light on the tonic. I feel a little giddy this evening."

"I only have Gordon's, sorry," Stacy said.

"It'll do," she said.

Stacy went to the mini fridge. He set the tie on it before taking out two miniatures and a bottle of tonic. He took two glasses off the top of the refrigerator, stopped and turned to her. "No ice."

"Not a problem."

Before he had a chance to stop her she had the ice

bucket in her hand and was out the door in her bra and panties. Oh Lord, he thought, what if someone sees her? He went to the door and poked his head out. The hall was empty as she curved and wiggled her way to the ice machine. She was still wearing her high heels. Christ, he hoped no one popped out of the elevator. He heard the machine rumble as the bucket filled. Then she sashayed back to him. A smile covered her face. The bra was as thin as the panties, making her pink nipples a beacon to his eyes. She might as well have been completely naked.

"Voila, we have ice." She handed him the bucket as he closed the door.

"Ice," he repeated as she reached behind herself and unhooked the bra. She tossed it aside and sat back down on the couch.

"You don't need it," he said, eyes fixed on her breasts.

"What?" she teased.

"The bra, you don't need it."

"Really? You think so?" She cupped her hands under her breasts, then released them. "They stand up by themselves. Kind of firm and soft at the same time." She squeezed them and Stacy gulped as her nipples expanded. "But a bra is kind of feminine, don't you think? And you did enjoy seeing me in it, didn't you?"

"I did." Stacy dropped ice into the glasses. "But I don't think I like the idea of others seeing you that way." He added the gin, then the tonic. "I was talking about your escapade in the hallway. What if someone had seen?"

"Oh, sorry. I wasn't thinking. I did it for you. It's all I had on my mind, pleasing you." He handed her the drink and she took a slow swallow. "That's good."

"You can't really tell the difference between Tanqueray and Gordon's, can you?"

"Not really, but I've found that if I order Tanqueray, rather than plain old gin, I get carded a lot less in bars. I guess they think if you're old enough to taste the difference, you must be old enough to drink." He sipped while she took another long swallow.

"That's pretty smart." He popped open the top button of his shirt.

"You look all stuffy and up-tight in that jacket." She set the glass aside, got up and sauntered over to him. "Let me help you take it off." She moved around behind him, breasts brushing his arm. Then her hands were on his shoulders. He set his drink down on the fridge, next to the tie, as she eased the jacket off. She tossed it on a chair and said, "There, doesn't that feel better?"

"Much," he said as she wrapped her arms around him. He felt her breasts against his back as she worked the rest of the shirt's buttons. In seconds it was off. Then her hands were at his belt. Then the zipper and his slacks were at his feet. He started to step out of them.

"No," she said as she slid around him, going to her knees. She pulled his boxers down. "So nice." She took him in her mouth.

He shivered with his own hardness. A delicious feeling ran through him. Delight coupled with shame. Better than Jennifer. Much better than Gayle. Then he pushed mistress and wife from his mind as his hands found the back of her head. He pulled her to him until she had it deep in her throat. Then he exploded and she was swallowing. It was over in seconds.

"I thought I could hold it," he said, embarrassed.

"That's alright. We have all night." She wiped her mouth off with the back of her hand. She still had her panties on. She stood, kissed him full on the lips and he tasted himself. Then she flopped down on the sofa and picked up the remote. He stood with his pants around his feet as she punched the power button.

He gasped when the screen lit up.

"Don't turn it!" he said as he saw his younger brother out on a balcony somewhere.

* * *

"Don't! Stay back! You might fall!" Gina yelled. Sandy stopped moving toward her. He was close, but not close enough.

"It's you I'm worried about," he said, whispering again, hoping that she'd move a little toward him so she could hear.

"I'm nobody, you help tons of people. It would be horrible if something happened to you," she said.

"You are somebody, Gina. You're a special person."

"Oh, Dr. Sterling, how can you say that? You're special. I know it. Everybody knows it. Even asshole Nesbitt knows it. And look how they attack you, just because you're black and your brother's not. But you stand up to them. What you told me about you and your family is true. You all have that special disease that makes you different. You all stick together, you have a bond with them. I used to have that with my brother, even kind of with my parents, but not anymore." No smile now. Not a hint. A tear trickled down a dimpled cheek.

"Gina, I know how you feel, but you have to tough it out. It gets better, believe me."

"How can you know? You've never lost your whole family, everyone you loved. You don't know what it's like to be so depressed that you don't want to go on living." The wind picked up. Her hair was flying. Strands of it seemed to be lashing her face, like tiny whips.

"I have kind of an idea what you're feeling. I lost my younger sister when I was sixteen. She was only fourteen years old. So pretty. She believed in God. She prayed, but leukemia took her anyway. It's true I had the rest of my family to lean on for support and you don't have that, but you have me. Let me help." He moved even closer. Only a foot away now.

"I didn't know about your sister. I'm sorry, I really am. But that was a long time ago and it wasn't your whole family. I don't have anyone. I can't get it out of my mind. I see their faces when I go to sleep at night. I see them when I wake up in the morning. I don't want to see them anymore. I'm sorry." She let go her hands.

"No!" Sandy kept his right hand wrapped around the rail as he lunged with his left. He grabbed her by the wrist and held on. Pain stabbed up his arm as she jerked to a stop. His hand was slipping off the rail. He couldn't hold her and he couldn't let go. If she fell, he fell.

"Help me," she wailed. He felt her slipping from his hand. He squeezed tighter, giving it everything he had. His arms were racked with pain. He was going to lose her. His right arm, the one holding their combined weight, felt like it was being ripped out of its socket. One last chance, his mind screamed. If he let her go, he could save himself. But he couldn't do it. All or nothing. Sterlings didn't quit. Not ever.

"It's okay, Doc. You can let her go. I've got her." It was Alvarez calling from the balcony below. Relief flooded through him. Some of the pressure was taken off as Alvarez supported some of her weight, but he couldn't let go. His fingers were frozen in place.

"Let her go, Doc." This time it was Norton, from

above. "I got you. You're gonna be okay. You did good." He had an iron grip on Sandy's wrist. He was stronger than his wiry frame suggested. "It's alright now. Let her go." Sandy opened his hand and watched from his unique position, dangling from the fifteenth floor, as Alvarez pulled her in. She wrapped her arms around the homicide detective. She was sobbing.

"Okay, Doc, your turn," Norton said and he pulled Sandy into the bar. He grabbed onto it with his left hand. He was drenched in sweat. Norton held onto him till he was over the rail and on the safe side of the balcony.

"You are the most beautiful man I've ever seen." Sandy wrapped Norton in a bear hug, squeezing him like a lost lover.

"Just doing my job," Norton said.

Sandy hugged him harder. He never wanted to let go.

"Easy, Doc." Norton laughed. "People might talk."

"Wouldn't want that," Sandy said, laughing too, his way to shake off the fear. He pulled out of the hug and stared into the albino's eyes for a second. They were pale gray and the only color other than white on his face. Hair, lashes, eyebrows, skin—pale as paper. To some a ghostly apparition, to Sandy, the hauntingly beautiful face of a savior. He would never forget it.

"It was a brave thing you did. Dumb, but brave." Norton smiled. He had a slow way of talking, almost a drawl. Sandy was surprised that he hadn't noticed it earlier.

"Thanks."

"No sweat." Norton turned and started through the sliding glass door. "Let's go see how your girl's doing." He had a slight limp, like one leg was shorter than the other, but that couldn't be it. You had to be in top physical shape to be a cop.

"How'd you hurt yourself?"

"Say again?" Norton stopped, turned back toward Sandy, looked him in the eyes.

"Your limp. How do you pass your physicals?"

"I'm pretty strong for my age. I just can't run as fast as the younger guys. Gunshot. So they promoted me to detective. I still had to pass the test, but it wasn't too hard. Most would kill for this job, but I loved working in a black-and-white. Just loved it. But I'm starting to get into being a detective. Every day I like it a little more."

"How long you been doing it?"

"Twelve years. I guess they keep me on 'cuz I'm good at it." He smiled, flashing those star-bright teeth again. "Come on, Doc. Let's go see this beauty you snatched from the jaws of death."

"Just doing my job," Sandy said, imitating Norton's slow drawl.

"You're a kick, Doc," Norton said. Then he turned again and Sandy followed him out to the elevator. When the doors opened on the fourteenth floor Gina rushed in and threw her arms around him. Alvarez and Quinlan were right behind her.

"Oh, Dr. Sterling. I was so scared. I don't know why I did it. Mr. Alvarez says I have to go to the hospital. Is that true?"

"Yes." Sandy eased out of the embrace. He was her doctor. He was black. His brother was running for president. Three good reasons why he didn't want these men to get any wrong ideas.

"You're dressed kinda funny, Dr. Sterling."

"This is my Clark Kent outfit." He plucked the small mike from her dress.

"From the old TV show, not the movie," Norton said.

"That's right." Sandy smiled. "I was at that charity showing of *Casablanca* when I got your call."

"And I made you miss it. I'm so sorry, Doctor," Gina said as Quinlan stepped into the elevator. Alvarez pushed the button for the bottom floor.

"Probably gonna be press, Doc. How you want to handle it?" Alvarez asked.

"No comment," Sandy said. "I'm used to it." He tossed the mike out of the elevator as the doors were closing.

"Alright, Norton and I'll be on each side of the girl, Quinlan in front. We'll wedge on through them. My unmarked is the lot. We can take her to Memorial or Community. It's your call."

"Community. It's farther. If you lose them, they'll all flock to Memorial."

"Me? Lose them? I like how you think," Alvarez said.

Norton laughed.

The elevator doors opened to lights, TV cameras and flashing cameras. Sandy wondered how in the world they could have gotten there so quickly, but then he remembered that Gina had been up on that balcony for awhile before he'd arrived on the scene.

"Dr. Sterling, how does it feel being the hero of the hour?" a petite blue-eyed blonde asked him. She was holding a mike in her right hand, shoving it forward.

"I'm sorry, I don't have any comment to make right now. Later on I'll be happy to sit down with you all, but not now."

"Gina, what were you thinking about when you let go?" the woman asked, shifting the mike toward Gina, shoving it toward her face like a sword. Alvarez knocked it aside and Quinlan pushed forward, leading them through the crowd.

"Dr. Sterling, can I have a word?" Sandy stopped when he heard Nick Nesbitt's Kennedy accent.

"I really don't have any comment, Nick," he said.

"Just a quick one. You owe me that." Lights glared in Sandy's face and he thought about the Nick Nesbitt-asshole remarks they'd made up on that balcony and figured that maybe Nesbitt was right.

"Alright, Nick. A quick one."

"What did she mean when she said that you and your family all suffered from a disease?"

"You're sure that's the one you want to ask?" Sandy feigned surprise.

"That's the one. Do you have some kind of genetic illness? Something like Lou Gehrig's disease?"

"Something like that," Sandy said. The lights moved in on him. Nesbitt's eyes were glassed over. This was his big moment. His exclusive being carried live world wide. He probably saw his star shooting skyward. Probably was thinking of the network and national news.

"Well what is it?" he pressed.

"We're color blind," Sandy said.

"What?" But Sandy didn't hear Nesbitt's startled shout, because he'd spun away and was jogging toward an unmarked Ford cruiser. Alvarez was standing outside the car, holding the back door open. The others were already inside.

CHAPTER FOUR

HALEY HARRISON WAS STRETCHED out on a chaise lounge when it happened. She'd been out in the sun for too long, but her honey brown skin, a mixture of her father's African genes and her mother's Swedish, kept her safe from the worst of the sun's rays. It was summer, the end of a blistering ninety degree day.

She was reading NIGHT WITCH, a Jack Priest horror story, and she was totally absorbed in the novel. The setting sun, the sound of the waves and the view of the beach all combined to combat the chills creeping up her spine. Jack Priest was a scary writer.

Taylor moaned and Haley glanced over at her friend

on the lounge chair next to her. She was sleeping and for a second Haley thought she might be having a nightmare, but she shrugged the thought aside. She was the one reading the scary story, not Taylor. Taylor had been reading a computer magazine, not the fare of nightmares.

Sweat glistened on Taylor's forehead as she stirred in her sleep again. She had a healthy looking Southern California tan that made her skimpy white bikini fairly glow. The bikini left little to the imagination, but that was okay, it was just the two of them. Taylor's dad was going to be gone for a few days and Haley was staying over till he returned. Haley was wearing a one piece, but then she didn't need a tan.

They were lying by the Sterlings' large kidney shaped pool. Two tall palm trees offered little shade. There were two large Cinzano beach umbrellas they could lie under on the other side of the pool if they'd wanted, but they preferred the side away from the house, which was located at the back of a cliff, because they had a clear view of the beach from there. It was Haley's favorite spot, between the pool and the beach below.

She turned away from her friend and went back to her book, but before she was able to get back into it Taylor moaned again, louder this time. Haley faced her as she sat up and grabbed her chest.

"What's wrong?" Haley set her book aside.

"Hurts, Hale. Oh, lord." Taylor hugged herself. Her eyes were squinted shut. She was in pain. "It really hurts." She started rocking back and forth. Her face had gone white.

"What?"

"I don't know, hurts, bad." Taylor was gasping, struggling for air. "Dylan, it's Dylan."

Haley shivered, cold despite the evening heat. She sat up, reached out and took Taylor's hand. She was shivering too. Haley grabbed her towel, moved over to Taylor's chair and wrapped it around her shoulders.

"We need to call someone," Taylor said. "We have to know how bad it is."

"Your father," Haley said. She'd grown up with Dylan and Taylor. She'd seen how they felt each other's pain. She didn't doubt.

"He's in San Francisco exploring, remember?" Exploring was what Stacy called his quest for the presidency. "Right now he's probably on his way to dinner with the mayor." Taylor was breathing easier now.

While Gayle and Dylan were in New Zealand, Taylor and Stacy were supposed to go to France. But as usual one thing led to another and the trip was put off a day, then shortened from three weeks to two, then canceled altogether. Taylor didn't seem to mind. She managed to squeeze a few hours of quality time into her father's busy schedule and that seemed to satisfy her.

"It feels like something's pushing at my chest," Taylor said. She was fighting for air. The shivers had turned to hot sweat. "Dylan's hurting." She pushed herself out of the chaise lounge, stood, hands on her knees, like a baseball player in the outfield, and took a few deep breaths. "The pain's going. We have to get to Dylan."

She hurried into her bedroom with Haley on her heels. Taylor turned on her PowerBook. In seconds she was online. Haley looked over her shoulder as she checked the airline schedules. "There's a Quantas nonstop to Auckland at 1:15 in the morning," Taylor said. "I'm gonna be on it."

"Me too," Haley said. "I'll call the airline." But when

she did she was told there were no seats available. "Now what?"

"I'll call Freddy Carson, Dad's administrative assistant in Washington." It was 9:30 at night there, so she called him at home.

"Fred, you're on the speaker. I have my friend Haley with me. We have to get on the Quantas flight to Auckland out of LAX at 1:15 AM. It's full. Can you work it out?"

"What's the matter?" Fred Carson said. "Is it your mother? Your sister?"

"I don't know. I just have a feeling. You know the kind Dylan and I get."

"I can't have someone bumped because you have a feeling," Fred said. He sounded relieved.

"It's more than a feeling, Freddy." She was interrupted by the sound of Stacy's downstairs phone. "Hold on, the official phone's ringing." That was the name Dylan and Taylor had given it when they were in grade school, because it was Daddy's work phone. Not for children. For official business only.

"I'll get it." Haley ran down the stairs, heading for Stacy's office off of the living room. She grabbed the phone and almost shouted into it. "Senator Sterling's residence." She clutched the receiver with sweaty hands. Taylor's apprehension had thoroughly infected her.

"The Sterling residence? The home of Gayle and Dylan Sterling?" The voice was male, nervous and it had a New Zealand accent. The bearer of bad news, she just knew it.

"Yes." She sagged into Stacy's easy chair. She was shaking too much to stand.

"Who's speaking please?"

"My name is Haley Harrison, I'm a family friend."

"Is Mr. Sterling at home?"

"No, I'm sorry. What's the matter? Why are you calling? Are they hurt?"

"Could I please speak to Mr. Sterling?"

"No, you can't. He's in San Francisco. You can tell me."

"Ma'am?" the voice questioned.

"Tell me!" Haley said. "Are they hurt?"

"There's been an accident. They're both in surgery at the hospital in Wellington and both expected to fully recover. That's all we know at the moment. Is there someone who can come down here?"

"We'll be there tomorrow."

"Senator Sterling?" the man said, but he didn't get an answer, because Haley had already hung up. She dashed back up the stairs.

"They've been in an accident and they're in the hospital," she said. "But the man said they're going to be okay."

"Fred, you still there?" Taylor said.

"I heard," he answered. "I'll take care of everything. And I'll get a hold of your father. With luck I'll be able to track him down and get him on a commuter flight out of Frisco in plenty of time to meet you at LAX."

"That would be great, Freddy. And could you call Simon and Gran, too? And don't forget, we need two tickets, Haley's going with me, you remember her, you met her last Christmas, you know, the girl with the alliterate name, Haley Harrison. She lives down the street."

"Not a problem. Pack your bags. I'll call you back ASAP with your confirmation."

"Thanks, Freddy. Bye."

Haley watched as Taylor pulled out a few changes of clothes from her bureau. "The seasons are upside down in the southern hemisphere," she said, "so it'll be cold in New Zealand. Remember how much fun Dylan had shopping for winter clothes in the dead of summer."

"Yeah," Haley said, "so we won't have to take very much, cuz no way can she wear all that stuff."

"You got it. I'm just gonna bring a couple pairs of jeans, a couple T-shirts and a sweat shirt." She pulled them out of her bureau and tossed them on the bed along with a ski sweater, then she dug a carry-on bag out of the back of the closet. In less than five minutes she was ready to travel.

"I better go and get my stuff and square it with Julia and Dad." Haley's mother hated being called Mom, but that was okay because Gayle had always been Mom to her.

"Yeah go, and don't forget your passport," Taylor said. Haley had been raised like one of the Sterling girls and all Sterlings had current passports, because they often traveled on the spur of the moment.

Fifteen minutes later she was back, packed and ready. She ran up the stairs, skipping every other step. Taylor was in her room, watching television. What's the deal?" she said.

"Joanie called while you were gone." Joanie was a friend of theirs from school. "She told me to turn on CNN. Uncle Sandy's out on a ledge. He's trying to talk a girl out of jumping.

"Holy cow." That was as close as Haley could come to swearing. Somehow those four letter words everybody else used couldn't pass her lips. "He's so brave." Her eyes were bolted to the television. Sandy was out on a balcony, many floors up. She recognized the Sterling Hotel site immediately.

"Oh, shit," Taylor said. On the screen, Sandy was jumping the balconies.

"Please, God," Haley said, heart racing.

"He made it," Taylor said.

"God, I love him. I just can't help it."

"Haley you're eighteen. He's thirty-five."

"The last time he was over he wasn't looking at me like I was a little kid anymore," she said, a note of satisfaction in her voice. "I'm old enough now. It's possible."

"You were wearing that skimpy bikini. What man wouldn't look?"

"Your dad wasn't staring at me the way Sandy was."

"Yeah, that's my dad. He only has eyes for Mom."

"Nesbitt, you're an asshole," the girl on the screen shouted down to the camera.

"He is an asshole," Taylor said.

"Fat, white and puckered," Haley said. They watched in silence for a few minutes.

"Look how he's sneaking closer. Hey, look at that!" Taylor jumped to her feet.

"He's got her!" Haley was standing too. "Hold on, Sandy, oh please, God, hold on."

"Please, God," Taylor echoed.

"There's a man in the room below. He has her. Thank you, God." Haley sighed as a man with a bleached white face was helping Sandy over the balcony.

"You're such a dreamer, Haley. It would never work."

"It would so. We're perfect for each other." She'd been in love with Taylor's Uncle Sandy since she was ten years old and someday he was going to love her back. He just didn't know it yet.

"Look, they're coming out," Taylor said.

On the screen they were coming out of the hotel. Sandy with his arm around the girl. Newsmen were shouting questions. Then he was there, sticking a microphone in Sandy's face. That scheming, back-stabbing low life that was after Gayle's job. Nick Nesbitt. From now on she would always think of him as "The Asshole Nesbitt." She smiled with the thought that everybody else in the country probably would, too.

Nesbitt was pestering Sandy. Sandy let the girl go on ahead with the policemen. Then Nesbitt was asking him something about a disease the Sterlings all had.

"Color blind," Sandy answered. Then he pushed past Nesbitt and was getting in the back of a car.

"Wow. Sandy just creamed him," Haley said. "I don't think he'll be so hot after your mom's job now."

The phone rang. Taylor grabbed it and pushed the speaker button. "Freddy?"

"It's me. I got you two tickets on that flight. But I can't find your father. He must be out at one of those arm twisting dinners he's so fond of. He's supposed to take his cell phone with him."

"He does," Taylor said, defending him.

"Yeah, but he turns it off. Never mind. He's the senator. I work for him. If that's the way he wants it, that's they way it is. Also, your Uncle Simon and your grandmother are on one of those photo safaris in Kenya. No way can I get a hold of them."

"Damn, I forgot about that."

"Don't worry about it, I'll figure something out. I always do."

"Thanks, Freddy," Taylor said.

"No problem, I've called a cab for you guys. It'll pick you up at 11:00. That'll get you to the airport at least an hour before the flight. If I manage to get a hold of your father, I'll have him meet you at the gate, but don't count on it. When he turns his phone off like this, he usually leaves it off all night."

"Why?" Taylor asked.

"He just forgets to turn it back on. He'll shut it off because he's in a restaurant or a bookstore and then it stays off till he needs to make a call."

* * *

Sandy slid into the backseat next to Gina. He pulled the door closed and rolled down the window. There was a slight breeze and it cooled the sweat on the back of his neck .

"Community? You're sure?" Alvarez said. He started the car.

"Yeah," Sandy said as Alvarez peeled out of the parking lot.

"That was a good piece of work back there Doc," Norton said as Alvarez took a right on Ocean Boulevard. "You should be proud."

"Of what? If I'd done a better job, she wouldn't have been up there."

"It's not your fault, Dr. Sterling," Gina said. "I thought it was, but now I know better."

"What do you mean?"

"I was in love with you and I wanted to hurt you because you didn't love me back."

"Gina, if I did or said anything to give you that idea, I'm sorry. You're a patient and I'm your doctor, nothing more."

"I know that now. I think I knew it then, but I was so depressed and you were the only one I could talk to. I don't have anybody else."

"But you will. We've been over that."

"Yeah, I know. It's just that I don't make friends easy. But now that I'm cured of both my depression and of you, I'm going to try."

"Cured?" Sandy said. "How do you know?"

"I was so sure I wanted to die when I let go, but right after I did it, I screamed for help. Then I knew I didn't want to die, but it was too late. I tensed up, waiting for the end, but it didn't happen. You grabbed my arm and that man up front grabbed me from below. It was a hell of a way to find out, but I want to live, I know that now. You won't find me out on any more balconies or on any more psychiatrist's couches either."

"Good for you."

"Yeah, good for me." She looked out the window toward the sea. "See that boat out there?" she said.

Sandy turned and saw a white sailboat backlit by the setting sun. "Yeah?"

"That's an Island Packet. They make good cruising boats. I wish I was on it and I wish it was setting out to sea. I'd give anything to be back out on the ocean again."

"Even though it took your parents?"

"The sea didn't kill them. It was that freighter. You can get killed just as easily in a car, but you don't blame the road, do you?"

"I never looked at it that way. When did you decide that you wanted to go back?"

"Right after I let go and fell off that balcony."

"She sounds pretty normal to me, Doc." Norton

laughed.

"She's sounding more normal every minute," Sandy said. Then to Gina, "I've got a niece, Dylan, who's into sailing like nobody's business. Has it into her head that someday she's going to solo around the world. She can sail the hell out of a boat in most any weather, but she doesn't know the first thing about cruising."

"What's cruising?" Alvarez said from the front.

"That's what we call long haul sailing," Gina said. "People who live on boats call it cruising."

"She just bought a thirty footer that she wants to sail to Mexico next summer," Sandy said. "It needs a lot of work. She's looking for someone to help her refit it and maybe go down there with her. Somebody who knows boats."

"I know boats," Gina said.

"I know you do. The pay wouldn't be great, but you could live on the boat so you wouldn't have any rent."

"Where is it?"

"Back there. In the Long Beach Marina. You can see it from the hotel."

"How come she just didn't buy a Swan or some other fancy boat? Your family's rich, right?"

"Nobody gets a free lunch in this family. Dylan worked three summers and after school to save up for that boat. It's been an all consuming passion with her."

"How much money does she have to put into it?"

"Not much. She paid twenty thousand for it. That's quite an accomplishment for a girl who's going to school and has to buy her own clothes."

"She has to buy her own clothes?"

"Only if she doesn't want to go naked in the world."

"Then how would she pay me? How would she pay to

buy the parts, epoxy, varnish and everything else she's gonna need? Refitting a boat can be pretty expensive."

"A hole in the ocean you pour money in," Alvarez said from the front seat as he hung a left on Redondo Boulevard.

"She won't be paying you or be paying for the parts," Sandy said. "She told me on her fifteenth birthday that she wanted to sail around the world. That's how long she's been into this. She worked at Sears during the summer and on the weekends during the school year, saving for her dream. In a year she'd saved five thousand dollars. She was so proud. So for her sixteenth birthday I gave her an IOU instead of a gift. A promissory note to match whatever she spent on the boat. On her eighteenth birthday she paid twenty thousand dollars for *Wind Song* and called in the IOU. I'm to match the funds in salaries and repairs. Do you want the job?"

"Why didn't you tell me about this earlier?"

"Earlier you weren't ready. I told Dylan about you. We've been waiting."

"For what?"

"For now. You're ready. You're cured, remember? No more balconies or psychiatrist's couches for you. How about I buy you dinner? Just friends and we talk about it?" He'd failed her up on the balcony, but he didn't want to fail her now. He desperately wanted her to take the job. It would be good for her and good for Dylan. Two birds with one stone.

"I'd like that," she said.

"Can you turn around?" Sandy said. "My car's parked by that theater on Fourth. The one that shows the old time movies."

"Sorry, Doc. No can do. We gotta take her to a

hospital and fill out a report."

"Is that really necessary?"

"Rules are rules," Norton said.

"Don't worry about it, Dr. Sterling. I'll go to the hospital. They'll observe me overnight and let me go in the morning, long as I don't foam at the mouth. I don't mind, because it's the last time head problems are gonna get me in trouble."

"Atta girl," Norton said.

"Then can you give me a ride back after?" Sandy said.

"No problem, Doc," Alvarez said.

The clock on his dash said a quarter to eleven as Sandy eased into the parking place across from the theater. There wasn't a soul around. The street light above was out and it was a moonless night. There were no lights coming from the theater, but there was enough light from the stars above for him to read the marquee. Casablanca and The Maltese Falcon. Just reading it flooded him with images. Morocco and spies, bad guys and private eyes. Since he was a child, Sandy had been able to lose himself in a good movie.

He'd been a closet hero all his life. Identifying with the good guys on the silver screen. Always afraid he'd never measure up. Maybe it was because, like Simon, he'd always lived in Stacy's shadow. Stacy had excelled at everything—school, sports, girls—leaving the younger boys in his wake. Simon had compensated by learning everything he could about the hotel business. When it got too much for Sandy, he lost himself in the movies.

The pressure had always been on the younger brothers. Teachers, coaches, friends. Stacy got all As. If he can do it, you can too. Stacy made the honor roll. Why can't you? Stacy was the quarterback, Simon and Sandy didn't even make the team, instead they ran track. But none of the criticism had ever come from their parents. And none from Stacy. Whenever one of them was in trouble, Stacy was there to bail them out. If a bigger kid picked on them, he faced Stacy's wrath. When Mrs. Pickett threatened Sandy with an F in typing, Stacy sweet talked her into giving him a C. When Simon sneaked out their father's Corvette and wrecked it on his sixteenth birthday, Stacy took the blame. Sandy and Simon worshiped Stacy and the ground he walked on.

Because of that, Sandy was looking over the last few hours, worrying about how they'd affect Stacy and his campaign. They were calling him a hero, but he knew better. He wondered just how long it would take them to see his failure. She'd let go. Only by lying was he able to get close enough. Luckily Alvarez got her from the balcony below. And luckily Norton got him from above. It worked out okay, but lying and luck, not his skill as a psychiatrist, had saved the day. And it worried him. When the heat of the moment had passed, when they were able to see, they'd see that he'd failed, that she'd let go. And Sandy wondered how that would affect Stacy.

His cell phone rang.

He picked it up off the seat, said, "Hello."

"Color blind!" Stacy shouted. "You son of a bitch, I think you just made me president! I didn't really think I'd get it this time around. No one did. But you've really put me in the race. You should quit that doctor job and be my campaign manager. You're smarter than all these guys I got working for me." Sandy wanted to interrupt, but Stacy was pumped and his excitement was infectious. It always had been. "You know if I make it, it'll be because of you and what you did and said tonight. I just wanted you to know that."

"I was just lucky," Sandy said.

"And you managed to scuttle that asshole that's been after Gayle's job at the same time. You are some kind of genius. I love you, little brother."

"So you liked the Asshole Nesbitt thing?" Sandy said.

"Liked it? No, I didn't like it, I bloody loved it. That dickhead has no business being in front of a camera. Besides, he hates my guts, has the hots for Gayle and is after her job to boot. You flushed him. You were fucking wonderful."

"This is a cell phone. Not too secure," Sandy said.

"I don't care. Nesbitt's a dickhead and you're fucking wonderful. I gotta go. I just wanted to say thanks. You're always thinking of me, you and Si. Without you two, I'd have to fold my tent and go home. Thanks. Thank you. I can't say it enough."

"See you when you get back," Sandy said and they hung up.

He saw a light come on inside the theater. An office door opened. He saw her through the glass, framed in a doorway of light. He assumed it was an office. There were two men and a woman with her. He saw them clearly as they moved like ghostly shapes through the lobby. One of the men opened the front door as Sandy was opening the door to his Toyota. He had a foot on the pavement when his cell phone rang again.

* * *

At 11:55 the cab pulled up to the Tom Bradley International Terminal at Los Angeles International Airport. Taylor paid the cabby and the girls took their carry-on baggage inside. Haley hoped Taylor's father would be there to meet them.

"This way," Taylor said, and she started off toward the Quantas counter.

"Taylor!" The voice rang through the terminal. Stacy had made it after all. Haley was glad. There was nothing he couldn't make right. She turned, but it wasn't Stacy Sterling charging through the lobby toward them.

"Uncle Sandy," Taylor said as he wrapped her in a hug.

"Sandy," Haley said, smiling.

CHAPTER

FIVE

GAYLE CAME OUT OF A GROGGY SLEEP unable to move, but conscious about where she was. She blinked her eyes against the light. She felt something in her throat. A tube. It irritated her, but it didn't hurt. She couldn't close her mouth. Instinctively she tried to swallow, but the tube prevented it. She felt a rising panic, fought to control it. Her heart was taking off. She closed her eyes.

Calm, she mentally told herself. You have to stay calm. She flexed her fingers, felt them curl. She wasn't paralyzed. Not the hands anyway, but she couldn't feel her toes. At least she didn't think she could feel them. She tried flexing them. Couldn't.

Again her heart started up.

Again she forced herself not to panic. It was going to be okay. It had to be okay.

"How you going?" She recognized Dave's voice, opened her eyes.

She tried to smile, but couldn't. She made a circle with the thumb and index finger of her right hand, signifying okay.

"Good, can you move your toes?" He lifted the sheet off of her legs. She wanted to tell him she'd just tried and couldn't. And she wanted to ask him why he was asking, but she couldn't talk.

"Can you move your toes?" He said it again.

She stared at him, worried now, but he didn't look too concerned, so maybe it was routine. She closed her eyes and focused. She tried to move the big toe on her right foot, but she couldn't feel it. Somehow the message wasn't getting through.

"Try the left," he said.

She opened her eyes. He didn't appear worried yet. He was wearing that same warm smile. She clenched her hands into tight fists, closed her eyes again and wiggled the toes on her left foot. All of them.

"Don't worry about the other one. It's stuffed full of pins. You'll get movement there soon enough." He had dimples in his cherubic cheeks. She still didn't think he looked very much like a doctor. More like a grown up Charlie Brown, with hair.

She tried to smile and felt that tube again. She put the thumb, index and middle finger of her left hand together and made a writing motion.

"She wants to write something." Gayle recognized Anna's voice and wondered if she'd fixed her eye. She raised her right hand and pointed to it. "Yes," she said. "You might have a slight scar, but it'll be hardly noticeable and with makeup you can hide it completely."

She made the writing motion again.

"Just a second," Dave said.

"Here, doctor." A nurse handed her a pad and pencil. She smiled down at Gayle. She was young. Dylan's age. She wanted to know about Dylan so she wrote,

My daughter?

"Dylan's fine," Dave said. "You don't have to worry about her. You were both very lucky."

Lucky, Gayle thought. Maybe lucky to be alive, but her luck sure took a turn for the worse when that car plowed into her. She put the pencil back to the paper and wrote,

Tube out!

"Sorry," Dave said. "If I take the tube out and you fall asleep, you'll die."

Won't Sleep!

He took the pencil and paper from her hand as she drifted off. He left the tube in.

* * *

"How'd you get a ticket?" Taylor asked. "The flight's sold out. Freddy Carson had to pull strings to get us on."

"I have a few strings of my own I can pull," Sandy said. They were in line at the Quantas desk. Incredibly, there were only a couple of people ahead of them. "I talked to your father just before I found out, but when I called him back I didn't get an answer. Just that recording saying that my party was out of the area. I hate that."

"Freddy told me he turns his phone off when he's in the middle of important appointments or dinner and forgets to turn it back on again."

"I'd just talked to him."

"Maybe he wasn't calling from his cellular," Haley said.

"That's probably it. Anyway, he doesn't know."

"I'm glad you came," Taylor said. Sandy hugged her. Haley stood behind him and she saw Taylor whisper something in his ear as they broke the hug. Sandy turned and Haley fell into his open arms. She hugged him too tightly, but she couldn't help herself.

"Our turn," Taylor said and Sandy released Haley from the hug before moving up to the ticket desk. The woman behind the counter was tall and Asian with jet black hair pulled into a ponytail. She had large, almond shaped black eyes and teeth to die for. Haley thought she was the most beautiful woman she'd ever met, face to face.

"Can I help you?" Not a hint of accent in her voice.

"I believe you have a couple of tickets for these young ladies," Sandy said. "Taylor Sterling and Haley Harrison. I love that name." He turned from the girl behind the counter to Haley and gave her one of his wide smiles. It was as if Sandy hadn't noticed the Quantas woman, as if he was giving all of his attention to her. She was in heaven.

"Yes, sir." The woman pulled the first copy from the

tickets, then handed them to Sandy, along with their boarding passes. "Thirty-four A and B. Non smoking."

"And I believe you've made arrangements for me? Dr. Sterling." Sandy was all smiles for the girl now.

"Yes." She pulled the first copy and handed him his ticket. "The plane will start boarding in about twenty minutes, enjoy your flight. Oh, and Dr. Sterling, if you like you can wait in the crew's lounge once you're in the terminal. Or you can make yourself known at the gate and board with the rest of the passengers. It's up to you."

"Thank you," Sandy said.

Haley was so happy. He didn't give the woman a second glance, not really. She was floating. He really was sweet, but she wondered why they were treating him so special.

"You didn't get a boarding pass," she said after they'd passed through security.

"I'm flying up front. With the flight crew."

"How'd you swing that?" Taylor asked.

"Connections."

"Really?" Taylor said.

"A patient of mine works for Quantas."

"Does he have a good job?"

"Good enough," Sandy said.

"And you called him in the middle of the night?"

"He's called me in the middle of the night often enough." Then he said, "Anybody hungry? I'm starved."

"I could eat," Haley said and she linked arms with him and started toward the cafeteria.

"If you two don't look like the perfect couple," Taylor said. Haley swelled with her words. Although they were dressed decades apart—Sandy looked as if he'd just stepped out of a gangster movie and she was wearing a chic silk blouse with tight Levi's and a pair of old Nikes, very New Millennium—they did make a picture perfect couple.

In the cafeteria line she took only a salad while Sandy heaped food on his plate. "I can't help it," he apologized. "I've had a rough day."

"We saw it on television. Haley said you were very brave." Taylor smiled as Haley felt the blood rushing to her head.

"Brave or stupid, it doesn't make any difference. I failed that girl. If I'd done my job she wouldn't have been up there in the first place."

"That's nonsense," Haley said. "You can't be responsible for every second of your patient's lives. Besides, you saved her life."

"Yeah, I guess." He set his tray at a table. Haley took the seat to his right and Taylor sat across from him. They spent a few minutes eating in silence, then Sandy said, "I'm thinking about selling my practice."

"What?" both girls said at once.

"I'm having a hard enough time taking care of myself. I need a break from everyone else's problems."

"You can do that? Sell your patients?" Haley said.

"I have a very good friend, Sandra Madrigal. She takes over for me when I'm on vacation, which is a lot. My patients all like her, it wouldn't be like I was abandoning them. Maybe I'll give her a call."

"The lady shrink you used to date?" Taylor said. Haley felt like her heart skipped a beat or two.

"We never really dated, we had dinner a couple of times," he said and Haley sighed.

"What about the girl that was up on that balcony? Won't she feel like you're cutting her loose?" Taylor said.

"Ah, Gina. Gina Sealy," Sandy said. "She'll still be in my life, probably for a long time."

"I don't get it," Haley said. "How, if you sell your practice?"

"Whether I keep my practice or not has nothing to do with it. She's no longer a patient. She had some emotional problems, but she's cured."

"Pretty big problems if they led her to that balcony," Taylor said.

"Yeah," Sandy said, "pretty big. Her parents and younger brother died when their boat sank off the coast of Mexico three months ago. That's why she was up there."

That's horrible," Taylor said.

"Yeah," Sandy said. "She's got no one, so she fell in love with me. Sometimes it happens, you have to guard against it. She thought I was using the vacation time to get rid of her, so she decided to end it all. Anyway, she's over it. I'm convinced she's better now."

"That poor kid. What's she going to do?" Haley said.

"Actually she's not a kid, she's eighteen. She's got a job in a video store on Second Street in Belmont Shore, but I guess she's going to quit."

"Why?"

"This is the good part. I've hired her to work with Dylan on *Wind Song*."

"You're kidding?"

"She's going to live on the boat while they're fixing it up."

"You're serious?" Taylor said.

"Never more. She's honest and she won't cheat Dylan by over charging for labor or getting her to buy parts she doesn't need."

"How do you know that?" Haley asked.

She doesn't need to work," Sandy said. "There was an insurance policy and her parents had a house and some money in the bank, but she won't touch it. She wants to give it all away."

"For God sakes, why?"

"She doesn't want money because her family died. She wants it all to go to Greenpeace. Fortunately I've talked her out of it. At least up till now. I got her to agree to put it in a bank and not to touch it for a year. Then if she still feels that way, she can give it away."

"Looks like they're getting ready to board," Taylor said. She started to get up and Haley saw her wince.

"What's wrong?"

"Nothing. It's not like before, just a little twinge, like an electric shock, Dylan must be thinking about me."

Sandy rolled his eyes, but Haley took Taylor's hand and gave it a squeeze. "You sure it's okay?"

"Yeah, I think so," Taylor said, then they boarded the plane.

Haley automatically took the window. She slept on flights, the twins didn't. They hated crawling over her every time they wanted to get out and true to form, Haley was asleep seconds after they were off the ground.

* * *

"You're back with the living," Dave said as Gayle opened her eyes. His smile was as large as ever and she wondered how someone could have a job like his and be so up all the time.

"You look a thousand percent better," Anna said. It was a relief to hear. Maybe it wasn't as bad as she'd originally thought.

"Do you still want the tube out?" Dave asked.

She made a thumbs up signal and closed her eyes. She felt the tube being eased out of her throat. It was an eerie sensation, like her insides were slipping up and out through her mouth.

"Do you know your name?" Dave asked.

"Gayle Sterling." Her voice was hoarse.

"If you turn your head a little to the left you can see your daughter. They're bringing her out of ICU."

She turned and saw Dylan as she was being wheeled by.

"Hi," she said, voice raspy, "how you doing?"

"Okay," Dylan answered, dreamy-eyed and obviously sleepy.

"They'll bring her by tomorrow," Dave said.

"Love you," Gayle said.

"Love you too," Dylan mumbled, then she was gone.

Gayle looked at the tube going from the IV into her left arm. There was another into the back of her hand. "Really hooked up, aren't I, Dave?"

"There's another one in your back, so be careful when you move around. I'll get that one out as soon as possible."

"Thanks," she said, then she drifted off to sleep.

"How do you feel?" Gayle was getting tired of that question. She opened her eyes as a young nurse was putting a blood pressure cuff on her arm.

"I don't know. Woozy, I guess."

"Here comes the doctor. Tell him about woozy," the nurse said.

"Hi."

"Hello, Dave," Gayle said.

"Want to know what I did?" He bent over and looked

at her eye.

"I guess."

"Anna did a nice job with those stitches. The scar will hardly show."

"And my leg?"

"I nailed it. That means I put a metal rod in it. Also I relocated your toes and set the bones. You're going to have to stay off it for at least eight weeks. Relax, enjoy yourself. You're gonna be fine."

"And Dylan? How's she doing?" Gayle said. "Really."

"She had a collapsed lung. They say she had a hard night. But it looks like she's past the worst of it."

She closed her eyes. Her last thought before she sailed back into sleep was of Dylan.

* * *

"Open your eyes, sleepy head. We're landing."

"What time is it?" Haley asked.

"Seven-thirty in the morning. We're an extra day older because we've crossed the Date Line," Taylor said.

Haley looked out the window as the plane lost altitude. The ocean looked the same, but she got a sense of cold. It was winter down there, winter in June. Then the wheels squeaked down on the numbers and the plane was slowing on the runway as the pilot applied the brakes.

"I can't believe it," Taylor said, "you've been in and out of sleep since we took off. It was like you shut down for the whole last half of the flight. Sandy came back a couple of times, but we decided not to wake you. You always sleep on airplanes, I wish I could."

"Flying scares me, so I turn off," Haley said.

"I never knew that."

"It's not something I'm proud of."

The plane stopped at the gate and the passengers unfolded themselves from their seats. Haley pulled their carry-on bags out of the overhead locker. She hated everything about flying, The take off, the flight, the landing, but most of all she hated the end of a flight, everybody standing in the crowded aisle waiting for the door to open. She felt like she was packed in, stuffed in a coffin. She shrugged it off as the door opened and people started to move, like moles inching their way out from under the ground.

They followed the crowd to immigration, where they spent fifteen minutes in line waiting for their passports to be stamped. Then they went through the green customs lane and found Sandy waiting for them. He'd cleared straightaway, going through with the flight crew.

"I just got off the phone with the hospital. Your mother and sister are both doing fine," he said to Taylor. "Your mom has a fractured femur and she broke all the bones in her right foot. It looks like she's going to be out of commission for awhile. I suppose that's good news for the Asshole Nesbitt."

"And Dylan?" Taylor asked.

"She had a rough go. She had a collapsed lung and they reinflated it. She's doing better now. I talked to Dr. Keith who did the procedure. He told me she's out of danger. She should be out of the hospital in about a week and good as new in less than a month."

"Thank God." Taylor sighed. "I was so worried. But I was pretty hopeful because I haven't felt anything since just before we left."

"I thought you said that was nothing," Haley said.

"It probably wasn't."

"Now we have another plane to catch," Sandy said as

Haley caught him rolling his eyes again.

"Another plane?" Haley shot him a look.

"Yeah, a small charter. They've been waiting for us." He winked at Haley. Then a uniformed flight attendant led them through the airport over to the domestic side. In minutes they were aboard a small twin engine craft, shooting down the runway. Haley hardly had the sense of being in a foreign country and she was airborne again, sitting in the back seat next to Taylor. Sandy was in front sitting next to a dashing young pilot with a movie star's face.

The flight took about an hour and Haley spent it looking out the window at the magical landscape below. So many blue harbors, snow covered mountains, farms and lots of very cold looking sheep. She wished she'd had more than just a small salad at the airport in L.A. because she'd slept through all the meals on the plane. Now she was hungry and looking forward to a big breakfast as soon as they landed. Dylan and Gayle were going to be fine. Relief flooded through her, cleansing the gloomy blues away.

"You're staying at the Sterling Hotel. It's right on the waterfront," the pilot said. He seemed young to be a pilot. Maybe twenty or twenty-one, but he was flying straight and level. He was square-jawed, blue-eyed handsome and Haley found herself attracted to him, despite the fact that Sandy was right there.

A taxi was waiting for them when they touched down. The driver, like the pilot, was young and good looking. Haley was beginning to wonder if all Kiwis were movie star material. "It's about a fifteen minute ride to your hotel. Check in has already been handled," the driver said and Haley realized he wasn't a taxi driver. He was some kind of policeman and they were in a plain clothes police car, not a cab. "Once you've settled your bags and had breakfast, I'll take you to the hospital. Dr. Collins is expecting you at 10:00, so you've got plenty of time to refresh yourselves." He pulled up in front of the hotel. The girls followed Sandy into the lobby.

"I have to use the bathroom," Taylor said. "I'll catch up with you guys."

"I gotta go too," Haley said and she followed Taylor into the restroom in the lobby. She was barely through the door when Taylor grabbed her chest and doubled over. "What is it?"

"Chest hurts, and I feel week. We have to go to Dylan." Sweat covered Taylor's forehead, her face had gone white, but last time it happened she looked scared and hurt, this time she just looked sick.

"Sandy," Haley said, but Taylor wasn't listening. She'd dropped her carry-on bag and was headed out the door. Haley dropped her bag next to Taylor's and followed.

The policeman was still outside, standing next to his car.

"Take me to the hospital. Now!" Taylor said.

He must have seen the look of desperation in her eyes, because he opened the door to the back and said, "Get in." Haley jumped in after Taylor as the handsome officer started the car. He jumped on the gas. Time turned to a blur as he sped through the center of town. Haley barely noticed anything outside her window. Then they were at the hospital. The policeman said he'd wait with the car and told them how to get the elevator up to the fifth floor and the heart and lung section, where Dylan was.

A doctor was sitting in the nurses' station pulling the

cellophane off of a sandwich when they stepped out of the elevator.

"Hello there, where can we find Dylan Sterling's room?" Haley said.

"Twins?" the doctor questioned, looking at Taylor.

"I was going to tell you," a nurse said to him. "Your patient is Mrs. Stacy Sterling as in Senator Stacy Sterling, maybe the next President of the United States."

"Senator yes," Taylor said. "President, maybe. But right now we need to see my sister."

"You came so quickly."

"We're close, Dr. Collins," Haley said, reading his name from the badge on his chest, "and in a hurry, could you show us to where Dylan is?"

"She's in room seventy-three. Second door on your right." The nurse pointed it out.

"Same name," Haley said, reading the nurse's badge. "Married?"

"Yes," Rachel Collins said.

Taylor turned and headed toward Dylan's room. Haley hurried after her. They entered the room and found four beds. Dylan's was the only one occupied. She was lying on her back, eyes closed. Taylor gasped and Haley went straight to the bed and took Dylan's hand. It felt clammy. Sweat ringed her forehead. Haley wiped it away. Dylan was cold, despite the sweat. Her lips had a blue tinge to them.

"Oh, Dylan, don't die," Taylor said. She'd moved around to the other side of the bed and was holding her sister's other hand.

Dylan opened her eyes.

"I'm here, Dylan," Taylor whispered through trembling lips. A single tear tracked down her cheek.

"I knew you'd come," Dylan said, voice soft, like she was under the covers and the sound was filtered through the blankets. She forced a tired smile. Her palomino hair was spread around her head on the pillow, like an angelic halo. Taylor ran her thumb back and forth on her sister's palm as she held her hand.

"Looking for that old electric feeling?" Dylan said.

"I found it," Taylor said. "That tingle is still there."

"But not too strong now," Dylan said.

"I love you, Dylan."

"Oh, Taylor," Dylan said. Her sweet voice pierced Haley to the heart. Haley squeezed her hand. Dylan gently squeezed back. "You too, Haley. I love you girls."

"Don't go, Dylan," Taylor said.

"It's not up to me."

"I know," Taylor said.

"Hold me."

Taylor climbed up on the bed. She lay next to her sister and Dylan rolled into her arms. Taylor hugged her in to herself. Haley ran her hand through Dylan's hair. Sweat oozed out from Dylan's body. She was so cold. Taylor and Dylan were cheek to cheek, tears mingling, holding each other like young lovers when Dylan sighed. "It's not so bad," she said. Taylor kissed her as she sighed her last breath away.

"Get off, Taylor! Now!" Haley pulled her off the bed. "I need a doctor!" Haley screamed.

"Help her, Haley!" Taylor cried.

Haley pinched Dylan's nose with her right hand, her chin with her left, pulling it down. She clamped her mouth over Dylan's and started to breathe in.

"What's going on?" Dr. Collins said, then he saw. "Crash cart! Stat!" He touched two fingers to a carotid artery. "No pulse. Hurry with that cart!"

Haley breathed in, counted to three and let the air out, then did it again. Over and over. Dylan's body jerked, but Haley kept breathing. The jerking stopped, but Haley kept on. Dylan shuddered a final time. Then she was still.

"She's dilated," Rachel Collins said. "She's gone."

CHAPTER SIX

HALEY FOUND HER SITTING in the nurses' station. She was in a red Naugahyde chair with stainless steel armrests, the kind of chair that belonged in one of those '50s diners that were being recreated all over America. She was bent at the waist, sobbing.

She took in the picture of her friend. She seemed so alone in this strange place. Lost. Crying. Taylor never cried, she just didn't.

"I couldn't stay," she said. "I knew she was gone. I saw them cover her up."

"It's okay," Haley said. "I'm sure she understood."

"She died in my arms."

"Oh, sweet Lord." Haley dropped to the floor at Taylor's side, knees hitting hard. She wrapped her arms around her. Taylor hugged her back.

"What's going on?" Sandy said. Taylor looked up, unable to speak. Tears streamed down her face. Sandy had his hands at his side, flexing his fingers. His lower lip was quivering. He must have rushed right to the hospital when he'd noticed they'd gone from the hotel.

"Dylan died," Haley said through her own tears. Taylor's hair hung in her face. Haley brushed it back with her hands. It was silky, soft, and slick with tears.

"But they said she was doing okay," he stammered. He stared at the girls for a few seconds, then sighed and nodded. "I'm sorry, baby."

"Oh, Uncle Sandy." Taylor jumped out of the chair, pulling Haley to her feet as she stood. "They covered her up and now they're gonna take her away. She's gonna be all alone. Cold and alone."

Haley didn't know what to say. She couldn't talk.

"Easy, baby," Sandy said.

"She was alive when I got here," Taylor said. "She was waiting for me so she could die. I tasted her last breath."

Taylor had an arm linked around Haley's waist. Haley tightened her grip on Taylor as shudders rippled through her own body, building to a crescendo. She was an only child and the twins had been sisters to her. They had always been the three musketeers. She couldn't remember her life without them in it and now Dylan was gone. "So sad," she said, and the tears came like rain, followed by racking sobs.

"Easy, Hale, easy. Come on, girl. It's going to be okay." Taylor was crying even as she was trying to soothe Haley's pain.

"I can't—" Haley sobbed, unable to finish. Taylor and Sandy helped her into the chair Taylor had been sitting in seconds ago. This time it was Taylor on her knees, arms around Haley. "I'm sorry." Haley sniffed, trying to stop herself, but her emotions were out of control. She didn't know humans could feel such pain, such grief. She bent over and buried her face. She hurt so bad. So bad.

And she could only imagine how Taylor felt.

"Come on, girls. Dylan wouldn't want this," Sandy said, but they stayed the way they were, Haley in the chair, Taylor on her knees, arms wrapped around each other.

After a few minutes Haley said, "I'm alright, now, I think."

"Me too," Taylor said. This time it was Haley who helped Taylor to her feet. She looked around the room. Dr. Collins and his wife were standing next to Sandy. Dr. Collins looked compassionate, caring. Rachel Collins had been crying and that struck Haley as odd. She must see death all the time.

"You're family?" Dr. Collins said to Sandy.

"Yes," Sandy said. Not whispering, but not his usual forward self either.

"Dr. Sterling," Dr. Collins said in recognition.

"Sandy. Have we met?"

"I'm Dave. No, we haven't met. I caught a rerun of American psychiatry in action on Headline News. That was a brave thing you did."

"I was lucky. Does Gayle know?"

"Not yet," Dr. Collins said. "I was going to tell her as soon as we'd gotten Taylor settled. I thought she might want to stay for the day. We have a couple of beds available in Mrs. Sterling's room, but maybe you have other plans."

"We have rooms at the Sterling," he said. He bit his lip. Haley thought he did it to keep from crying. He wouldn't cry. Not him. "I'll tell her."

"I'd like to be there. She's my patient."

"Of course," Sandy said.

"We should do it as soon as possible. Mrs. Sterling is awake and alert," Dr. Collins said. Haley wondered how many times he'd had to do this, tell someone that a loved one had died. She was going to Stanford in the fall. Premed. But right now she didn't think she wanted to be a doctor anymore. Dr. Collins looked down at Haley and Taylor. "My wife will stay with you, and if you need anything, she'll see that you get it."

"No," Taylor mumbled. "I have to go, too."

"Alright," Dr. Collins said, "I understand."

Haley and Taylor embraced tightly, cheek to cheek. Haley tasted her friend's salty tears. "You can't go like this." She pulled out of the hug. "Does someone have a washcloth or a towel?"

"Here," Rachel Collins said. She was holding a damp washcloth.

"Thank you." Haley took it. Gently she wiped the tears from her friend's face. "We can't go to Mom crying," she said. Gayle Sterling had always been Mom to her. Although her parents loved her in their own way, they'd always been kind of distant. She'd had the best of everything as she'd grown up, but the love money can't buy came from Gayle Sterling, who'd loved her and cuddled her as if she had been one of her own.

"Now let me do you." Taylor took the cloth. Haley closed her eyes as Taylor wiped her face. "Okay, Hale, we're ready. We can go now." The girls linked hands and followed Dr. Collins and Sandy as they walked through the halls.

A young male nurse was coming toward them, pushing an empty gurney. Dark black hair cascaded over his shoulders. His light brown face was covered with geometric, blue tattooed swirls. "Taylor, did you see that?" Haley whispered, squeezing her friend's hand after he wheeled the gurney past.

"Yeah," Taylor said.

"He's Maori," Dr. Collins said by way of explanation.

"Do they all do that? Tattoo their faces, I mean," Taylor said.

"No."

"He was beautiful," Haley said.

"Yeah," Taylor answered.

"Most foreigners don't think so," Dr. Collins said. "It usually takes a while for them to get used to it." He made a left and they were walking down a long hallway between wings. Glassed windows on both sides reminded Haley of a concourse at Heathrow airport in London. Clouds were moving across a dark morning sky. It started to rain. It was turning into a blustery day.

They turned right at the end of the hallway and passed another nurses' station, where an elderly nurse looked up from behind a counter. Dr. Collins nodded to her. She nodded back, then looked away. Bad news travels fast in a hospital.

"We're here." He stopped. "This isn't a private hospital. There's three other women in the room with her. Right now they're strangers, but they're about to become friends."

"What do you mean?" Sandy asked.

"Death brings people close," he said.

Then he was through the door and in the room, Sandy at his side. Taylor hesitated. Haley felt her tension. Any second she was going to break.

"Come on." Haley gave her friend a firm squeeze, fighting her own tears, as they stepped into the hospital room.

Sunlight streaked through the high windows. There were three hospital beds with retractable rails on each side of the room. The center bed on each side was unoccupied. A porcelain basin was on the back wall, next to a television on a movable stand. The room was clean and antiseptic.

"Dave. Oh, Sandy," Gayle said. "Taylor, Haley. I was expecting you, but not so soon." She ran a hand through her mussed up hair. "I look a mess."

"You look fine," Sandy said. "You always do." He spoke softly, almost a whisper.

"I don't. I look like I just lost a fight with Godzilla. I have a horrible black eye and my hair looks like a rat's nest. Oh, girls, you've been crying," She said. "It's bad, but it's not awful. We're going to be fine."

"Dylan didn't make it," Sandy said. The girls were still holding hands, standing shoulder to shoulder. Taylor stiffened with her uncle's words and for a second Haley thought she was going to crush her hand, but then she relaxed her grip with a sad sigh. She was crying again, silent tears.

"Dr. Dave says I'll be good as new in seven or eight weeks and Dylan—" She stopped in midsentence. "What do you mean?"

"Dylan's dead, Gayle." He took her hand. The woman in the bed nearest the window gasped. She was older, with silver hair. She'd been sitting up, reading. She dropped the book in her lap and wrapped her arms around herself.

"No, it's not true," Gayle said. "I saw her. She was sleepy, but she was alive. She talked to me."

Haley was crying now as she saw a shudder ripple through the frail woman in the bed. She loved Gayle. This was too much. She was feeling light headed.

"I'm sorry, Gayle," Dr. Collins said. "It's true."

"No, you told me she was going to be fine. You said not to worry." She tried to push herself up, but Dr. Collins held her down. At first it looked like she was going to resist, to fight him, but then her shoulders sagged and she lay back.

"I was wrong."

"Help me," Haley murmured. Then she was falling.

"Haley!" Taylor jerked on her hand, trying to hold her up. The room was spinning. Hot. Taylor pulled her into herself, holding her tightly. "Don't fall."

"I'm okay, now," Haley said. Her knees felt wobbly. "Maybe I should sit."

"Let me help." Sandy moved to her other side. There was another of those red chairs by the television and they started to lead her to it.

"Maybe she should lie down," Dr. Collins said.

"No, just a few seconds and I'll be okay," Haley said and they helped her take the few steps to the chair. She sat and bent forward with her head between her legs to try and keep from passing out. Taylor took her hand.

"You gonna be okay?" she asked. Haley nodded, took a deep breath and straightened up. Dr. Collins was holding Gayle's hand. She had tears in her eyes, but she wasn't crying. Somewhere a phone rang.

"Yeah," Haley said. "I guess."

"Mr. Sterling's on the phone." The speaker was an older nurse. Silver hair and a thin lipped smile, but despite her spinster looks, Haley got the sense of a caring person.

"Stacy?" Gayle said.

"Your husband, ma'am," the nurse said. "I can wheel your bed to the phone." Haley looked around the room. There were no phones by the bedsides as in American hospitals.

"Bring one in here," Dr. Collins said. "And get his number. We'll call him back."

"Yes, doctor." She backed out of the room. A few seconds later she pushed a phone on a wheeled table next to Gayle's bed and plugged it in. "Here's the number," she said, handing Dr. Collins a slip of paper.

"Oh, God, what can I say to him?" Gayle said.

"He has to be told," Sandy said.

"I can't do it. I just can't."

"I'll do it." Sandy took the number. Haley was glad he was here to take charge, because there was no way Taylor could tell her father and stay in one piece. And she sure couldn't do it. She watched Sandy dial the number as if she was in a fog looking through a window into a dimly lit room. Wispy gauze curtains covered the window, flowing back and forth from an unfelt breeze. She was floating, barely able to make out his words as he told his brother about the accident, his wife's injuries and his daughter's death.

After a few minutes Sandy handed the phone to Gayle. Haley teared up as she watched her cry into the receiver, then she gave it over to Taylor. She heard her friend murmur that she was alright. Taylor was crying again. Sandy took the phone, said something, then hung up.

"He's still in San Francisco. He'll catch a flight out

today. He wants to bring Dylan home," Sandy said.

"No," Taylor said. "She wants to be buried here." Everyone turned toward her as she spoke. "There's a Maori girl buried all by herself in a small cemetery in a place called Onerahi. She's been alone so long. Dylan wants to keep her company."

"How can you know this, baby?" Gayle said. Haley was coming out of her fog. Now everything was crystal clear. Colors were vibrant, edges sharp, words crisp.

"She told me about her last week when we talked. She said she felt so sorry for that little girl, cold and alone. She wondered about her family. Dylan's her family now. It's what she wants."

"I remember that cemetery. It was beautiful. Tall trees swaying in the breeze. There was a street called Church Street, but there was no church, at least not by the cemetery." Gayle was speaking softly, almost in her television voice, but as if she was afraid someone not far off camera might hear. "We spent an afternoon there, walking among the graves, reading the tombstones. I remember that little girl. Her name was Charlotte and she died in 1838. She was buried in the back of the cemetery, one of the first to be buried there. She was only four years old. I got the impression that later they started putting them up closer to the street. Dylan cried when she read her tombstone."

"We should let Dylan sleep next to Charlotte," Taylor whispered.

"I can take care of it, if that's what you want," Dr. Collins said.

"It's what we want, Dave," Gayle said.

"Shouldn't we check with Stacy first?" Sandy said.

"Daddy would want what Dylan wants," Taylor said.

"And Dylan wants to be with Charlotte." Haley shivered. Taylor was talking about her as if she were still alive.

"Okay, if that's what you want," Sandy said. Then to Dr. Collins, "Is there anything I can to do help?"

"No, it's pretty straight forward. I'll make the calls and take care of it."

"I'd like to go there and handle the arrangements personally," Sandy said. "It's important to me."

"Onerahi is a small town close to Whangarei up in the north," Dave said. "Whangarei's the big smoke up there, but it's really a small city compared to what you're used to. The people are close, but warm. You won't have any trouble. Anyone you meet will want to help. You can fly up on one of the commuter planes."

"How far is it?" Sandy asked.

"About four hundred miles. I can have someone check the flight schedules," Dave said. Sandy nodded and Dave left the room. He returned about fifteen minutes later to say, "I booked you on a three o'clock flight, coming back tomorrow at two. I've written down all the numbers and addresses you'll need and arranged for Hertz to have a rental car waiting for you at the airport."

"That's above the call," Sandy said, "and I appreciate it." Then Dave left and the four of them were alone.

Taylor and Haley spent the day in the hospital. They had lunch with Sandy in the cafeteria before he left for the airport and afterwards they went back to Gayle's room. One of her roommates had been released. That left the woman with the silver hair, whose name was Helen. She was in the hospital because she'd been trying to get her granddaughter's cat out of a tree. Somehow she'd gotten up the tree, a branch broke and so did both her legs when she hit the ground. The other patient was a Maori woman in her middle thirties, another victim of a drunk driver, like Gayle and Dylan. She was suffering from a dislocated shoulder and a broken arm. Both women did their best to help comfort Gayle.

They'd been back with Gayle for about fifteen minutes when Dave and a young nurse came into the room and over to Gayle's bed. "I'm going to take that needle out of your back."

Haley took Taylor's hand and they clutched tightly as the nurse helped Dave roll Gayle onto her side. Haley flinched as he pulled out the needle.

"Didn't feel a thing, did you?" he said.

"Just a chilly sensation running up my spine," Gayle said.

They helped her back onto her back so that she was staring at the ceiling. "Okay, I've got a pin here." Dave showed it to Gayle. He lifted the right side of Gayle's hospital gown and ran the pin across her thigh. "Did you feel that?"

"Yes."

"Good." He moved the pin lower, tickling the side of her leg as he ran it down to her knee. "Feel it?"

"Yes."

"Very good." He ran it below her knee, down toward her bandaged foot. Haley shivered when she saw the spikes sticking out between her toes. "Still feel it?"

"Barely."

"Good, good."

"Good that I can hardly feel it?"

"Good that you feel it at all. You had a local. I'd expect it to be numb." He dropped the pin into a wastebasket that was sitting by the side of the bed.

"Not going to poke me?"

"Not today," Dave said. "But I'm going to send you down to get a cast put on your foot."

"Is that necessary?"

"Very. You broke all the bones in it. It's the only way it'll heal."

"Will I be able to go to my daughter's funeral?" Tears misted her eyes.

"We'll work something out." He turned toward the girls. "You're welcome to spend the night here. We have the beds. If you don't want to do that, we can have a cab take you to your hotel."

"We'll stay," Haley said.

"Yeah, we'll stay," Taylor echoed.

"I'm your taxi driver, Mrs. Sterling." The Maori nurse with the tattooed face pushed a gurney into the room.

"You can call me Gayle."

"Okay, Gayle." He wheeled the gurney next to the bed and two other nurses appeared. The girls stood aside as the three of them slid Gayle from the bed to the gurney. The handsome man with the tattoos turned to the girls. "You're welcome to come, too." His smile was real. Never in all her life would Haley have dreamed that tattoos could make a man so beautiful.

"I'm Haley."

"Danny." The Maori extended his hand. She took it and shivered with the electricity of his touch.

"And this is Taylor."

"I'm sorry about your sister." He took her hand. Taylor nodded. Danny nodded back, then took the gurney and wheeled it out the door, with the girls following.

Six hours later Haley lay looking at the ceiling. Taylor

was asleep in the bed next to hers. Gayle had been moved to the bed next to the window. She was sleeping too. The hospital was quiet. A nurse slipped in, softly not to wake the patients. She checked Gayle's IV and took her blood pressure without waking her. She glided over to the two women on the other side of the room and checked on them, then she slipped out as quietly as she'd entered.

The curtains on the windows were parted and Haley was able to see stars. The Southern Cross was bright in the southern sky, beacon to aviators and sailors. She'd never thought about it before, the fact that the night sky in the southern hemisphere was different from what she was used to. She'd always been a stargazer and now she gazed in awe.

No way could she sleep. She slipped out of bed, shucked the hospital gown and put on her Levi's and blouse. She skipped the shoes. Babies. The new babies. That's just what she needed to feel good about life again. She didn't know where they were, but they were here. All hospitals had them.

The nurses' station was empty. Everybody must be attending patients. Rather than wait around for someone to ask, she decided to take off on her own. She'd find the babies. How hard could it be? In a few minutes she was back in that long corridor between wings. She stopped in the middle and looked out the window, watching the headlights go by outside. She felt like she was alone in the world. She looked up to the Southern Cross and was caught in its majesty.

"Oh, Dylan," she whispered, "we miss you so much."

She felt a hand on her shoulder and jumped.

"Sorry. I didn't mean to scare you." It was Danny the young Maori nurse.

"It's kinda spooky here. So dark outside. The headlights look like shooting stars below and the real stars look like heaven."

"Like you're alone in the middle," he said.

"I was saying a prayer for my friend."

"I saw you crying earlier. You must have been close."

"Yeah. I miss her so much and the day's not even over yet."

"I've seen what you're going through lots of times. It gets better, it really does." He put his hands in his pockets, started rocking on his feet as he talked. He seemed nervous and maybe a little shy.

She reached out and touched his face. He took a hand out of his pocket and pressed it to the back of hers as she felt his cheek, then his chin, then his nose. She dropped her hand and he let go of it.

"I'm sorry. I shouldn't have done that."

"It's okay," he said. "Some foreigners find it disgusting, some think it's amusing, but you're the first that ever liked it."

"It's so beautiful," she said.

"You think?" He smiled.

"Oh, yes."

"Can I buy you a cup of coffee or something?" he said.

"Sure, on one condition. You gotta show me the babies first."

"That's a great idea," he said. "This way." He led her back the way she'd come. "You should have turned right and taken the elevator instead of the way you went. You were headed to the heart lung ward."

"I guess I went that way because it's the only other part of the hospital I know." The elevator doors opened. He pushed a button and in a few seconds they stepped out onto the maternity ward.

There were seven babies behind the glass. Four white and three Maori. Haley put her hands and face to the window. She smiled, roving her eyes from child to child. They were so beautiful.

"This is what it's all about," he said.

"What?"

"Life. People end their lives in all the other parts of the hospital, but here's where it all starts. I love it here. There is nothing prettier than a mother who's just given birth. When you see her eyes when she holds her new child, it's like nothing you've ever seen. It's indescribable. And the new fathers, especially the young ones, all nervous as hell. Then how they puff up after the baby's born, like they did all the work. It's so funny, so touching. It's why I work in a hospital. It renews your faith."

"I wanted to be a doctor," Haley said, "but I don't know if I can do it now. Not after today. I saw Dr. Collins' wife and how Dylan's death hurt her. I couldn't go through that day after day. It would destroy me."

"But she helps a lot of people. She's a good nurse, one of the best. She's never detached the way some get. Every patient's like her own child. She's dedicated, but you're right, I don't think she'll last too long. Burn out rate's pretty high for people who care that much."

"How about you?"

"I keep coming here to get a sense of what it's really all about. Nothing like a new baby testing out his lungs to make me smile and forget all the hurt in the world."

"I should get back," she said. "Can I take a rain check on that coffee till after the funeral?"

"Sure," he said. "I'll walk you back."

Haley eased herself back into the room and changed

back into her hospital gown. She was chilly in it. They were so thin, and open in the back. She was about to crawl into bed when she heard Taylor moan. She was crying in her sleep. She padded over to her friend's bed.

"Taylor," she whispered, gently shaking her. She was shivering in her sleep. Haley shook her a little harder, but she didn't wake. Then she remembered that they'd offered them each a pill to help them sleep. She'd declined, but Taylor had taken the pill and fallen asleep shortly after.

She climbed up onto the bed.

"Shhh, it's going to be okay. Please don't cry."

Her friend rolled over and faced her, eyes closed. Her arms were open and Haley fell into the hug. Like before, she tasted Taylor's tears. Then something happened. Taylor pulled her in tightly, hugging her fiercely. Haley stroked her hair, concentrating on the silky feel of it when all of a sudden Taylor's lips were on hers, her hand was behind her head, pulling her into the kiss.

She quivered as Taylor's tongue snaked into her mouth and she felt like she was going to explode when she felt her friend's hand slide between her legs.

"Taylor," she whispered. "Don't."

Taylor opened her eyes.

"Oh, Hale, I'm so sorry. For a minute I thought you were Dylan."

CHAPTER SEVEN

"I JUST DON'T UNDERSTAND how it could have happened," Stacy Sterling said. Haley and Taylor were still in their hospital gowns. The sun had barely risen, winking through the partially opened curtains when Taylor's dad and Sandy burst into the room. Stacy was tan and handsome. He looked distraught.

"She had a tear in her aorta," Sandy said. "Because it was such a small tear the tube held for awhile. The doctor was new, he saw the chest trauma, treated it and was satisfied that she was out of danger. The next day the aorta ruptured, pouring her entire blood volume into her chest cavity. It was just one of those things."

"An American doctor wouldn't have made a mistake like that." Stacy was angry and Haley thought he needed to be mad at somebody.

"He is an American doctor," Sandy said. "But even an experienced doctor in the best of hospitals could have missed it. I saw the chest x-ray. She didn't have a widened mediastinum, that's the middle compartment of the chest that contains the heart. Not seeing that danger sign, he didn't order an arteriogram."

"What's that?" Stacy asked.

"An x-ray of the heart and aorta performed with special dye," Sandy said.

"So you're saying nothing could have been done?"

"I don't know," Sandy said. "Sometimes these things happen. Medicine's an art as much as a science. If I believed in God, I'd say that it was her time. She wasn't neglected. She didn't get bad care."

"I want to take her home," Stacy said.

"We want to bury her here," Gayle whispered. Tears glistened on her cheeks.

"I don't," Stacy said. "If we bury her here, her death won't mean a thing. I want to take her home and show the world what happens when you drink and drive. Maybe if some kid sees Dylan's face in his mind he might call a cab. Or maybe he won't drink at all. I think that's what Dylan would have wanted."

"Stacy, you're running for president. It'll be a media circus. Not to mention a campaign event," Gayle said. "Your people, their people, everybody will be putting their spin on Dylan's funeral. I'm sorry, I don't want that. Taylor's right, she wants to stay here, with Charlotte."

"Honey, Dylan doesn't care anymore." He was speaking softly, but Haley heard the irritation in his voice.

She couldn't believe it, they seemed to be fighting. "Taylor," Stacy said, rounding on his daughter, "What do you think? Really? Wouldn't it be better if Dylan were buried back in the States, so that her death could mean something?"

"Daddy, please don't. Her *life* meant something. She was good and kind and we all loved her and that's enough. It really is. It's enough." She sounded like she was twelve years old again. Like that girl Sandy had been trying to talk off that balcony. She was lost and her father wasn't making it any easier for her. Couldn't he see what he was doing?

"Honey, what if knowing about her kept some other kid alive, because someone didn't take that drink?" Haley heard his words as she gazed into his sky blue eyes. He was so attractive, so enchanting. Everything he said seemed to be right, even though she knew it was wrong.

"Daddy, I don't care about anyone else and Dylan does care where she sleeps. She wants to be here, with Charlotte. Please, let's just let her sleep in peace." She was crying again. More of those silent tears. Haley's heart went out to her. She got out of her bed and climbed up next to Taylor. She took her hand, letting Stacy and the others know that she was taking sides.

"She's right," Gayle said, closing the subject. "Dylan will be buried next to Charlotte. It will be a quiet and private funeral. We don't have to let the public in on our sorrow, even if you are running for president, Stacy."

"Okay, Gayle, I was just trying to do what I thought was right, but if you and Taylor want her to rest here, then here is where she's going to stay."

"I'm staying, too," Gayle said.

"What?" Stacy's soft whisper went through the room

like a gunshot.

"I want to recover here. Dr. Collins said that I can leave the hospital after a couple of weeks and be an out patient if I want. He says I'll have to do physiotherapy when the cast comes off."

"How long are we talking about?" Stacy asked.

"Six weeks for the cast. The same for the therapy, maybe a little longer."

"We've never been apart that long."

"You could stay here with me."

"I've got a campaign to run. We've got momentum now. It'd be suicide if I took a three month holiday."

"It's not exactly a holiday for me, you know. Wait, I'm sorry, I shouldn't have said that. It wasn't fair."

"It's okay," Stacy said. "We've all had a major shock. None of us is thinking too clearly."

He bent over the bed and kissed her. Haley thought he looked like he was stretched to the limit, so she wasn't surprised when he said he had to go to the hotel and make some calls.

A nurse came in and told the girls that they were welcome to use the showers down the hall. Haley picked up her clothes and left Taylor with her mother. She dropped her hospital gown in the shower room and padded on the cold floor toward the middle of the three showers and pulled the curtain. She stepped into the white tiled stall with a hand on the stainless steel rail. The first blast of water was shivering and woke her right up. She adjusted the spray to warm, then to as hot as she could stand it. She'd always liked showers in hotels, and this was the same, because you could use all the hot water you wanted.

"Are you going to save some for me?" Taylor said. She

was in the shower room, and instinctively Haley's hands went to her breasts. Then she dropped them. She was being stupid. She'd showered naked with Dylan and Taylor plenty of times in gym class. But still she shivered in the hot water, because last night changed everything.

"No way, I'm going to use it all," Haley said. She half expected Taylor to step into the shower with her. She didn't want that, but she didn't want to hurt Taylor either.

"It's a good thing I like it cold then," Taylor said. Haley heard a curtain being drawn. Thank God it wasn't hers. "Brrr, but not this cold," she squealed from the shower stall next to hers.

"It's winter in July." Haley sighed. She'd been worried over nothing.

With that exception, the girls weren't alone together the whole day. They spent the rest of the morning with Gayle, then Dr. Collins dragged them to lunch in the hospital cafeteria, then it was back to Gayle's bedside until 4:30, when Sandy came back to the hospital room. He spent a few minutes talking with Gayle, then asked the girls to dinner.

"We've got some business to take care of at the marina, then dinner at the Sterling. I'm sure you're tired of that hospital food," he said as soon as the elevator doors closed.

"But Sandy, Mom's all alone," Taylor said.

"Dr. Collins will be there. Besides, she said she wanted some time by herself." He was out of the elevator before the doors were completely open, hustling through the hospital.

"Hurry girls," he said, looking at his watch and Haley wondered what business they could possibly have to take care of at a marina.

* * *

Gayle hated using the bedpan, so she waited till she absolutely had to go before ringing for a nurse. She had to go now, was about to ring when Dave came into the room.

"The girls are gone?" He was dressed in jeans and a sweater, not his usual white coated doctor's garb. It was just after five. He was stopping by to check on her before going home.

"Sandy dragged them off to an early dinner. I could tell they didn't want to go, but he has a way about him."

"So for now you're sans family."

"For now. Actually I kind of needed the quiet."

"I don't want to pry, but I'm curious about you all."

"Most people are," Gayle said. "You've heard of Stewart Sterling?"

"Who hasn't?"

"He wasn't the richest man in America, but he wasn't hurting for cash by any means. His first wife died giving birth to her second child, Simon. Less than a year later he created quite a scandal when he married his pregnant housekeeper, Adele."

"And she was black and the kid's Dr. Sterling." He seemed pleased that he'd puzzled it out.

"The Sterlings are a very close knit clan. Bite one and the others bite back. Color has never been an issue with them. In their minds, there are only two kinds of people in the world. Sterlings and everybody else. There's nothing they wouldn't do for each other."

"That explains Dr. Sterling, but your daughter, Haley?"

"Oh, she's not my daughter, although it seems like she is most of the time. She's been calling me Mom since she could talk. Her own parents are very into their respective careers and since they live down the street and since Haley got on so well with my girls, I sort of wound up raising all three."

"But you work?"

"Yeah, I know, but I seem to find time for the kids. It's something you have to want to do. I love them very much and fortunately I had enough love left over for Haley. She needed it and I had it, so it worked out all the way around."

"So if the Sterlings are so rich, how come you work? I'm sorry, that was a dumb question. My family has money and I work."

"That's alright. I work because I have a job I love and I'm good at it. But it wasn't always like that. Stacy and I married during our first year of college. I was a journalism major and he, of course, majored in business. After graduation he went into real estate, and I went to work for the *Los Angeles Times*. Stacy hasn't taken a cent of his inheritance. Neither has Sandy. They've turned it all over to Simon to reinvest in the family business, the Sterling Hotel Group."

"It doesn't sound like they had a falling out. So what's the deal?"

"They're Sterling men. They have to make it on their own. The money was always there in case they failed, but for them, failure was never an option."

"But their brother Simon's a Sterling man and from what you say it looks like he's very much involved in the family business."

"Simon didn't have the luxury of making his own way

in the world. Besides, someone had to stay home and take care of the business. Maybe it was because he was always Adele's favorite, I don't know, but there was never any question about who was going to run the hotels. Simon lives in a castle in Malibu, drives a Ferrari, and works twenty hours a day keeping the family rich. Stacy and Sandy don't begrudge him a thing. He could spend the whole fortune and they'd shrug it off, but of course, he never would."

"You'd think Sandy, her natural son, would be her favorite. "He pulled the red Naugahyde chair up to the head of her bed and sat down.

"Stacy and Sandy were very much like their father, men's men. They were into sports, guns and hunting. Simon's into books and he's a vegetarian, as is Adele. Besides, you have to remember that she had him in her arms months before Sandy was born."

She was uncomfortable now and needed that bedpan, but she didn't feel she could go with him right there. Maybe if she shifted her position, it wouldn't be so bad. She tried to push herself up on her elbow and fell right back on the pillow as if someone had slammed a fist into her head. All of a sudden the room was whirling out of control.

"Dave, help me," she whimpered. The floor was on the ceiling, then the wall, then back where it belonged, then up again. She fought to keep from vomiting.

"Gayle, what's wrong?" He jumped out of his chair.

"Just a second," she said, between breaths. "When I tried to get up the room started spinning. It's settled down now."

"It sounds like you have a concussion," Dave said. "I'm going to order a CT scan, right now. I'll get you a nurse while I make the arrangements."

Within minutes she heard that friendly voice. "Hey, Mrs. S., we're going for a little ride again."

"Drive careful or no tip, Danny." She needed to pee and thought about asking them to stop by a bathroom, but decided she could hold it a little longer.

"Nobody in New Zealand tips." He laughed as he helped Dave and the nurse with the pursed lips ease her onto the gurney.

Gayle watched the ceiling as it rolled by overhead. High and white, with acoustic tiles, some cracked, some not as old as others. A slight chill pricked her as Danny wheeled the gurney around a corner and she felt a blast of air-conditioning. She couldn't see where it was coming from.

"Hold the elevator," Danny yelled out and the high ceiling shifted into the low overhead inside the elevator. Dave edged around the gurney, the doors closed and her stomach told her they were going down.

Concussion, what did that mean, exactly? She'd done a story last year about the trauma center in Long Beach. She knew what a concussion was and she knew what else it could be. Brain contusion, a bruise on the brain. Or worse, a skull fracture. She could be hemorrhaging. She could die. She felt a tingling at the back of her neck with that thought, even though there was a pillow snug up against it.

"You're tense," Dave said. "Don't worry. I'm sure it's just a mild concussion. We're only going down here to confirm it. We don't like to take chances."

"I can't help it. A little knowledge is a dangerous thing."

"You know about head injuries?" Dave asked.

"A little, that's why I'm scared out of my wits."

"There's nothing to worry about. If it was serious, we'd have known about it by now. We're just playing it safe."

"Really?"

"Absolutely," Dave said as the elevator bottomed and the doors started to open.

"Still, I'll be glad when it's over."

Danny wheeled the gurney out of the elevator as Gayle had visions of a subdural hematoma. She just knew they were going to shoot her straight into surgery and she shivered with the thought of it.

"Almost there," Danny said.

"Hold it, Emergency." Gayle looked sideways and saw the ashen face of an older woman who was obviously unconscious. "She fell," a gray haired doctor said.

"We'll have to wait," Dave said.

"Sure, I understand." Gayle really had to go now, but she was too embarrassed to say anything in front of the men. She'd just have to tough it out. She closed her eyes and tried to think of something else. Dylan came first to her mind and she struggled to turn her thoughts away. She didn't want to cry now. She focused on the only other thing she could think about, the head injury.

* * *

"Keep the change," Sandy said as the cab pulled up to the marina. He was out of it as quickly as he'd left the elevator, speed walking toward a dinghy dock at the water's edge. By the time Haley and Taylor were out of the car they had to jog to catch up.

"He's in an awful hurry," Taylor said.

"Seems to be," Haley said.

"See it out there?" Sandy pointed to a sailboat, painted black, resting peacefully at anchor just outside the marina. "That's where we're going." He stopped at the end of the dock, faced into the wind and inhaled through his nose, like a bird dog sniffing the breeze. The air was crisp and clear. Haley smelled the sea on it. Gulls screeched in the distance.

"That boat's a Phoenix 60, mine's a 45. I'd give anything to sail on her. For sure she's faster than *Sea Hag.* The Phoenixes are real cruising boats, all built in the early '70s. Seven in California, and the last six here in New Zealand. Flush deck, sloop rigged, deep keeled, fast. You can do two hundred miles a day easy in one of them. The first eleven were forty-five footers, the last two were sixty feet."

Haley looked out at the sloop. "A Darth Vader boat, like *Sea Hag.*"

"Yeah, black's not such a good color in the tropics," he said. "Too hot. But Gerald Ronstadt painted them all black, with that big, white phoenix bird on the bow."

Haley saw a red Zodiac dinghy cutting through the boats moored in the marina. It was making its way toward the dock and Sandy was waving to it.

Haley studied the occupants as it came closer, splashing through the waves. A young woman sat up front. She didn't look like she was much older than twenty. She was wearing a halter top and shorts that did little to cover her suntanned body on this cold winter evening. Haley could just imagine the goosebumps that must be running up her arms and legs. She had long, blonde hair tied in a ponytail that whipped around in the artificial breeze created by the rubber boat as it shot through the water. The driver had even lighter hair.

Haley guessed he was in his middle to late twenties. He was also dressed lightly in a white tee shirt and a pair of khaki shorts. Why were they dressed like that? Didn't these people get cold?

"That's Bill and Linda Ronstadt. Old Gerald's grandson and his wife."

"Like the singer," Taylor said.

"I don't know if she sings," Sandy said."

"Different hair. Linda Ronstadt's not a blonde," Taylor said.

"They live on that black sloop. They're setting sail in three days for Noumea. That's the capitol of New Caledonia, a French island about a thousand miles north of here. Just the two of them. Their boat sleeps six comfortably, so they've got plenty of room."

"Room for what?" Taylor said, but Haley thought she knew.

"Why for you guys, of course," he said.

"I'm not going anywhere on any boat," Taylor said, giving her uncle a look.

"Don't say anything now. We'll just go out and look the boat over. Then we'll talk about it over dinner. If you still don't want to go, then you don't have to, but for now, just play along. Okay?"

"Sure, if it's what you want. But I'm not going. No way."

"I don't think I'd like to go either, Sandy," Haley said.

"I get the point. Just humor me and pretend. They think you're going, so let's keep it that way till after we talk about it."

"Sure, Sandy," Taylor said.

But Haley didn't like it. Pretending to do something

you had no intention of doing was like lying. It was dishonest.

"Hey, Sandy," Bill Ronstadt said.

"Hello, Bill, Linda. These are my girls, Taylor and Haley."

"Are you ready to go out and see her?"

"We are," Sandy said.

Bill held the Zodiac steady to the dock as the girls climbed in. Haley sat on the rubber tube and grabbed onto the safety rope. She was used to riding in a dinghy, having sailed on *Sea Hag* a few times. And she'd studied up a little on sailing, because Sandy loved it so much.

The gray sky was rapidly turning dark as it does in the winter, but Haley reveled in the ride. She loved the ocean, the smell, the spray, the thrill. It went on forever, a moving blanket that covered most of the earth. It refused to be tamed or predicted and the mere thought of it sent smiles running through her. She almost wished she could go sailing off into the sunset, but she knew it just wasn't possible. College was only six weeks away and she still had a lot to do to get ready.

They pulled up to the port side of the sloop. Sandy was first off and he offered a hand to Linda, who didn't need it. Haley boarded next and offered a hand to Taylor, who took it, and she helped hoist her aboard.

"She's sixty feet, as you know," Linda said. "She's not really a sloop now that we've roller furled the staysail. Technically, because the mast is so far forward, you'd call her a cutter rigged sloop."

"So the staysail is your storm sail," Sandy said.

"Exactly," Bill said. "When my grandfather built it he had racing in mind. He figured you'd just take a triple reef in the main if you got in trouble, but with a shorthanded crew that's almost impossible. So we added the staysail."

"It ruins her for racing," Sandy said.

"Yeah, but she's over thirty years old. She wouldn't win anything anyway."

"Be lots of fun though," Sandy said.

"Linda and I don't actually like the sailing part of it that much," Bill said. "It's the being there we like, not the getting there."

"What does that mean, exactly?" Haley said.

"You know. Being at anchor with all the cruisers. The good friends, the parties." He sniffed. No wonder he had a cold, the way he was dressed.

* * *

In the dream Gayle faced a row of toilets, all waiting with the seats down. But there was a puddle of slippery oil between her and them and every time she took a step, she slipped and fell. She pushed herself through the black ooze, but could get no closer. She was like a floundering fish out of water, flapping, slipping and sliding.

Then the oil was gone and she was standing again, but the toilets were gone, too. In their place was a rundown, stinky, fly infested outhouse. She reached out and opened the door. It fell off, but she didn't care. She stepped into it.

The seat was up.

She lowered it.

She raised her dress as she turned.

She wasn't wearing panties.

The stench was terrible, but she had to go too badly to pay it any attention. She felt a cold breeze from overhead. She shivered. She wasn't alone. Stacy and Sandy were watching. The Sterling men with their crossed arms and stern gaze. Taylor and Haley stood behind them. They were all here to watch her pee in the outhouse. She couldn't do it. Then a thought pierced her. Where was Dylan?

She shivered again and woke up. She felt the cool breeze from the air-conditioning. She had to go so badly that she felt that she was going to wet herself. She looked around the room. She was alone. Where were they?

"Dave? Danny?"

No answer. How could they do this? She really had to go.

"Dave!"

"Here," he said, coming out of a door. Danny was with him. They'd left her in the hall. How could they do that? "Just a few more minutes," he said.

"So what's the difference between a CAT scan and a CT scan?" Gayle said, trying to take her mind off of her bladder.

"Same thing, CT is just a short way for saying computerized tomography. It just means that we're going to take pictures of your brain in layers. You won't feel a thing, but it'll sort of seem like something out of a science fiction movie."

"Is it going to be soon?" she said.

"We're going in now." Danny wheeled the gurney. Two nurses, Dave and Danny lifted her onto a table. She closed her eyes and clenched her fists against the pain in her bladder.

"It's nothing to be afraid of," Dave said.

She opened her eyes as the table started to slide. It was like science fiction, but it was science for real. In a few seconds her head was encased in a sort of high tech, plastic cave. It kind of reminded her of getting x-rays at the dentist, only this was, in a word, awesome. And a little scary.

"Can you hear me?" It was a woman's voice coming through a speaker somewhere.

"Yes." Gayle was breathing fast. She clenched her fists, tried to slow it down.

"It's okay, honey, try to stay calm," the woman's voice said." This is all routine."

"I know."

"Would you turn your head a little to the right.

Gayle did.

"Fine, hold it there, that's perfect."

Gayle closed her eyes and followed the woman's commands and before long the table slid her out from the scanner. She opened her eyes. Her fists were still clenched.

"It wasn't that bad," Dave said.

"I have to go to the bathroom."

"We'll have you back up on the ward in a few minutes," Dave said.

"Now!" Gayle said.

"There's a bathroom right over there. I'll help her." Gayle recognized the voice. It was the woman who had been giving her the commands when she was under the scanner. They helped her into a wheelchair and the lady technician pushed her toward the bathroom.

"How'd I do? No subdural?"

"No," she said. "Nothing at all. Perfectly normal. You probably just have a mild concussion. It'll go way in a couple of days and you'll feel fine."

But I won't be able to go to my daughter's funeral, she thought.

"I can take it from here," she said after the woman opened the door. Inside she pushed herself out of the wheelchair and using the stainless steel rails on the walls, got on the toilet. Tears ran down her cheeks as she urinated.

CHAPTER EIGHT

"OKAY, WHAT'LL IT BE, GIRLS?" Sandy buried his face in the menu as soon as they'd taken their seats and that surprised Haley. It was like he was hiding from them. They were on the top floor of the Wellington Sterling, in the Seaview Restaurant overlooking the marina. The sun had just gone down. It was overcast and gray outside.

He raised a hand and a young waitress appeared instantly. Everyone on staff knew that the Sterlings were in the hotel. She had green eyes, shoulder length black hair and she was wearing the form fitting long black dress that waitresses in all the Sterling restaurants wore.

"What can I get you?" She was nervous.

"Coke for me," Haley said, "and that hamburger with the three different cheeses you get in all of the Sterling Restaurants."

"Yeah, Uncle Simon's famous Sterling Burger," Taylor said. "Same for me."

"He should have called it the Cholesterol Burger," Sandy said. "Make it three, all the same."

"Okay," Haley said after the waitress left. "Now can we talk about why you thought we'd just take off on a sailboat?"

"Yes, that," Sandy said. "I think we should just forget it. It was wrong of me to suggest it and now that I've thought about my reasons for wanting you to go, I feel pretty crummy about myself."

"What do you mean?" Haley said.

"I'm supposed to know better. I've been dealing with feelings and emotions my whole professional life, but when I have to deal with my own I just blow it."

"Come on, Sandy, what are you talking about?" Haley said.

"I wasn't thinking about you guys and your grief. I was just thinking about myself and Dylan. It would have been the best cure for her, me too. A long sea voyage. And if you want to know the truth, I guess I was hoping that you'd love it and we'd go sailing on the weekends back home. Like I did with Dylan."

"You wanted us to take her place?" Haley said.

"No, I don't think so. Not the way you think. There was this special thing about Dylan and the sea. The way her eyes glowed when the wind picked up. The way she laughed when a pod of dolphins swam in the bow wake. The pure joy in her smile when she was sailing in the groove. Somehow, in the back of my mind, I must have thought I could get that back. I just didn't want to let it go. I'm sorry." It looked like he was going to cry.

Then for the next two hours they talked about Dylan. The little things she did. They way she flicked the hair from her eyes with her left hand when she was angry. The way she changed boyfriends like old shoes. The way she scrunched her eyes together when she studied French. And after they were talked out, Sandy fished a key out of his pocket and handed it to Taylor.

"The room is on the top floor, the fifteenth. It's a double off of the Sterling Suite. You can catch a cab to the hospital in the morning."

"We're not going back now?" Taylor asked.

"It's pretty obvious your folks need some time," Sandy said.

"You mean, alone?" Taylor said.

"Yeah, they seemed a little uptight earlier, don't you think?" Sandy said.

"Oh, yeah," Haley said.

"Have you ever heard of anyone working out their problems with the whole family around?" Sandy said.

"I didn't know they had any problems."

"Come on, Taylor," Haley said. "I've never seen them like that. It's almost like they were fighting."

"I'm sure it's the grief," Sandy said. "It messes with everyone's judgment. Look what it did to me. I was going to send you guys off on a strange boat in a big ocean to a faraway place, because I wasn't thinking clearly. They just need a little time alone to work through this." He pushed his chair back from the table. "I've got to go by the marina and tell Bill and Linda you guys aren't going.

"He's pretty great," Haley said ten minutes later as she punched the button for the fifteenth floor.

"Yeah," Taylor said. "He is."

"And maybe he was right," Haley said, "maybe going off on that sailboat would've been the right thing for us to do. Can you imagine it, sailing off into the South Pacific?" The doors opened and they stepped out into the hall.

"Fifteen-seventeen," Taylor said, looking at the key. "This way."

"It can't hurt to at least think about going," Haley said as she followed Taylor to their room and watched as she unlocked the door.

"I suppose." Taylor turned on the light and stepped into the room. "It's not like we have jobs or anything. This is probably the only time in our lives that we'd be able to pick up and go off on an adventure like this. We could do it if we wanted."

Haley looked at the two large beds and all of a sudden that kiss from last night loomed large in her mind, shoving away all thought about what they'd been talking about. They were going to have to talk about it. But not here. "Let's take a walk," she said. "I saw an ice cream stand on the corner. I could use one, how about you?"

"Yeah, I could." Taylor was probably as nervous as she was.

It was chilly out and Haley felt invigorated by the short walk. She was awake and alive. Her skin tingled. She quivered with the anticipation of the unknown and it unnerved her. She was excited and ashamed at the same time as they approached the small ice cream store.

"Can we still get ice cream?" Taylor asked as they walked up to a take away window.

"I was just about to close, but sure," a happy faced woman said. She was a plump lady with bright green eyes and red hair in Viking braids.

"What's hokey pokey?" Haley asked, reading from a list of flavors on the wall behind the ice cream lady.

"It's hard to describe, sort of a caramel ice cream with bits of butterscotch candy in it. It's very good."

"I'll have chocolate," Haley said.

"I'll try the hokey pokey. Make mine a double." Taylor had never been afraid to try new things and she'd always liked ice cream.

"Uh oh, no Kiwi money. Only US dollars," Haley said.

"That's alright, pay me tomorrow," the woman said as she handed over the double hokey pokey to Taylor. Haley watched while she took a big bite. She couldn't imagine any business back home giving two total strangers credit.

"It's delicious. My new fave," Taylor said. The ice cream lady beamed.

"Could you change mine?" Haley said. The woman made it a double. Haley took her cone and the girls started walking toward the marina. "Let's sit here." She stopped at a park bench facing the water.

"Sure," Taylor said. "It's nice."

"I want to talk about last night," Haley said.

"I know you do," Taylor said. Then she took a long lick of her ice cream.

"So tell me about it."

"It's no big deal," Taylor said. "It wasn't for us anyway, but other people wouldn't understand, so we kept it secret."

"You and Dylan were like lesbians or something," Haley whispered, shocked.

"Not lesbians. We liked boys, we dated. We're not virgins. We just love each other, too." Haley found it eerie the way Taylor slipped between past and present tense when she talked about Dylan.

"But you slept together?"

"We slept together. But we've slept with you, too, one or both of us. Lots of times."

"Not sleep, sleeeep. You know what I mean."

"Oh, that."

"Yeah, that."

"We did that. Sometimes."

"My God, why?"

"Why not? We never hurt anybody. It was between me and her, no one else."

"But it's wrong."

"Says who?"

"Everybody, that's who."

"You know the world would be a lot better off if everybody took care of their own selves and left people like me and Dylan alone. What we did was our business and ours alone. If I wasn't so out of it last night, you never would have found out."

"Are you sorry I did?" Haley asked.

"Yes."

"Why?"

"Because it's going to come between us."

"Nothing could ever come between us. Nothing, not ever," Haley said. She saw the tension ease out of Taylor's shoulders.

"Look, Haley, what Dylan and I did doesn't mean I want to do it with you. It's different. Besides, I don't think I could do it with another girl. I'm as hetero as you and so was Dylan."

"Whew," Haley sighed. "That's a relief to hear. Let's just forget about it, okay?"

"Deal," Taylor said and they shook hands on it just

like they used to do when they swore to keep a secret when they were little girls.

They walked back to the hotel cold in the night as they wandered around in their thoughts. They took the elevator in silence. Taylor opened the door with the key and hit the light switch.

"Gorgeous room," Haley said as she took in the salmon carpet and original seascape paintings on the light green walls.

"Yeah," Taylor said. "You know Uncle Simon, Sterling Hotels are done with class, but they still have to look like home." She laughed. "Sandy's probably staying next door in the suite, let's check it out." Taylor started through the room, toward the connecting door, then stopped. "Look," she said, "Dylan's things."

"Brrr," Haley said, staring at the three suitcases at the foot of the beds. "It seems so cold."

"We don't have any clothes," Taylor said. "She'd want us to wear hers. She didn't shop that much, she wouldn't have wanted the effort to be in vain."

"Yeah." Haley laughed, but tears were running down her cheeks.

* * *

"How's it going?" Haley looked up. It was Sandy. He was dressed in street clothes—Levi's, Nike running shoes and a thick sweatshirt.

"Not so good," she said. It was morning. She was nursing a black coffee alone in the hospital cafeteria. "Taylor's upstairs, her dad's there, too. It's so sad. I just needed some time by myself."

"Mind if I join you?"

"It's okay," she said.

"So about the great sailing adventure." He pulled a chair away from the table and sat down.

"I thought you were gonna tell Bill and Linda last night that we weren't going," Haley said.

"I went down to the marina office and tried to raise them, but I guess they didn't have their radio on, so you guys have another day to think about it. Unfortunately I mentioned it to Gayle yesterday. I'm sorry."

"Why are you sorry?"

"Because she kind of wants you guys to go, but she's afraid, too. It would kill her if anything happened to you out there."

"Yeah," Haley said.

"But she knows she can't baby you forever. She knows you and Taylor are going off to college in September and that you could just as easily be killed by a drunk driver as you could drown on a sailboat. She's pretty philosophical."

"Yeah, she is."

He was silent for a minute. The clink of silverware coming from the kitchen echoed through the cafeteria. A chair across the room scraped as someone got up to leave. She was melting into his eyes. A warm glow tingled her. She had been in love with him for so long.

"I've rented a small day sailor for the time I'm going to be here, twenty-two feet. You want to go out on it?"

"When?"

"Right now. I was gonna spend a couple of hours behind the tiller to clear my head."

"I don't know. It seems wrong somehow."

"It always seems wrong to go on living, but you do it anyway. We're five minutes from the marina. We'll be back by lunch."

"Alright, I'll go," she said and thirty minutes later she was sitting in the cockpit as he turned the small boat into the wind so he could raise the main. She'd felt guilty when she told Gayle that she was going sailing with Sandy and almost changed her mind, but Gayle insisted, saying that it would do her good. She'd asked Taylor to come along, but she begged off, saying that she didn't feel very well. Haley knew she was just being a friend by letting her have this time alone with Sandy.

"You don't need instruments to know which way the wind's coming from," he said. "You can see it on the ripples on the water, or feel it on your face, or hear it."

"Hear it?"

"Yeah, face the direction you think it's coming from and listen. When you hear the stereo sound of the wind flowing past your ears, you're facing right into it."

She tried it, slowly turning her head till she heard it. "It works."

"You've been sailing before and didn't know that?"

"You and Gayle are the sailors, and of course Dylan was. Taylor and I only go along for the ride. We enjoy ourselves, but we're not really into it."

"How can you go out on the water and not be into it?"

She took in a deep breath, tasting the sea air. "I could ask you the same thing. You've been riding before. How can you sit on the back of a horse and not love it?"

"Touché," he said.

"But I do kind of see why Dylan was so into it. And I've read a little about it. She gave me a beginning sailing book. I wish I could say it was interesting, but it was kind of dry."

"I know, why don't I give you a lesson. I'll explain

everything I do as I do it. Maybe it'll help you see what Dylan knew, what I know, what all of us who love the sea know."

"What's that?"

"I can't tell you. I'm not eloquent enough to put it into words. I'd have to show you."

"Alright, I'm willing."

He tied off the tiller, then went to the mast where he took a line off of a cleat and hauled up the main, then came back to the cockpit.

"Now we're going to sail." He unlashed the tiller. They turned to port and heeled over. The little boat skimmed over the waves as he unfurled the jib, then she heeled more as she picked up speed.

"How do you like it so far?" He said.

"It's great," she said.

The water was so close, she could reach out and touch it. Adrenaline sparked through her. It was like being on the back of a motorcycle, holding on to an unknown driver as he weaved through the traffic at a hundred miles an hour. And it continued for the next two hours as Sandy tacked back and forth, explaining everything to her as they went along. He moved the boat through the waves as if it were a part of himself and he made it a part of her too.

Then all too soon it was time to head back. He furled in the jib as they neared the marina, then put the boat back into the wind and lowered the main.

He sat next to her in the cockpit after the boat was safely tied to its mooring. It was so quiet, just the sound of the wind and the gentle lapping of the sea as it splashed against the hull.

"What did you think?" he asked.

"I loved it."

"Have you thought any about the trip?"

"I'm thinking about it, but not too seriously." She smiled. She didn't know if this outing counted as a date, but it was the first time she'd ever been alone with him for any length of time. And he'd asked her. That was pretty much like a date. "Well, maybe a little seriously." She laughed.

He laughed too.

"My God, I was laughing," Haley said.

"It's not a sin," he said.

"Yeah, it's not. It just seems too soon."

"Dylan's funeral is tomorrow." He changed the subject. "That's why I sought you out in the cafeteria. To tell you."

"Why didn't you?"

"I thought this would be a better place. Out on the ocean she loved so much." He smiled and her heart warmed.

"Gayle can't go, can she?"

"No, we're flying out tomorrow morning in a small plane. Gayle can hardly leave the hospital, much less be crammed into one of those tiny seats."

"She's going to be so hurt." Haley didn't feel so happy anymore.

"Stacy said that Dylan wanted you and Taylor to share everything she had. That includes *Wind Song*."

"She wanted us to have her boat?"

"There's something else. Dylan had an insurance policy. You and Taylor are the beneficiaries."

"Oh my God," Haley said. "Why would she have life insurance? She was so young."

"That's what I thought at first when she came to me about it. I told her it was stupid, but she insisted. She was going to sail around the world and she knew how dangerous it was. She told me that if anything happened to her, she wanted to leave you guys something to make a dream come true. I was supposed to tell you that. You have to spend the money on a dream."

Haley was crying now. Her tears glistening.

"Oh, Sandy," she sobbed and she fell into his warm hug.

* * *

The next day, on a wintery New Zealand afternoon, they stood with bowed heads as a minister prayed over Dylan's grave. Dark clouds, threatening rain, hovered overhead. Haley picked up a handful of damp dirt when he finished. It chilled her soul as crumbs of it slid through her fingers.

The others scooped up a fistful of earth as well. Dark earth, dark as the inside of a coffin. Stacy scattered the dirt into the grave, almost throwing it, as if he was mad at God, or maybe mad at Dylan for dying. His tortured face as he turned away from the damp hole in the ground was like a knife to her stomach. His eyebrows scowled around light blue eyes that in this funereal light had gone gray. He frightened her. At this moment he could kill. If that drunk driver hadn't died in the accident, Haley would fear for him.

Sandy tossed the dirt up a little, watching it rise some before it started its descent to the grave. The look on his face was just sad, there was no other way to describe it. Just sad.

Taylor was shaking, more of those silent tears. She'd borne up well, till this moment. She dropped the dirt, then turned away without a look, her tears no longer silent. "I wish it had been me," she cried. The look on her father's face softened as he opened his arms to his daughter and Taylor threw her arms around him so tightly that she chased away the hate from his face.

Haley stepped up to the grave. So unfair, she thought. She tried to open her hand, but it was frozen around the wet earth. If she didn't drop the dirt, Dylan wouldn't really be dead. Tears streaked down her cheeks. She felt a hand on her shoulder. It was Sandy. She held her shaking arm over the pit. With effort she stretched out her fingers and let go of the dirt, shivering as it splashed over the casket.

"Sleep in peace," she whispered. "And look after Charlotte."

They had a charter plane waiting for them at the small airport in Onerahi and thirty minutes after saying amen, they were on it, winging their way back to Wellington, the hospital and Gayle. Dr. Collins had been insistent that she was in no condition to travel. Haley knew how it broke her inside. To lose a child was a horrible thing, it didn't seem fair that she wasn't able to say the final goodbye.

She looked out the widow, but didn't see the landscape below. Her eyes were misted over and her thoughts were mingled with Dylan, Taylor and that kiss. Nothing more had been said about it after the conversation on that bench, but it burned in Haley's mind. Dylan and Taylor, lovers as well as sisters. She shuddered at the thought. She'd known them so well, but she'd never imagined that. There'd never been a hint. They'd been close, but it was only natural, they were twins.

On the surface, Taylor hadn't changed any. She still looked the same, still behaved toward her the way she always had. Like a sister. But Haley sensed a tension, a thin thread stretched taut. The others didn't notice and Taylor acted like it wasn't there and maybe for her it wasn't. She'd just buried her sister, after all. But Haley felt it.

"Haley," Taylor said. Haley felt her friend's hand on her shoulder. "I'm going to sail away on that boat. Please say you'll come, too."

"I'll come," Haley said, still looking out the window.

"I knew you would," Taylor whispered. Then she lay her head on Haley's shoulder and went to sleep.

CHAPTER
NINE

THEY SET SAIL THREE DAYS LATER, on the fourth of July, at noon. The Ronstadts had been waiting for two things—a paying crew and a stationary high over the southern part of the Tasman Sea. They were counting on the high to generate east winds further north to speed them on their way and to give them a six or seven day weather window. The girls wanted to stay with Gayle a few more days, but it was late in the season and the Ronstadts were ready to go.

"Wellington is located in the center of the Cook Strait," Linda said from behind the wheel, "and Bill's decided to go up the east coast instead of out as the crow flies." Haley turned toward Linda, antennae aware. Was she disagreeing with Bill's decision?

"Usually the winds are pretty brisk through here," Bill said, "but it's unusually calm today, that's why we're not waiting for tomorrow morning and shooting straight across the Tasman."

"So we're not going north like we talked about yesterday?" Haley asked.

"Eventually. Linda's right, under ordinary circumstances it would be quicker if we continued on through the strait and shot a straight course for Noumea, but the local forecast calls for winds out of the southwest along the east coast. It'll be a much nicer sail with the wind at our backs. We'll sail flat and fast and won't have to beat against the westerlies for the first couple hundred miles."

"Oh." Haley didn't understand a word, but the look in Linda's eyes told her that she definitely disagreed.

"So, if we're going to sail along the coast, will we be anchoring for the night?" Taylor asked.

"No, we have our weather window, so we're going for it." Bill took the line off of a large winch on the port side and started hauling on it. Haley gasped as the big jib unfurled. The boat heeled over and they picked up speed.

"I gotta pee," Taylor said. She went below and came up a few seconds later. "I smell something down there."

"What?" Bill asked.

"I don't know, exhaust maybe," she said. Bill secured the jib sheet in the self-tailing jaws and went below. Haley followed.

"I don't smell anything," he said as he stood in the center of the salon sniffing the air.

"I coulda swore I smelled something," Taylor said.

"Sorry."

"Okay," he said, going back up through the hatchway. "Let's shut off the engine and let the wind take us to New Caledonia."

Haley stayed below while Taylor used the head. She sniffed the air. Maybe she smelled something like exhaust. She couldn't be sure. But if Bill wasn't worried about it, then she wasn't either.

"Excited?" Haley turned. It was Linda. Her blonde ponytail was hanging over her right shoulder and her bangs almost covered her eyes. She stuck out her lower lip and blew the hair away. "I really gotta do something about that. I'd love to cut it, but Bill won't let me. He likes it long."

"Who's driving the boat?" Haley asked. She wondered why any woman would need a man's permission to cut her hair.

"It's on autopilot," Linda said. "We're all passengers now. In a couple of hours we'll change course and it'll be flat and level sailing all night long."

"We're hardly heeled now," Haley said. The salon seemed only a little out of kilter. Moving about the inside of the boat was fairly easy. There were teak hand holds on the white bulkheads, but Haley found that she didn't need them. The gentle sea offered them a ride smoother than she would have thought possible.

"Yeah, it's kind of nice." Linda sat on the port settee. She made a comb out of her fingers and pushed her bangs back over the top of her head. She reminded Haley of a sturdy Midwestern playmate of the month.

"Are you guys having a fight or something?"

"Just a little disagreement, it's nothing." Linda folded her hands in front of herself and set them between her legs. Her thumbs were at war with each other.

"I just didn't want to get in the way of anything."

"Don't worry, you won't," Linda said.

Haley wasn't sure how to take that, so she changed the subject. "You have a beautiful boat." She sat on the settee opposite. "I like way the white bulkheads and ceiling show off all the teak. And the brass lights really give it an old time look."

"Bill's grandfather wanted a fast, modern boat, but he kept the traditional look inside." She smiled now, apparently talking about the boat took her mind off of whatever it was that was bothering her.

"I really like the galley," Taylor said, coming out of the head. She sat next to Haley and Haley felt a small electric tingle shoot through her when their legs touched. Almost like the feeling she got during a scary movie. She scooted a couple inches away.

"Granddad didn't like those poky little kitchens you see on most sailboats," Bill said, coming down the companionway. "The two Phoenix 60s have huge galleys, almost like a gourmet kitchen."

Haley nodded, the galley was beautiful. Two full sinks, a gorgeous white counter made of some kind of synthetic that resembled marble. The counter was surrounded by teak cabinets. The stove was gimbled and the microwave was built in. Opposite the galley was a breakfast nook that would be at home in a mountain condo. Behind the galley was the huge salon with opposite facing settees. And unlike most boats, there was no table in the salon for the crew to gather around. Instead one got the impression of space. Lots of it. You could dance in the salon.

"Granddad wanted to build a cruising boat as

comfortable as a house, but he wanted it to sail, too. She has a fin keel and a spade rudder, like the race boats. Her mast is seventy-six feet high and she sails like a witch. The Phoenix 60s were his dream, unfortunately they weren't anybody else's. Cruisers want a shallower draft, a small galley, and on a sixty foot boat, more cabins. He built *Dark Witch* and showed her at all the boat shows. He got exactly one order and he lost money on that. He went bust, but it wasn't such a bad thing. He went into computer software and made a fortune."

"Where's the engine?" Taylor asked.

"There, under the sink." Linda pointed to false teak cabinets that surrounded the two sinks and the galley work area. "Just open those doors and voila, there she is, an eighty-five horsepower Perkins four-two-three-six."

"So the exhaust I smelled could have come from there?" Taylor had her hands on her knees, almost like if she let go they'd start shaking. She really was worried about that exhaust gas, Haley thought.

"But it didn't," Bill said, meeting Taylor's gaze. Haley saw sweat ringing his forehead and wondered about it, because it was chilly out and he hadn't been exerting himself..

"Now let's talk about watches," he said after a few seconds. "The boat will pretty much steer herself all the way. And once we get to the open sea we'll set the radar alarm to go off if anything gets within five miles of us. But we should still have someone on deck at all times, just in case the alarm fails or we run into a problem with the sails. None of that's going to happen, but it's a good policy to be prepared."

"Absolutely," Taylor said, nodding.

"So I think one hour watches. That's not too long

and it'll give us three hours rest."

"Sounds fine," Haley said. She looked at his hands. They were shaking a little. Maybe he was coming down with the flu.

"We won't worry about it during the daytime, because we'll all be up and about, but let's always try and keep someone on deck, okay?"

And on deck is where Haley spent the rest of the afternoon, watching New Zealand's craggy green landscape as they sailed by. The smell of the sea, coupled with the brisk wind, exhilarated her and she wondered where her mind was those few times she'd gone out with Sandy or Dylan. She couldn't believe that she hadn't loved it and she wondered how much of her new appreciation of the sea and things nautical she owed to Sandy and that little boat he'd rented in Wellington.

"It's beautiful, isn't it?" Taylor said, coming up from below as the sun was setting.

"Welcome to the world, sleepy head." Haley blinked as her friend came into the cockpit. She'd obviously taken a quick shower to wake up. Her palomino hair was damp and glistening. Framed with the sun at her back, she looked angelic and kind of sexual. Something stirred in Haley, a feeling like when she saw Harrison Ford on the big screen. She fought it away.

"I can't help it." Taylor said. "It was just so peaceful. I zonked out, but the shower perked me right up."

"Maybe it was those exhaust gases that knocked you out." Haley laughed.

"Very funny."

"Well it's probably a good thing you got some sleep, 'cuz you have the first night watch," Bill said. Then he pointed. "That's Cape Palliser off to the left. We're going to jibe around it in about fifteen minutes. That's a turn with the wind at our backs."

Haley laughed.

"What's so funny?"

"I know what a jibe is. When we go sailing with Sandy or Dylan it seems like they're tacking and jibing all the time."

"That's what you do when you're day sailing for pleasure, but a cruiser will look at the sails, study the waves, glance up at the sun and then say something like 'We should think about a left turn in about half-an-hour.' We generally get lots of time to plan our moves. So what we're going to do is shift the sails to the other side as we go through the turn. Taylor, you can work the mainsheet and Haley, you can work the wheel."

"Us?" Taylor said.

"Sure. You want to learn, don't you?"

"Yeah, but—"

"Then there's no time like the present." He punched a button on the autopilot. "There, she's free. Okay, Haley you want to come back here and get the feel of her before we do the jibe?"

"Sure." Haley took the wheel. Excitement zapped through her at the thought of so much boat under her control. She turned the wheel a little to the left, then back to the right, getting the measure of her. "I like it," she said.

"You're a natural." Bill took the mainsheet off its winch and took two wraps off of it. "Here, it won't bite." He handed the line to Taylor. "As Haley starts the turn, you pull slightly on the line. Don't worry about it getting away from you, there's two wraps left on the winch, just keep some tension on it. When the wind hits the sail from the opposite side, the boom will want to slam from starboard to port. It's your job to see that that doesn't happen."

"How do I do that?"

"Just before she's halfway through the turn and the boom starts to move, you pull like hell on that line. You should be able to stop the boom dead center, then as she goes through the turn you gently ease it out, till it's all the way over on the other side."

"Got it," Taylor said.

"Okay, it's time," he said. "Haley start your turn to port, that's left."

"I know that," she said as she gradually eased the wheel around.

"Get ready, Taylor," Bill said. "You can do this, it's a piece of cake."

"Shouldn't Linda be up here?" Taylor said. "Just in case."

"Naw, you'll be fine. Okay, she's moving, haul in on that line." Taylor started pulling. "All the way, Haley, spin it fast." Haley did as she was told and the boat responded, whipping around faster than she thought it would.

Taylor pulled on the rope. Her biceps, honed by years of horseback riding, rippled as she struggled with the line, but she held the boom centered till Haley was halfway through the turn. Then she eased it out until the boom was on the other side and the mainsail was full.

"Perfect. You girls are going be top notch sailors by the time we get to Noumea." Haley beamed even as she wondered why Linda stayed below through the maneuver.

Darkness fell soon after they'd rounded the cape. The boat was back on autopilot. Bill and Linda were down below. When Haley went down to use the head she heard them fighting. Although they weren't shouting or anything, she could tell by the tone of their voices that they were arguing. She did her business and went quickly back up on deck.

"They're not getting along too well," Taylor said.

"Doesn't sound like it," Haley said. "I wonder what it's all about."

"It's about none of our business, that's what it's about," Taylor said. "We have to live with these people for the next two or three weeks. We can't get involved in one of their arguments right off the bat. That's a recipe for certain disaster."

"You're right," Haley said. "I'll just ignore them."

"It might be hard, being the busybody you are, but that would be best."

"I am not a busybody."

"Oh, Hale, you're such a liar."

"Okay, so I'm a little curious sometimes," she said, and they laughed.

"Isn't it beautiful, Hale." Taylor looked up. "Millions of stars, way more than anyone could ever count. Now I know what Dylan saw in it."

"But it's not a horse," Haley said.

"Yeah, it's not a horse, but maybe we're getting a little old for riding."

"Speak for yourself, I happen to love it."

"But you're not really free. You're tied to a dumb animal and dependent on the stables to care for it and you have to work to support it. Much as I love Blaze, I'm selling her when I get back."

"Who'll I ride with?"

"Sorry, Hale. Besides, how can I keep a horse and go

away to school at the same time? She'll be better off with a little girl who loves her and I'll be better off not having to worry about her."

Taylor's words cut Haley to the quick. She hadn't given any thought to her own horse, Suzy Q. She didn't want to lose the animal, but she didn't want to be tied down to her either. It was something to think about. And she was still thinking about it when the sun came up. She was alone on deck, her watch about over, admiring the orange sunrise when Linda popped up with a cup of coffee.

"Black, right?"

"Yeah, black. Thanks." She took the hot cup and sipped at it. "That's good."

"There's nothing better than that first cup of coffee in the morning," Linda said.

"So, what's on the agenda for today?"

"It's a straight shot right up to East Cape. Then a jibe and another straight shot up to North Cape. We could do that, just take it easy, but that would be kind of boring. Or we could do several jibes back and forth with you and Taylor doing the work, so that you'd get a good feel for the boat, the wind, the sails, everything. What do you think?"

"I'd like that, and I know Taylor would, too."

"Then that's what we'll do," Linda said. And that's what they did. The wind stayed out of the southeast so they got plenty of practice jibing and Bill assured them that when they passed the North Cape and were out in the blue Pacific they'd get to practice tacking.

"That'll be easy peasy," Linda said, "because you already have the hard part down pat and you're starting to understand how it all comes together." Haley thought she was going to explode with pride.

They had the sailors grog, rum and coke, at sundown. They were all in the cockpit watching the yellow ball as it slowly melted into the sea. The sky overhead was clear, but a band of wispy clouds surrounded the sun, glowing pinkish in the western sky.

"I don't know when I've ever seen anything so beautiful," Taylor said.

"There's nothing prettier than a sunset at sea," Linda said. Haley nodded as Linda took a sip of her drink.

Haley was tired and turned in right after dinner. She found it easy to sleep her second night at sea. She stargazed during her watches, but when they were over she was back in her cabin, eyes closed before her head hit the pillow. The morning came with her slowly wakening to the smell of coffee, bacon and eggs. She stuffed herself, loving every bite of the high cholesterol breakfast.

"Boy, you really wolfed it down," Taylor said.

"Without a guilty thought. I could get used to this life."

"Me too," Taylor said.

The wind picked up from fifteen to twenty knots, gusting to twenty-five, so they made better time, cruising along at ten knots, but right after they passed Great Barrier Island the wind died with the setting sun.

"Gonna have to motor," Bill said.

"Maybe we should wait a bit," Linda said. "We shouldn't use any more fuel than we have to."

"The wind's being blocked by the island behind. If we motor for ten or fifteen minutes we'll get it back." He started the engine.

"I think you're wrong." Linda crossed her arms.

"Linda, this is a stupid thing to fight over." They

were all in the cockpit.

"It's just another thing we disagree about."

"I think I'll go below," Haley said.

"Me too." Taylor followed Haley down the hatchway.

"Let's go to my cabin till they cool off," Haley whispered.

"Good idea." They made their way to the forward cabin and shut the door after themselves and sat on the bed. "Kinda small with two of us in here, isn't it?" Taylor said.

"And it was designed as a double cabin, can you believe that?" Haley felt a strange kind of anticipation, like when she was a little girl under the covers on Christmas Eve. She was excited, like something was going to happen. But what? Was it because she was shut up so close with Taylor?

"I smell that exhaust again," Taylor said.

"You're imagining it."

"No, I'm not. And I wasn't the first time either. Just smell."

Haley sniffed. "You're right, I smell it."

"I guess we should go out and tell them," Taylor got off the bed, opened the door and screamed, "Oh, my God. Fire! We have to get out of here. Come on, Haley!" Smoke drifted through the boat and it was flowing into the cabin. Haley chased after Taylor. But all of a sudden Taylor stopped. "Wait."

"Why?" Haley said.

"It's not a fire. It's exhaust. The exhaust I smelled earlier, that's what it is." Haley watched while Taylor opened one of the cabinet doors beneath the galley. Hot exhaust smoke steamed out from the engine compartment. "Tell them to shut it off."

"Okay." Three steps and she was at the companionway. "Shut off the engine. The boat's filling up with exhaust." She saw Bill's startled expression as Linda stabbed the shutdown switch with her index finger. The engine coughed and died.

Taylor backed away from the hot engine and opened an overhead hatch.

"What happened?" Bill was down in the salon now, hands shaking, as he surveyed the situation.

"Some kind of exhaust leak," Taylor said.

Bill looked into the engine compartment.

"Think you can fix it?" she asked.

"No. We'll have to have a mechanic look at it."

"But we have no wind," she said.

"It'll come back, it always does."

The flogging sails sounded like someone was pounding against the mast with a hammer.

"I'll go take care of that," Linda said.

"I'll help." Haley went up the companionway after her.

"When there's little or no wind," Linda said, "there's not a lot you can do to keep the sails from flogging, short of bringing them in and we can't do that without an engine. All we can do is to adjust them so that they make the best use of the little wind there is." She turned into the slight breeze. "The wind's shifted some."

"I can feel it." Haley turned her face to the west. "Barely." She looked at the speed log. "We're not going very fast."

"Two knots," Linda said. "It'll take awhile, but it'll get us there."

"How far do we have to go?"

"It's about a hundred miles northwest to Whangarei

or the same if we go southwest to Auckland. The way the wind is right now, we might make a little better time if we made for Auckland, but it's the wrong way. I'm guessing Bill will want to make for Whangarei. And he's right, the wind will pick up, and if it stays out of the east, it'll be a broad reach all the way in."

At noon the next day they had the mouth to Whangarei Harbor in sight. It was odd, Haley thought, the further north they went the warmer it became. Just the opposite of what she was used to.

"That's Bream Head on the right," Bill said. "And Marsden Point on the left. The entrance is between them. It's a little tricky, even if you have an engine, which we don't, so we're going to have to be on our toes."

"Tricky?" Taylor said.

"Yeah, we have to stay directly in the center of the channel. It's marked so it's usually not a problem."

"It looks plenty wide to me," Haley said.

"We have to avoid the sand banks."

"What's so hard about that?" Taylor said.

"They're under water. We can't see 'em."

"Oh."

"There's two right after we pass Bream Head. We have to make a straight in approach, jog to the right, then back to the left toward the oil docks. We have to stay well off the land on the port side because of the shallow shoal and if we drift too far to starboard we'll run aground on Snake Bank. That's an underwater sand bank over a mile long."

"Swell. Just how far in there do we have to go?"

"About twelve miles. You girls think you can do it?"

"What?" Haley said.

"Think you can do it?"

"No," Taylor said.

"Sure you can. I'll be right here giving directions. Haley can steer and you can work the sheets."

And to Haley's amazement they didn't have any trouble. He helped them through the first two sand banks, and from then on he just pointed out the hazards and let the girls figure out what to do themselves.

"We want to head straight for the left side of that point," Bill said after three hours of sailing up the river. "Right after we get around it you'll see a long pier. That's where we're going."

The girls were tired, but Haley felt like she could go another three hours, she was so pumped. And Taylor had been working the sheets, keeping the sail full, like a girl with a mission. It was almost as if she was her old self again.

"I see the pier," Haley said. "There's a white sailboat tied to the left, but the right side's empty, we can just coast her in."

"We're gonna have to get some fenders out." He got three from below. "Just keep doing what you're doing," he said. "I'll take care of these." He tied them to the lifelines, then flipped them over so that they dangled alongside, a buffer between the boat and the pier.

"Okay, Haley," Bill said, when he finished. "Take her in."

"Me?"

"Practical experience. The best way to learn. All you have to do is drive us right up next to the pier." Then to Taylor, "And all you have to do is gradually slow us down until we're at an almost dead stop alongside it. Then I'll jump over with a line and cleat us off."

"We can do this, Haley," Taylor said.

"I'm here, girls. I'll talk you through it."

"We don't need any talk," Taylor said.

"What?" Haley said.

"We can do it!" Taylor jumped out of the cockpit, dashed to the mast, took the main halyard off the cleat and let the sail drop. "Bill, you and Linda can tie it off," she said as she came back into the cockpit, where she was a whirl of activity. She slammed a winch handle into the furling winch. Haley watched as she bent over the top of it, breasts bobbing under the tee shirt, muscles rippling as she ground in the jib. Again she felt a queasy feeling and again she fought it away.

With the jib furled, Taylor jammed the line and took it off the winch like she'd been doing it all her life. "How's the speed?"

"Four knots, way too fast," Haley said.

Taylor wrapped the staysail sheet on the furling winch and ground in half of the small sail. "Now?"

"Two-and-a-half knots and slowing." Haley said. But she was sluggish, reminding Haley of her father's ten-year-old station wagon. She'd loved that old car, but then it was all she'd ever got to drive till she graduated and her dad gave her the Targa.

"A little to the right," Taylor said.

"I'm doing it." Haley turned the wheel. She found she had to turn it just a little farther then she wanted to get the boat to respond, but she was quick to bring the wheel back once she was on the new course. She checked the speed log. A knot and a half. Still too fast, but Taylor had seen it too, and she was already cranking in more sail, till only about a third of it was left out. The speed dropped to point-seven knots. They were closing fast. Taylor cranked in more sail. "Bring it all in," Haley said.

"Yeah," Taylor said, grinding on the winch as Haley kept her eyes on the speed. Point-five knots, point-four, point-three, point-two-five. They were barely moving. For a second it appeared they'd stopped too soon. She didn't know why, but she felt like she'd been defeated in some kind of sporting contest.

Then Bill yelled out, "You've done it!"

Dark Witch was still moving, approaching the pier so slowly it was almost as if they were standing still. Haley held the wheel steady, elation running through her. Watching, waiting. Then they kissed the side of the pier and Bill was over the lifelines, tying them off.

"I'll be damned, that sailboat. It's *Ghost Dancer*." Linda was looking at the boat tied on the other side of the pier.

"The thirteenth Phoenix?" Haley asked.

"Yeah, the thirteenth Phoenix."

"I thought they were all painted black."

"All except her. White's the color for a ghost."

CHAPTER

TEN

STACY GOT OUT OF THE CAB in front of the motel on a cold New Zealand evening. He doubted its two star rating, but it was out of the way and private. The sun was going down, glowing orange in the western sky. He barely noticed. A chill tingled the back of his neck as he approached the room.

He opened the door with the key Randy had sent over to the Sterling. It was risky flying her over from San Francisco, but he couldn't help himself.

"What?" He almost left, but the girl sitting on the bed was exquisite, very young, and blindfolded.

"Surprise." She sounded like a child.

"Where's Randy?" Stacy said.

"She's gone for a while." The girl stood from the bed. She was unsteady without her sight, but she managed to face him. "Do you like me?" She kind of pouted and put her hands on her hips.

"Sure." Stacy felt an erection building. "But I don't understand."

"She said that I have to leave the blindfold on because I'm way under age and you could get in trouble if I could identify you."

"How old are you?"

"Fifteen."

"And you're my surprise?"

"Yeah." Her hands went to her blouse and she started working the buttons. Fifteen, the thought sent shivers to his erection. He'd never had one so young.

"What's your name?" His hands were at his belt as she shrugged out of the blouse.

"Carol." She wasn't wearing a bra. Her small, perky breasts were shivering, betraying the fear. She was terrified. Stacy slipped off his shoes and stepped out of his pants. He was ready.

Two hours later he opened the door for Randy. "I'll be back as soon as I drop Carol," she said. Then he was alone.

He spent a few minutes staring at the ceiling, then decided on a shower. He set the spray hot as he liked it and stepped in. A few minutes later Randy stepped under the spray with him. She had a bar of soap in her hand and she started to lather him up.

"How'd you find her?" he asked.

"Trade secret. Did you like her?"

"She was a scared little kid."

"So did you enjoy yourself?"

"Immensely."

"You wanna tell me about it?"

He did and he found himself getting hard again during the telling.

"That's what I like to see." She grabbed him around the erection and led him to the bed.

* * *

Gayle stared at the stainless steel bars that ran around the toilet. It seemed to be getting harder for her to move herself from the wheelchair to the toilet seat. The opposite from what she would have expected. For a second she wished she'd used the bedpan, but that would be giving in. She pushed herself to her feet and felt a flash of quick pain as blood rushed into her foot. Then she was on the seat. By the time she was finished her foot was screaming. She pushed the buzzer, stood and plopped back into the wheelchair.

"Ready for the ride back, Mrs. S?" It was Danny.

"What a pleasant surprise," Gayle said. "I was expecting Gwen." She'd long gotten over being embarrassed in front of him. In a very short time she'd become used to her backside and other parts of her body being exposed to hospital personnel. In fact, she didn't think anything could ever embarrass her again.

"Night shift now," Danny said, "right in the middle of your toilet." He laughed as he pulled the leg brace out and set it in place, then he gently lifted her leg onto it.

"I didn't know you could do that," Gayle said.

"They've been wheeling you around with your foot down?" Danny asked.

"Just to the toilet. It hasn't really started hurting till last night."

"It'll get worse," Danny said. "It's because you're on your back all day. When you stand or even sit with your foot down, it's gonna hurt. You should keep it elevated as much as you can until after the pins come out."

"That's what Dave said."

"Dr. Collins is a good doctor."

"I think so," she said.

"Is that why you're staying in New Zealand, because you like Dr. Collins?"

"I suppose so, but it's more than that. I can be myself here. Nobody knows me."

"So you're famous back home?"

"Yeah, but it's even more than that. Look at us. We're having a conversation in a bathroom. I'm an attractive woman and you're a young man with a tattooed face. Back home I'd be afraid of you. Even if we were in a hospital."

"It's that bad there?"

"Oh, yeah. In a lot of ways we've become prisoners in our own homes. I've been in your country for almost a month and haven't seen one window with bars on it. Your homes aren't patrolled by private security guards. You don't have gated communities or cops with guns. Heck, you don't even have hand guns. People are safe here. Nobody's afraid of anybody. Nobody has any reason to be."

"It's not all roses," Danny said.

"Go to L.A. or New York for a month, then come back and say that."

"You don't paint a very pretty picture of America."

"No, I guess I don't. You know, I met a nice woman

at a bookstore in Auckland. We got to talking and she invited Dylan and me over to her home for tea. We'd only been in her house a short while when it started to rain. After a few minutes someone knocked on her door. It was the mailman. He wanted to come in out of the wet until it stopped. He had lunch with us. That could never happen in Los Angeles. You just don't knock on a stranger's door to come in out of the rain. Not if you don't want to be shot. I don't think I'll ever be happy there again."

"Come on, Mrs. S. you're just feeling lousy because of your loss and because of your leg. You'll be all better in a couple of months and you'll feel the pain of your loss less and less each day as time goes on."

"My brother-in-law is a psychiatrist, you should talk to him. There might be a future in it for you."

"Why, Mrs. S. flattery will get you everywhere." His smile lit up his face and Gayle could swear that his dark eyes sparkled. "And right now it's going to get you back to your bed." He moved behind the wheelchair and started to push her toward the door.

"Come talk to me again, Danny," she said, after he'd helped her into bed. "You're like a breath of fresh air and I need all of that I can get."

"You can count on it, Mrs. S., but right now I think you should close those misty eyes of yours and get some sleep."

"I have misty eyes?"

"Yes, you do," he said. "Now close them and I'll see you later."

"Yes, sir." She closed them, but it took her a long time to fall asleep.

* * *

"Good morning, gorgeous." Gayle opened her eyes to the sound of her husband's usual cheerful voice. She'd missed it lately.

"Morning, Stacy." He bent to kiss her, but she turned her head and his lips found only her cheek.

"Morning breath, bad." She put a hand in front of her mouth and pantomimed breathing into it. "Oh, yeah, bad." His lips curled up, quivering as he tried to conceal a laugh. "Bad, bad," she said. The smile broke and he laughed.

"I love you, kiddo," he said.

"I love you, too."

"You know you can still come back with me. You'll be on a stretcher the whole way. And you'd have your own nurse for the flight." His hands were shaking, just a little. He seemed nervous and that wasn't like him. Nothing got to Stacy Sterling. He could handle anything.

"I couldn't. I'd rather be here by myself than back there. I couldn't stand the stories. And the pictures. My puffed up face would be on the cover of everything. The press would hound me to hell and back. They'd dredge up Dylan and that would depress me. It's better that I stay. Better for me and better for you. You'd worry yourself to death when you should be out there giving them hell. You'd cut dinners, rallies, and fund raisers short so you could rush home to your sick wife. Worse, you'd cancel out of town engagements till I was better. This way you're free to run around without worry."

"What makes you think I won't worry? I'll be worried sick."

"Yeah, but I know you. You put things out of your mind that you can't do anything about. If I'm home, the ailing and recovering wife, you'll have it in your head that you have to cheer me up and you'll think you could make me better faster if you waited on me hand and foot. I'd get my meals in bed, you'd be there to fluff my pillows, read to me, draw my bath and a thousand and one different things. I won't have it. You go home. Run around the country. Do what you have to do to get your name on the ballot next year. Just do me a couple of favors."

"Anything. I'd do anything for you."

"Call me every day."

"Of course. What's the other thing?"

"Don't let them drag Dylan into it. Just say no comment whenever they bring her name up."

"That could be hard," he said. "They're going to want to know."

"Don't tell them. Let Dylan be. Please, for me, for Taylor." He didn't answer immediately. Oh, God, she thought, he was going to make a big deal out of Dylan's death after all, use it to get votes.

"Alright," he said. "This is what I'll do. I'll start my next speech saying, 'Tragically my daughter, Dylan, lost her life in New Zealand. My family misses her very much and I hope that in this matter you'll respect my privacy. From this point on all questions about her, or the accident that took her life, will be answered with a *no comment*. I'm sorry but that's all I'll say publicly about this.' How's that?" Stacy took her hand. "That way I won't seem quite so cold."

"That's fine, Stacy." She felt a slight tremor in his hand.

"So now all we have to do is get you better. And you're right. If you recovered at home, I'd worry morning till night. I'd never get anything done. But you're wrong to think I'd put you out of my mind just because you're so far away. I'd still worry and I'd still not get anything done. I'd feel like I was abandoning you. So I'd probably fly down here every weekend, and since it's so far I'd lose four days out of the week instead of two. I'd be so jet lagged the rest of the time that I'd be useless. I'd be better off dropping out of the race."

"That's the last thing I want. You've worked so hard for this."

"So in typical Sterling fashion Sandy and I have come up with the perfect solution."

"This I have to hear," Gayle said.

"I talked to Dr. Collins and he said that you could leave the hospital this afternoon."

"Stacy," she said.

"Wait, let me finish. He said you could continue treatment on an out patient basis, if you have the proper care and can come in on occasion for a check up. So, I've arranged to have you moved to the Sterling."

"Stacy."

"I'm not finished yet. Sandy's going to stay. Dr. Madrigal can continue seeing his patients, so he doesn't have to go back right away. He'll be bunking in the next room, just a connecting door away."

"I don't want Sandy waiting on me hand and foot all the time."

"I know that. We hired a nine to five nurse. I knew you wouldn't want some stranger, so we worked it out with the hospital."

"What do you mean?"

"You can come in, son." Stacy turned to the door.

"How you going, Mrs. S?"

"Danny, how come you didn't tell me?"

"Mr. S. made me promise to keep it a secret. He

wanted to be the one to tell you."

"I love the way he calls me that," Stacy said. "Do you think I could get my staff to do that?" He laughed and Gayle found herself laughing along with him. He was right, in typical Sterling fashion the brothers had gotten together and come up with the perfect solution to a problem. There was nothing Stacy and Sandy together couldn't do.

"They have to teach you how to use crutches before they'll let you out of here," Stacy said. "And I have a few political things to do."

"Like what?" Gayle said. She couldn't believe how Stacy was taking care of everything, putting her first. Her heart swelled with the love she had for him.

"I'm a United States Senator and I'm running for president. It'd be rude if I didn't go by and see the prime minister. Besides, he's kind of a friend."

"I understand."

"But I'll be by to see you before they take you to the hotel. I love you." He bent to kiss her. This time she offered her lips. To hell with the morning breath.

"I love you, too," she said when he pulled away.

"See you later," he said.

"*Hasta entonces,*" she said.

"Yeah, till then." He flashed a smile. Then he was gone. Danny left, too. But he was quickly replaced by a woman with a pair of crutches.

"I'm Katy. I'll be your physiotherapist." She had a sweet voice, green eyes, red hair and freckles. Gayle thought she looked like a female Tom Sawyer. Freckles and Midwestern innocence, until you looked into those eyes. "I'm going to teach you how to use the crutches."

"I thought I was supposed to keep the foot elevated."

"Dr. Collins said that it's okay to use them for short trips, like going to the toilet."

"Well I don't think I need a teacher. How hard can it be?"

"That's what everyone thinks," Katy said, "but you'd be surprised. Now, the most important thing to remember is not to stick them up into your armpits. Keep your arms stiff and let the crutches hit you in the rib cage, like this."

"I can do that," Gayle said.

"Let's see."

Gayle used the overhead bar to prop herself up and hung onto it as she slid out of bed. She stood, holding onto the mattress for support.

"Give me those babies and watch me go."

"Okay, they're all yours." Katy handed them over and Gayle held them the way she'd been shown and took a slow tenuous step. Then another.

"It's harder than I thought and my foot feels like it's gonna explode."

"Pretty good for a first try," Katy said. Then, "We'll work for five minute intervals, then you can sit and rest your foot. It's gonna hurt, but it's the only way they'll let you out of here. If you can't walk on the crutches, you gotta stay."

"Then let's get started," Gayle said.

Katy worked with her for the next couple of hours and by the time they'd finished Katy told her that she'd passed Crutches 101 with flying colors. Then the big test. She walked to the bathroom by herself. No help. Her foot throbbed and her arms felt like they were on fire, but she made it. And she made it back to the bed by herself. No more calling on others so she could pee. She was already starting to be independent.

She'd just climbed back up into bed when Danny was back, pushing a wheelchair. "The ambulance is downstairs. They're ready for you."

"Now?"

"Now," he said. "You want to walk or ride?"

"I'll ride, thank you very much." He helped her into her robe and then into the wheelchair. She said goodbye to her roommates. He handed her the crutches and she held them to herself as he wheeled her out of the room for the last time.

They took an elevator down to the garage level, where Danny and the driver helped her into the back of the ambulance. It wasn't until they were pulling up to the Wellington Sterling when she realized Stacy hadn't come to see her. Oh well, the meeting with the prime minister must have gone on longer than he'd planned. He'd probably come by the hotel on his way to the airport and say goodbye.

Danny was first out of the ambulance and unfolding the wheelchair when an older man approached. Sandy was with him. He smiled at her and it looked like he was about to say something, but the man spoke first. "My name's Geordie Champion. I'm the manager of the hotel. It's going to be my job to see that you're as comfortable as possible, Mrs. Sterling."

"Gayle, call me Gayle."

"Okay, Gayle. I'll show you to your room." He talked as he walked. "You're in the Sterling Suite on the fifteenth floor. It connects to the double next door where Dr. Sterling will be staying."

"I don't want the suite," Gayle said. "Sandy can take it."

"But Gayle," Sandy said, "you'd probably be more comfortable in the larger room."

"I only need three things. A bed, a toilet and a television. Do you have those in the double, Mr. Champion?"

"Yes."

"Then I'll take the double."

"It's yours," Geordie Champion said. "We also have twenty-four hour room service." He went on as if she hadn't interrupted him. "You probably know that, but what you don't know is that I'll personally take the head off anybody who doesn't drop what they're doing and respond to your requests with all possible haste."

"I don't want to be any trouble," Gayle said as Danny wheeled her into the elevator.

"Don't be silly. Cause trouble. That's what we're here for. As far as your meals are concerned, you'll find Seaside Cafe and Seaview Restaurant menus in your room. You can order breakfast from the cafe menu and lunch and dinner from either one. We have satellite TV. CNN is on channel ten, Fox News is on twelve. Those seem to be the only channels Americans ever watch." Gayle wondered how he knew that. He was still babbling as he unlocked the door and Danny was wheeling her across the threshold.

The room was nice, she thought, two queen-sized beds, separated by a nightstand with a telephone on it. The remote for the television was next to the phone. The television was on a chest of drawers on the wall opposite the foot of the beds. The carpet was salmon and plush. The light green walls were almost a pastel color.

"You're sure you don't want the suite," Sandy said.

"No, this is fine."

The phone rang in the next room.

"I'll get it," Sandy said and he went through the connecting door to the suite. "It's for you, Gayle," he said, coming back into the room a few seconds later, "Stacy. I had it transferred here." And as he finished saying it the phone rang.

Danny pushed her between the beds to the nightstand as Sandy picked up the phone and handed it to her.

"Hi, honey, things took longer than I thought and now I barely have time to make the airport. I hope you understand."

"Yeah, sure."

"I'll call you as soon as I get to L.A."

"Okay," she said, disappointed.

"I love you."

"I love you, too." She put the phone down after she heard his hang up.

* * *

She clicked the television off with the remote. She was lying naked on top of the covers. The heater was on high and the room was hot. She had to pee. She looked at the clock. Eight-thirty. Six hours since the last time. Whatever was wrong with her in that department appeared to be getting better. Thank God. The crutches were beside her on the bed. She pushed herself into a sitting position with her legs dangling over the side.

"I can do this," she said. She struggled to her feet. "Keep the arms stiff, don't dig them into the arm pits," she told herself as she crutched her way to the bathroom.

"Double damn!" The toilet faced her, seat up and she didn't know what to do. It didn't have those bars around it like the ones in the hospital. She stood there staring at it. The toilet was next to the bathtub. If she backed up next to it, then gradually lowered herself, she could use the bathtub rim for support, kind of like she did with the bars.

She scooted around to its left side and lowered the seat. That done she moved around so that the back of her legs were up against the bowl. She shifted her weight to the crutch on her left and dropped the other one into the tub. She grabbed onto the rim as she lowered herself and to her great satisfaction she made it.

She did her business, flushed, then leaned over and plucked the crutch from the tub. Then she pushed herself to her feet, lost her balance and went tumbling forward.

* * *

Sandy sat at the kauri wood desk. It reminded him of dark, gnarly oak. It was a magnificent piece of furniture. The suite was tastefully done. Plush salmon carpets, walls painted eggshell white with original paintings by local artists. The sofa and matching chairs were trimmed in the kauri wood and the coffee and end tables were made of it as well. He was staring at Dylan's PowerBook.

She'd kept a journal and he thought it would be good for Gayle if she could read it. That way she'd have a personal part of her daughter with her forever. But the laptop was another casualty of the accident. It wouldn't boot up.

Tomorrow he'd take it to an expert, he told himself. He got up from the desk and was about to head for the bedroom when he heard Gayle shouting his name. He ran to the connecting door.

"Gayle!"

"In here, the bathroom."

"What happened? Oh, shit." She was naked.

"I fell and couldn't get back up," she said. Then she laughed. "That's funny."

"Where's your robe?" He tried not to look as he helped her to her feet.

"Just help me back to bed."

"Okay, lean on me." He wrapped an arm around her waist and led her back to the bed. She sat on the edge of it as he looked away.

"It's funny," she said. "I fell and I can't get up. Like in that stupid commercial."

"I get it," he said as she pulled the bedspread around herself.

"It's okay, you can turn around now. I'm covered." He did, but he couldn't get the picture of her lying naked on the bathroom floor out of his mind. He'd tried not to look, but he'd seen too much.

Chapter

Eleven

SANDY LAY ON TOP OF THE COVERS, perspiring in the old
sweats he used for pajamas, and watched her sleep. Her
blonde hair was splayed around the pillow, highlighted by
the early morning sun streaming in the windows. The
thermostat was set too high and it was hot. She'd thrown
off the covers during the night. She was lying on her back.
Two of the buttons on the flannel pajama top had come
undone and they did little to conceal the rhythmic rise
and fall of her breasts. But it was the fuzzy, brown triangle
between her legs, barely hidden by the thin panties, that
captured his eyes as surely as the trap snags the rat.

They'd talked last night, really talked. And that was

unusual for him, because he was Sanford Sterling, the world's greatest listener. All his life he'd been absorbing other people's problems and making them his own. It was habit.

But Gayle had listened to him ramble on. And ramble on he did, telling her of his love of old movies, old blues and old cars. He told her how he'd often felt that he'd been born too late. He loved everything about the '40s and '50s. It was a time when you knew your neighbor, could fix your own car, could count on the post office, didn't have to lock your door. A time before metal detectors in airports, libraries and schools. A simpler time.

"Also a time of segregation, burning crosses, Nazis and World War," Gayle had said. And Sandy had agreed. He knew about the bad, he just chose not to think about it.

"That's why I love you so much," she'd said, "because you only see the best of things." He knew she'd meant that she loved him like a brother, but still it charged him, filling him with the kind of glow a teenager feels when he falls in love for the first time, and it was wrong, because she was his brother's wife.

He could still taste the lemon flavor of the Sterling Chicken room service had brought up for dinner. Chicken breasts, crispy and brown, sautéed in a lemon butter sauce, perfect with the Australian Chardonnay they'd had with it. By the time room service had cleared away the dishes, they'd finished the first bottle of wine. An hour later, with the second bottle of wine half gone, they were reliving their childhoods. Another hour and another half bottle and it didn't seem strange at all when she'd asked him to sleep in the opposite bed.

"That way if I need help during the night, I won't

have to shout to you in the next room," she said and when she'd suggested it, it seemed natural, so he went next door and put on his sweats. When he returned, she'd asked him to turn up the thermostat and in seconds she was asleep, looking like an angel.

And she still looked angelic. He sat up, unsure if he should wake her. He decided against it, she needed all the rest she could get. He covered her with the bedspread, then made up his bed. He didn't want anyone to suspect he'd slept in her room. Then he went next door, where he showered, shaved, put on his running shoes, a pair of faded Levi's and an old sweat shirt with cut off sleeves, almost the twin of the one he slept in, then he remembered Dylan's computer and decided against an early morning run.

He poked his head into Gayle's room and found her still asleep. He wasn't worried about her, Danny was due at 9:00. Downstairs, he found Geordie and asked him for directions to the nearest Apple dealer. Geordie looked it up in the phone book. There was one close by.

Sandy found the computer store after a brisk walk. It was cold out and Levi's and a sweatshirt weren't enough. He pushed through the door and found himself in a warm waiting room decorated with posters of Apple Mac products on the walls, but not a computer or a soul in sight. He checked his watch. Five after eight.

"Are you open yet? Is anybody here?"

No answer.

"Hey, customer out here."

"Oh, hi, sorry." The speaker had slipped into the waiting room from a side door. He was young and wearing jeans as faded as Sandy's Levi's, a blue work shirt and a red tie, along with black high top tennis shoes. He wore his stringy hair long and it covered most of his face. He pushed it back, revealing restless green eyes that took in and recorded everything.

Dylan had restless eyes. That was how he was able to tell the twins apart. Dylan saw things others missed and she had had an uncanny ability to know the whole of a thing by seeing only a part. Show her a piece of the puzzle and the jigsaw of life unfolded before her like magic.

"You okay?" the kid said.

"Yeah, sure," Sandy said. "Just lost in thought for a second."

"I do that a lot." He pushed his hair out of his eyes again, but it fell right back. Sandy wondered if he was old enough to shave.

"I got a PowerBook that doesn't want to boot up."

"Then you came to the right place," the kid said.

"It was in an auto accident, so it probably took quite a shock."

"If it's possible to fix, I can make it work. I'm sort of a PowerBook junkie. I've got seven that work, all given up by their owners as hopeless."

"When can I come back for it?"

"Give me an hour. If it's simple, it'll be done by then. If it's impossible, then I'll need an extra day." The kid was smiling, eyes bright. He didn't look like he got out much.

"You want a deposit?"

"No, I have the machine. That's better than cash money any day."

* * *

Gayle couldn't believe it. She'd slept the night through without having to go to the bathroom, and she'd had wine last night, but she had to go now. She sat up and threw the bedspread off. She heard gulls outside, sunlight was streaming in the window and it was almost too hot, even for her. She noticed that the top had come undone on the PJs. It was a good thing she was under the covers, or Sandy would have gotten another eyeful.

She looked over to the other bed. It was made up, but she knew Sandy had slept there. She wondered why she'd suggested he sleep in her room. She could easily pick up the phone and call next door if she needed anything. But it didn't seem wrong, him sleeping there. They were adults, after all, but still others might not understand.

She heard a knock on the door. Then, "It's me, Danny. Are you decent?"

"Just a second." Her robe was at the foot of the bed. She put it on and tightened it up as all thoughts of Sandy in the next bed fled from her mind. "Okay, you can come in now." She heard the lock click as he used his key.

"It's a sauna in here, Mrs. S." He set a backpack down by the door. It looked heavy.

"Yeah, I know. I had asthma when I was little. Sometimes nights were very bad and I found that if I slept with the heat up it was easier to breathe. The asthma's gone, but now I can't sleep unless it's real hot. It took Stacy a long time to get used to it."

"I'll bet."

"It's not dark any more, you can turn the heat down."

"You got it, Mrs. S." He went to the thermostat and fiddled with it.

"You can call me Gayle."

"Don't want to. I like Mrs. S. It fits you."

"How do you mean?"

"It's got kind of a mysterious sound to it. Sort of like that look in your eyes. Mystical, magical and mysterious."

"Why Danny, I think that's a compliment, but I thought I had misty eyes."

"You do, sometimes. And it is a compliment."

"Thanks. I don't get many."

"Then you're hanging out with the wrong men. Stay in this country for awhile and some Kiwi is going to sweep you off your feet."

"Danny, stop." She laughed.

"We all need compliments now and then," he said. "Now what can I do for you?"

"You can help me up. I need to use the bathroom."

"Just this once," he said, offering her his arm. "Katy told me not to baby you."

"No, it's alright, you can baby me."

"She said it would be that much harder for you later on, after the cast comes off."

"You baby me now. We'll worry about that, then. Okay?"

"You're the boss, Mrs. S. If you want to be babied, I'll be your babysitter. And I'll stand by your side when Katy vents her wrath."

"She's that tough?"

"You'll find out."

"Brrr," she said, then they were in the bathroom. "It's so ignoble." She sat on the toilet. "I'll call when I'm finished."

"Sure thing, Mrs. S." He left her alone, shutting the door on his way out. She pulled up the robe and wondered why such a basic human function had to be so embarrassing.

Back in bed, she picked up the remote and clicked the power button. "If you've got something you want to do, I'll be alright for a couple of hours," she said as the screen lit up with the CNN news.

"They're paying me to be at your beck and call, but I can see where you might want some privacy. Dr. Sterling said I have free access to the room next door, so I'll go over there and study."

"Study what?"

"I'm brushing up on my chemistry and calculus. I'm thinking about going back to school."

"Really?"

"I've come this far. I might as well go all the way."

"So when would you start?"

"Next year. I need to save some money. I can get help from the government. They want Maori doctors, but it won't pay for everything."

"Go study. If I need anything, I'll yell." He picked up his backpack. Now she knew why it looked heavy. Chemistry and Calculus, big books. He slung the pack over his shoulder and left the room, leaving her alone with the news.

She studied the newscaster before she turned up the volume. It was an old habit, studying the competition. He was a young man with hair that looked like plastic. His perfect teeth reminded her of piano keys. She wondered if he could close his mouth. He looked like a hyena with big eyes. She laughed. They always looked silly with the sound off. She pressed the volume button and listened to his Walter Cronkite imitation. Maybe she was being overly critical. After all, he was reading before the world while she was still stuck in a local market. True, Los Angeles was a big market, but it was still just the local news. It wasn't the network and it wasn't CNN.

"Senator Sterling came back from New Zealand early this morning where he buried his daughter, Dylan, tragically killed by a drunk driver," the newsman said. She'd been so caught up with mentally abusing him that she hadn't been paying attention to what he had been saying. "We go now to a tape of Christine Coffee at Los Angeles International airport with the story."

The image on the screen changed. She recognized the airport lounge at the Tom Bradley International Terminal. The camera zoomed in on Stacy as he came through the gate. He looked haggard. Freddy Carson was there with a hand out. Stacy shook it. Then the two men embraced. Stacy broke the hug, then he was hugging a young woman with flowing auburn hair. It seemed like they hugged a little tighter and longer than appropriate, but Stacy had always been emotional. That's what made him such a good politician. He kissed the girl on the cheek as he broke the hug. Then he hugged old Gloria Grisham, one of the women on his San Francisco staff. It seemed everybody who worked for him was there. The San Francisco and Los Angeles crew, Freddy from D.C. and there was Janis, also from the Washington office. This was going to be a big deal.

"Senator Sterling, I know this is a hard time for you, but do you have a statement?"

"Yes, Christine, I do. A week ago today my daughter, Dylan, was killed by a drunk driver. This is a problem that plagues New Zealand as well as America. And sadly it's a problem that we tend to ignore. If the drunk makes it safely home, we put him to bed and laugh it off. Only when something like this happens do we take notice, but then we quickly forget. Not this time. If elected I will see that federal highway funds are cut off from any state that doesn't introduce mandatory six months sentences for first time drunk drivers. If they do it again, I want them put away for a year.

"I know there are those that will say this is an abuse of presidential power. I disagree. I intend to act. The way I see it, either we allow drunk drivers on our streets, endangering our kids, or we don't. This is the way I intend to lead, by action, not talk. That's all for now."

Gayle punched the power button and the television flickered off. She was saddened that he appeared to be using Dylan the way he was, but she supposed his staff told him he had to say more than they'd agreed upon or else the press would hammer him to death with questions. Stacy probably felt that he didn't have any choice.

* * *

Sandy was back in the computer store on schedule and the kid came up front right away.

"Got you fixed up." He had Dylan's computer bag hanging over his shoulder.

"Lots of steamy stuff on there."

"You read it?" Sandy said.

"Just glanced at it."

"How much do I owe you?" Sandy didn't know what was on there, so he didn't know what the kid had seen, but he felt if he didn't make a big deal out of it the kid would forget all about it in a couple of days. The kid quoted a figure. Sandy paid him and left with the computer.

Outside, he inhaled the cold air. He'd spent the last hour shivering and walking. He needed warm things. He ducked into a touristy shop and bought a wool sweater with a baby blue and beige weave that seemed nautical to him. He put it on over the sweat shirt. Then he was on the street again and he found that he was hungry. He'd missed breakfast and he didn't feel like going right back to the hotel. He still felt guilty about watching Gayle as she slept, so he found a restaurant with a waterfront view. He ordered bacon and eggs and wolfed them down the way only a hungry man can.

He ordered a second cup of coffee and while he was waiting for it he took the PowerBook out of its bag and set it up on the table.

"Going to do a little work?" the waitress said, bringing his coffee. She was older than his mother, Maori, and friendly.

"Just checking on work already finished," he said.

"Take as long as you like, we're between breakfast and lunch." It was a polite way of telling him that he couldn't sit there all day.

He opened the computer, heard the chime as it started up. He fingered the trackpad, moving the pointer to *Journal* and double clicked. Another window opened showing three folders labeled, *Sixteen*, *Seventeen* and *Eighteen*. He moved the pointer and double clicked on *Sixteen*. There were nine documents in the folder, all labeled with a date. He picked one, double clicked again and started reading.

> *Last night was the best and the worst. Taylor and I kissed. Not a sisterly kiss, something deeper. I love her so much. If what we did is wrong then there's something fucked about the way life works. I shivered and quivered like a little girl when her tongue slinked into my mouth, but when I felt her down there, how her body shimmied beneath my hand, that was the best, the most absolute.*

He looked away from the screen, palms sweaty. He was getting aroused. He'd sampled *Sixteen* so he double clicked on *Seventeen*. Unlike *Sixteen*, *Seventeen* was broken down into twelve folders, labeled *January* through *December*. The twins' birthdays were on January the eighth. He'd given Dylan the computer for Christmas two years ago. Apparently she'd started writing right away, because the dates in *Sixteen* went from the 27th of December till the 7th of January. He double clicked on *July* and was surprised to see a document dated for every day of the month. She never missed. He double clicked on *15 July* and read:

> *I wonder if anybody but me knows that Dad wants to be president. I wonder if he knows himself. I see the way he stares at the television whenever the real president is on and I see the thirst in his eyes. He wants that job, he just doesn't know it yet, but I know. I wonder what Jennifer will have to say about it, or that other girl. I wonder if the skeletons in the back of the Sterling closets will come out to haunt him. How thorough will the press be when they sneak through the pages of his past? Will they find out what should stay hidden and buried? If he knew about those old bones, would he chance it? Would he risk destroying everything the Sterlings have built? I see the thirst. He's like a man who's been too long in the desert. Can anything quench it?*

Sandy shivered. What was Dylan talking about? They

had all been at the Castle when she wrote that. The rest of *15 July* was about how they'd rented all three *Star Wars* movies and lazed the day away. Sandy remembered that day. He clicked on another date. It was all trivial family stuff. But he'd read enough to know that he had to go through it all.

He chose *June*, going back a month, and read for an hour. Mostly stuff about school and boyfriends. Nothing that could harm the Sterlings. Then he opened *20 June* and read:

> *Day seven of summer vacation, day five at the Castle and last night Taylor and I made quiet but passionate love. We've done it plenty of times, but never anywhere but in our own beds. This was the first time in the Castle. I don't know why we've never done it here, but somehow with the whole family around it just seemed, not wrong, but not right either.*
>
> *At home our rooms are right next to each other, with a connecting door. Here they're separated by Gran's room, Uncle Simon's, and the upstairs library. Miles between them. I don't know why it worked out that way. It just did.*
>
> *When we were younger we used to scoot back and forth between each other's rooms with wild abandon. Maybe that's why we haven't slept together here. Sneaking around makes it seem dirty. I don't know why, but it does.*
>
> *Anyway, I was sneaking out of Taylor's room around three in the morning. I wasn't sleepy so I ducked into the library for something*

*to read. It's not a real library. The real one,
with the hardcover books, is downstairs for
everyone to see. The upstairs library is just a
den full of bookcases and paperbacks. Uncle
Simon is a speed reader and he reads
everything. I left the door open a crack and was
quietly looking through the books by the light of
the moon that, like me, had sneaked into the
room.*

*I heard a creaking hinge, so I went to the
door and peeked out, and, much to my surprise,
I saw Gran coming out of Uncle Simon's room.
And she was sneaking. I know. It takes one to
know one. She was sneaking.*

*What was she doing there? Was she doing
what I think she was doing? I'll find out
tomorrow.*

Sandy looked up from the computer. Sweat ringed his
forehead. If what he'd read was true and not the
imagination of a seventeen-year-old girl, then Dylan was
right on track when she talked about skeletons in Sterling
closets. This could destroy Stacy. His mother sleeping
with his brother. His daughters lesbians. How could it get
any worse? But maybe there was a logical explanation for
what she'd seen that night. He was about to click on *21
June* when he noticed the time in the upper right hand
corner of the screen. Eleven forty-five. Almost lunch time.
He looked up and saw his Maori waitress staring at him.
He'd overstayed his welcome. Time to go.

He speed-walked to the hotel. He nodded to the girl
at the front desk as he made straight for the elevator.
Although it wasn't unusually warm in the hotel, it seem

sweltering to him, having just come in from the cold out-of-doors. He set the computer on the floor in the elevator and took off the sweater. He was sweating like he'd just run a mile in the Caribbean.

He was surprised to find Danny on the couch with his nose buried in a chemistry book. He'd have to wait till later to check the computer. He stashed it in the closet, made a few minutes worth of small talk, then went next door to visit with Gayle, leaving Danny to his studies.

"Hey, big guy," Gayle said when he poked his head through the door.

"How you feeling?" He came into the room and sat on the opposite bed.

"Like there's this tiny little man stabbing my foot with a nail." Her brow was furrowed and her fingers were balled into fists. She was in pain.

"Why don't you take the pills?"

"They make me nauseous. I'd rather have the pain."

"That's barbaric," he said.

"I'll get through till dinner, then I'll take something. Hey, I have an idea, why don't we order up a bottle of one of those New Zealand Cabernets from the Marlborough wine country?"

"I don't think you should mix the pills with alcohol."

"I agree. I'll have a couple of glasses of wine with dinner to help me sleep. That way I won't need the pills."

"What are you watching?"

"Some British sitcom. I think I'd like a video."

"I heard that, Mrs. S." Danny said, peeking his head in the door. "I can take care of that for you. I'm sure the hotel could get you a player, but forget it. Tomorrow I'll bring mine in. State of the art. Surround sound. You'll think you're at the cinema. And don't worry about movies, let me be your video guide. If it's worth having I've got it. I'm the biggest movie junkie south of the equator."

"That's nice," she said.

"If you have any preferences, let me know."

"I'll leave it to you."

"Good." Then to Sandy, "You want to leave us alone for a bit, Dr. S. It's bath time."

"You are not going to wash me," Gayle said.

"Oh yes I am. Relax, I'll keep my eyes closed." He was laughing. "No, seriously you can do the private parts. I'll just do your back and legs. How's that?"

"I saw a small wine store down the street, I think I'll go and check it out, maybe find something a little unusual." Sandy winked at her, then retreated to his room and closed the connecting door. He wondered just how much of her Danny was going to bathe, then chased the thought from his mind as he pulled the sweater back on.

He took a long walk before buying the wine. He had a lot to think about. Part of him wanted to trash everything on Dylan's hard drive. Gayle would assume it happened in the accident. But part of him didn't want to destroy her last link with her daughter. He'd have to clean it up. But he wasn't sure he could stand any more of Dylan's revelations.

At the wine store, he settled on a California Cabernet and a New Zealand Cab from the Marlborough area that Gayle had suggested. He thought it might be a good idea to compare them.

He got back to the hotel just before five, in time to say goodbye to Danny. Then he picked up the phone and ordered a couple of wine glasses from downstairs.

"I got one of ours and one of theirs so we can

compare. You want a glass before dinner?"

"Or two," she said. "My foot is fairly screaming. I ordered dinner for 6:00. Steak Diane, medium rare. Is that okay?"

"Perfect," he said. He opened both wines and they'd finished half of each by the time dinner arrived. They spent the meal in small talk and when it was over so was the rest of the wine.

"Should I call down for another bottle?"

"No, I don't think so. I'm pretty sleepy, I took a couple of those pills Dave gave me to help me sleep."

"I thought you weren't going to take any pills with the wine."

"Pain pills. I wasn't going to take any pain pills. Besides, I didn't drink that much, I'll be fine."

"I've got some work to do next door to keep me company, so I'll leave you then."

"Could you just turn the heat up some before you go?"

"Sure. Night."

He set the thermostat the way she liked it, then went back to his room. It had been his intention to read more from Dylan's journal, but he'd had more to drink than he thought. So had Gayle, despite what she'd said. He flopped on the sofa, picked up the remote and turned on the television. He went through the channels till he found *African Queen* in mid movie. He watched it with the sound on low till it was over. Then he went to check on Gayle.

Again the room was hot and again she'd thrown the covers aside. She was still wearing that PJ top and another pair of those wispy panties. He slipped off his shoes and sat on the bed opposite, his eyes filled with her body. He watched her for the longest time. She was so white. Milky white. Then he got up and went to her bed. He dropped to his knees and inhaled the scent of her. Never had he had such an erection. He bent over, lowering his mouth over that fuzzy triangle between her legs and took in a deep breath. Then he kissed her through her panties while she slept.

He pulled himself away from the scent of her. She smelled like heaven. Woman mixed with talcum powder. The room was hot and sweat ran down the back of his neck, but it wasn't the heat that caused him to sweat. Still on his knees, be leaned forward and kissed that silky triangle again. He shivered, like someone was sliding cold ice up and down his spine. He inhaled her again and involuntarily fondled himself. She was so delicate and fragile and broken. His erection throbbed. He squeezed and it blew up, shooting semen all over the hand he'd slid into his pants.

She moaned and he pulled back. Fear and shame gripped him like a butcher's hand on the neck of a chicken. But she didn't wake. He stood, careful not to make a sound, and backed out of the room. What had he been thinking? It was as if he had no control over himself. He was acting like a child, worse, like a sex starved sixteen-year-old pervert.

He went to his bathroom, kicked off his running shoes and carefully slipped off his Levi's. He hadn't ejaculated in his pants since he'd snuck into the porno theater in downtown Long Beach just before he went into the service, and then he'd had the good sense to wrap it with toilet paper he'd taken from the restroom.

He grimaced as he dropped his boxer shorts. He had the stuff all over himself. He turned on the shower, dropped the shorts to the floor of the tub, then stepped under the spray. He soaped himself down as he swished the shorts around with his feet. He was an idiot. What if she'd woken? He turned down the cold, letting the hot water prick his skin. Almost too hot. He was punishing himself.

Out of the shower, he put on a clean pair of boxer shorts and his sweats. Never again, he told himself. Then he remembered he was going to sleep in her room. But it wasn't like he was uninvited. She'd asked him to do it.

He padded out of the bathroom, past the fine desk and the expensive kauri wood furniture and stepped softly toward that connecting door. He gasped when he saw her as he held onto the door jamb. He felt faint and again his eyes were drawn to her milky white skin and that triangle. It was a magnet for his eyes and it was making him into what he wasn't. He slinked into the room and sat on the edge of his bed, eyes glued to her like a hungry fox glues his gaze to what he can't have.

He watched her sleep for awhile. Then he pushed himself from the bed and went to the thermostat and lowered the temperature so that she'd be cold and keep covered up. The room started cooling right away. He tiptoed to her bed and raised the blanket up to her chin. She looked so helpless. His heart cried out for her and he realized that he was falling in love.

He sighed, lay back and closed his eyes, but it was a long time before sleep came.

CHAPTER TWELVE

"YOUR EXHAUST ELBOW IS MUSH," the mechanic said to Bill. "And since it's a custom job, I'll have to make one from scratch."

"What's it do, the exhaust elbow?" Haley asked.

The mechanic favored Haley with a smile. He had fierce blue eyes, a protruding forehead, a hawk's beak for a nose and a two day stubble over a square jaw. His name was Hank and Haley thought he looked like a Hank.

"The gases coming out the back of that engine are hotter than my wife's beef pies. In a car or truck you just let 'em go out into the air, but you can't do that here, because the engine's in the middle of the boat. See, you got this long hose taking the gases all the way aft, where they go out that hole in the back. You with me?"

"Kinda," Haley said.

"Those gases are so hot they'd melt the hose, so they've gotta be cooled. That's where the exhaust elbow comes in. Seawater meets the gases in the elbow, cooling them down. That's why you see water coming out the back of the boat."

"So why did it go bad?"

"They all do after awhile. The seawater corrodes 'em. They should be checked every other year or so."

"How long before you can fix it?" Bill asked.

"I can build you one in a day."

"Great."

"But I can't get started for a week or so. You can go somewhere else, but it's gonna be the same all over. Lot of work right now."

"I'm in a hurry," Bill said.

"Tell me something I don't hear ten times a day," Hank said.

* * *

"Think they're upset?" Taylor asked. They were walking along a two lane road with carry-on bags slung over their shoulders. They were headed toward town. Everything was so green. Haley actually saw pines growing next to palms, like a giant greenhouse. The air was fresh and delicious.

"About what?" Haley said.

"About us looking for a motel."

"No. They're upset about something, but that's not it. I think they're actually kind of glad they won't have to deal with us for a few days. They've got something coming between them and they need to work it out. We'd only be in the way."

"Yeah, I kind of sensed that," Taylor said. "Hey," she pointed, "a car lot. The sign says used and rentals. Can you drive on the wrong side of the road?"

"How hard could it be?" Haley said and Taylor laughed.

Ten minutes later Haley was confusing the turn indicator with the windshield wiper stick when Taylor said, "No, no, the other side of the street."

"I'll get it." Haley swung back.

"Turn in there." It was a Mobil station.

"But we don't need gas."

"I'm going to ask for directions to a good place to stay."

The attendant suggested the Park Side Motel at the edge of town, and five minutes later Haley shut off the engine in the motel parking lot. They grabbed their bags, locked the car and entered the lobby.

"Do you have a room for a few days?" Taylor asked the man behind the desk.

"Sure do, we're mostly empty. It's still early," the man said. He had a nervous tick in his left eye, and he smelled like fresh earth. "Excuse the clothes," he said, handing her a registration card, "but I'm the gardener, too." He picked at the dirt under his nails with a clean card.

"I'm gonna go jogging and work up a sweat," Taylor said once they were in their double room. "Then I'm gonna shower and drink this." She pulled a bottle of champagne out of her carry-on bag.

"Where did you get that?"

"I liberated it from *Dark Witch*. Along with this." She took out another bottle.

"Taylor, that's stealing."

"Nope, we paid. Food and drink, remember?" She dropped her Levi's and changed into sweatpants. "Come on, kiddo, get a move on."

"I'm hustling," Haley said as she was changing into her running clothes.

And for the next hour they ran hard. Haley let her mind wander as she always did when she ran. At home the girls ran every day. It had been over a week since she'd done it and Haley was surprised how hard it was to get up the energy to really pour it on.

Back at the motel, Haley took an extra long time under the spray soaking up the steam. And when she was finished and out of the bathroom, she saw that Taylor was under the covers, asleep. The champagne unopened.

* * *

Haley got up early and took a long shower, letting the hot water steam her tired muscles as she soothed them with a soapy massage. The last few days at sea had been like a never ending workout. She'd bent and stretched muscles she didn't know she had. It was easy to see why people who lived on the sea were so thin and hard-bodied.

"Hey, save some for me," Taylor said from the other side of the shower door. The door was made of clear glass, but she'd been so rapt in thought that she hadn't seen her come in. Taylor was in the middle of the bathroom, still in her pajamas. Haley felt her friend's eyes on her body as she caressed herself with the soap. It was an awkward situation. She wanted to rinse off right away, grab a towel and let Taylor have the shower. But that wouldn't be normal. She'd never been shy before, but everything was different now. Her nipples hardened under Taylor's gaze.

"I'll be right out." She set the soap in the soap dish, turned away from Taylor and into the spray. She rubbed her body all over with her hands, helping the hot water as it washed the soap away. In a few seconds she was squeaky clean. Taylor was still in the bathroom, holding a towel. There was nothing for it but to open the door and step out of the shower.

"I hope you didn't use it all." Taylor handed Haley the towel. She took it and dried herself as Taylor slipped off her pajamas and stuffed them onto the towel rack. "I mean it. I really hope there's some hot water left, cuz if there isn't, you're going to get it."

"It's a motel, they never run out," Haley said. She took in Taylor's body. Firm breasts, not large, like hers. Pink nipples, not brown, like hers. Slim waist with that downy fuzz between her legs, not black and wiry, like hers. "I'm gonna see if I can find us some coffee," she said.

"Good idea." Taylor turned on the water and Haley left the bathroom. Something was happening to her. It was like Taylor's body had bewitched her. She needed to be dressed, and fast. She jumped into her old Levi's, fetched her bra and put it on. Then a cotton tee shirt, followed by a heavy sweatshirt. She was out the door and into the cold before Taylor finished her shower.

"Good morning," she told the clerk-slash-gardener as she entered the motel office. "That coffee smells good." She took a Styrofoam cup from the counter and filled it with coffee from a large urn. She took a sip and sighed. "It is good." He was smiling and his eye started blinking like it did yesterday when they checked in. "Why does it do that? Your eye, I mean."

"I fell down when I was a kid and hit my head. It's been like this ever since. When I get excited it goes out of control. I can't play poker." He laughed.

"You could wear a patch."

"I did, for years, but I've pretty much got a handle on it now."

"I don't think so. It's blinking like crazy."

"Pretty girls set it off."

"You dirty old man." She laughed. "Do you ever get lucky with that line?"

"Sometimes."

"I bet there's nothing wrong with your eye at all." Haley laughed harder when his eye started blinking like a telegraph key. The man fished his hand into a drawer and came up with an eye patch.

"I think I'll keep this on while you're around." He put it on. "Don't forget, if there's anything you need, just ask for Phil." He emphasized his name.

"I think the man with the blinky eye tried to pick me up," Haley told Taylor once she was back in the motel room.

"You should get used to it. You're a beautiful woman."

"No one's called me that before."

"What? Beautiful?"

"No, woman."

"Can't be a little girl forever," Taylor said. "Now, what should we do today?"

"I think we should take the champagne back."

"You're kidding."

"If we kept it, I'd feel like a thief. I can't help it. It must be the Catholic in me."

"Then let's get it and go," Taylor said.

Fifteen minutes later Haley braked at the end of the pier. "Think I can drive on it?"

"Sure, those big forklifts are on it. They weigh a lot more than this car."

"No, I mean do you think it's alright?"

"Hale, you can't go through life afraid of breaking the rules. Take your foot off that brake and live a little."

"We could get in trouble."

"Get real. If anyone says anything, you're just a pretty girl who doesn't know any better."

"Earlier I was a woman, now I'm a girl?"

"When you look like you do, it's okay to have it both ways. Now, let's go."

Haley eased off the brake and slowly drove forward. She parked next to the white Phoenix, *Ghost Dancer*. There were two men aboard. One was older, gray hair, balding at the top. He was wearing a suit and tie. The other looked to be about twenty-five. He was dressed similar to the girls, faded jeans, sweatshirt and running shoes.

"Good morning," Taylor said.

"You looking or thinking about buying?" the older man said. He was American.

"Neither, we're on *Dark Witch*."

"You must the be the guests. I'm Kevin Kirk, come aboard."

"You're selling her?" Haley stepped over the lifelines.

"Sure am. She took us around the world and now it's time to move on. Besides, the money's running out."

"It's a great boat, but it's more than I can afford," the younger man said. He used the girls as an excuse to cut the sales pitch short, said goodbye and left.

"Sorry if we chased him away," Haley said.

"He wasn't going to buy anyway."

"How much are you asking?" Taylor said.

"A half million. That's Kiwi. But I'd take a hundred and seventy-five thousand US, cash money. I'm in a hurry to sell."

"What fixing does she need?" Taylor asked.

"She needs a new windlass. The refrigerator compressor is shot. The generator is on her last legs. That's the downside, but it's not really so down. She's just had a total refit, everything else is good to go. All of the wiring is new as are all of the electronics, even the autopilot. The main engine's just been rebuilt. The whole interior looks like the day she left the yard. The bottom job is only a month old. All of the gear aboard goes with her, including the brand new dinghy and outboard."

"Those things that have to be replaced. How much do you think that would run?" Taylor asked.

"Maybe another ten or twelve grand or so, to do her right."

"That's a lot of money." Haley whistled.

"I have over twice that into her the way she sits, of course that's over five years and I've had my use out of her."

"Could we see below?" Taylor said. Kevin Kirk was halfway down the companionway before she finished the question.

"Unlike the other Phoenix boats, she has a kauri wood interior." He was talking even before the girls were down. "The wood's hard and strong, like teak, but as you can see, has a darker finish. And it's much more rare."

"Rare?" Haley said, stepping off the ladder.

"The trees live over a thousand years. They're huge things. They get to be fifty feet around and the lowest branches are often that high or higher. They are really something to see. New Zealand used to be full of them, but when the Europeans came they cut most of 'em down."

"Why?" Taylor asked.

"Masts for the English warships, white man's buildings, then they started exporting it. Now they're protected and only allowed to be used in specialized furniture and ship building."

"She's beautiful." Haley admired the way the white bulkheads showed off the wood.

"Her layout is the same as *Dark Witch's* with the exception of the front cabin. *Ghost Dancer* has a single large double cabin up front instead of the two tiny ones on *Dark Witch*. *Dark Witch* may sleep more, but *Ghost Dancer* sleeps 'em more comfortable."

"I wish we were in a position to buy her, but obviously it's only a dream," Taylor said. "I'm sorry we took so much of your time."

"Oh, I don't mind showing her off." He had a sad smile. Haley got the impression that he really loved that boat and if circumstances were different he wouldn't be selling.

They returned the champagne, then spent the rest of the day walking around the small town of Whangarei. They wound up at an ice cream stand in a small outdoor mall in the city center. Taylor stayed with the hokey pokey, Haley ordered chocolate and they found a bench to sit and watch people as they ate.

"I saw the way you were looking at me this morning," Taylor said. "Like I was some kind of dragon lady or something." She took a bite of her ice cream, but she kept her eyes on Haley as she licked the cone.

"What do you mean?" Haley said. "No, I'm sorry. I know what you mean. I try not to, but sometimes I can't help it. At first it shocked the heck out of me, but with everything else that was going on, it was easy for me to push out of my mind, plus you were acting more like your old self every day, so it was easier not to think about. But then all of a sudden, you're in the bathroom and I'm in the shower without any clothes on, and I can't not think about it." She sighed and licked her own cone. The chocolate ice cream was sweet and wonderful in her dry mouth.

"It was between me and her," Taylor said. "Just because I'm a girl who's made love with another girl doesn't mean I'm after any pretty thing in skirts. It's not like that." She took another bite of her ice cream and Haley heard the crunch as Taylor bit into the cone. A young Maori boy bladed by, graceful on his in-line skates. A little girl was frantically working a pair of roller skates, trying to keep up. His little sister?

"How is it then?" Haley asked.

"You really want to know?"

"I think I have to know. Otherwise I might be afraid of you forever and I don't want that. You're my best friend. Like a sister. Closer. I don't want anything to come between us, least of all the love you had for Dylan. I just want to understand it so I won't be afraid." The boy on the Rollerblades turned and dropped to his knees. He opened his arms and the little girl skated into them. It was his sister.

"It's sort of like Mom. Just cuz she loves Dad doesn't mean she wants to go to bed with every man she meets."

"Yeah, I understand that. But you love me, don't you?"

"But not like that. Like a sister, not like a lover."

"Dylan was your sister."

"Yeah, she was. What can I say? What happened, happened. Look, Mom loves Uncle Simon and Sandy, but she doesn't sleep with them. See, there's more to it than love. Besides, I'm not a lesbian or anything. It's just that Dylan and I discovered we could make each other feel good. So we did. It's no big deal, really. I loved her, she loved me. She's dead, it's over. Besides, it was boys that really turned us on."

"Was?" Haley said.

"Nothing much turns me on now. I think maybe that part of me died with Dylan. Now I have this big hollow spot inside of me that all the ice cream in the world won't fill." She took another crunchy bite of cone.

"So when you made love, what did you do?"

"We did what girls do to each other. That's all." Taylor looked out across the small outdoor shopping center, like she was lost in a dream. The Maori kid took the little girl by the hand and was pulling her along as they skated. "We kissed." She sighed and was quiet.

A pair of young lovers walked out of a bookstore, holding hands. They looked happy. Haley wondered if that was the kind of happy Taylor had had with Dylan. She hadn't known that kind of happy yet, but she knew it was out there.

"Did you do the other stuff?" she asked.

"We hugged and slept in each other's arms and we used our hands and fingers to make each other feel good." She had a wistful smile on her face as she looked out across the mall.

"Did you, you know, go down on each other?"

"No, never. Like I said, we weren't lesbians or anything."

"That's good," Haley said, wondering just what the

definition of a lesbian was.

That evening they watched television and turned in early. The next morning Haley took a quick shower and was out and dressed before Taylor woke up. Taylor caught her in the shower the following day, but Haley found she wasn't nervous at all. She was over it. She sighed as she accepted the towel from Taylor that morning and both girls laughed. Things were back to normal. The way they were meant to be.

They settled into a routine of running in the morning, breakfast of beef pies at a little place in the mall, long wandering walks in the afternoon, a phone call to Gayle, another run before dinner, then TV and bed. They were both ready to go when Bill showed up at their door on the seventh evening and said that the exhaust elbow was in place and they could be on their way as soon as the girls were ready.

"We're ready now," Haley said, and she went to settle the bill with the man with the twitch in his eye. She smiled as he flirted with her and told him that she might be back again someday.

They set sail at dawn with Haley again at the wheel and Taylor working the sheets. They shifted places after six miles, halfway to the sea. They rounded Bream Head about an hour before lunch without incident and Bill took the wheel, allowing the girls some rest. They lunched on ham and cheese sandwiches as they sailed on autopilot with the long Ocean Beach off their port side.

Morning found them with North Cape, New Zealand's northernmost point, in sight. The autopilot had been moving them along with favorable winds. And although they were making good time at ten knots, the three hours it took to pass the cape seemed like forever to

Haley. The wind shifted to off their starboard side as soon as they passed the point and they picked up some speed. At first she could hardly wait to leave the land behind, but then she wished for its comfort when she was confronted with the reality of the open sea. Nothing ahead but water, water and more water.

They continued on, making between ten and twelve knots, sailing on a beam reach in moderate seas for the next two days. Then, late in the day, the wind died and they were becalmed.

Linda furled the jib and Bill went forward to lower the main. Linda had the jib in and was furling the staysail while Taylor and Bill tied the main to the boom.

"I don't get it," Haley said after Bill was back in the cockpit. "One minute we have wind and the next it's gone." The water was flat calm, as far as her eyes could take her.

"They don't call them the Horse Latitudes for nothing," he said.

"Why do they call them that?" Haley said.

"Because when the old sailing ships got becalmed in them, they'd throw their horses overboard. They say the sound of the panicked animals was like a thousand banshees, and remember those ships were becalmed, those horses were swimming right alongside, whining and dying.

"My God, why."

"They were afraid of running out of water."

"Swell," Taylor said.

"But not a problem for *Dark Witch*. God was kind by giving us strong winds most of the way through them. We're almost halfway to Noumea. We could motor from her on out if we had to."

"We could?" Haley said.

"But we won't have to. With luck we'll catch the southeast trades by tomorrow morning and the wind will be at our back all the way to New Caledonia."

"So, should I start the engine?" Haley said.

"Not just yet. How'd you like to go swimming?"

"You're kidding? Here?"

"I don't know if that's a good idea, Bill," Linda said. Haley caught a hint of that underlying tension that had been between them since they'd started back in Wellington.

"We can get in the water here? Out in the middle of nowhere?" Taylor said. "Neat. I'm getting my suit." And she went below without further discussion. Back on deck she took one look at Linda and Haley, still in the cockpit, and said, "Come on girls, don't spoil the party," and she dove over the side.

"I am hot." Linda got up. And in a few minutes the three of them were in the water, splashing and having fun.

"Look at that sun," Taylor said after a bit and Haley, treading water, turned to look.

"Sunsets on the ocean are so beautiful," Linda said.

"The sky is so orange," Taylor said, "and it goes on forever."

"Like a dream," Haley said.

"Yeah, like a great big Tangerine Dream," Taylor said."

"I like that," Haley said. "Tangerine Dream, I won't forget it."

"Perfect for you, Hale, 'cuz you're such a dreamer."

"Nothing wrong with being a dreamer," Linda said.

"No, there isn't," Taylor said. "If there were more of 'em, this world would be a better place."

"Hey, you!" Haley shouted up to Bill who had been watching them from up on deck, "aren't you coming in?"

"Someone has to watch the boat," he said.

"Like there's someone around to steal it. Come on in!" she yelled.

"Ready or not!" He pulled his shirt off, stepped back, then attempted a flying leap over the side, but he didn't make it. One of his feet caught on the lifelines and he went tumbling forward.

"Bill!" Linda screamed. His body smacked into the hull and he slid into the water. Taylor was the closest and first to him.

"It's my arm," he said as Taylor maneuvered behind him, helping to keep him afloat with her kicking legs.

"Can you get up the swim ladder?"

"I think so," he said. Linda swam to the ladder as Taylor helped him over to it.

"I'll go up first." Linda hurried up the ladder. On deck she looked down and said. "If you can get him started I can grab his good arm and help him up." Haley swam over to help hold the swim ladder in place as he grabbed onto it with his good left arm. He got a foot in the bottom rung and Taylor went up the ladder, almost on top of him, so that he wouldn't fall.

"Stupid thing to do," he said when he was halfway up.

"Give me your hand," Linda said from on top. He extended it as Taylor held him in place on the ladder. Between the two of them they managed to get him up on deck and Haley came right up the ladder after them.

"I think it's broken," he said.

"We'll have to splint it." Linda went below and in less than a minute was back with a Cruising World magazine and an ace bandage. "It's probably only a simple fracture," she said as she folded the magazine around his right forearm. Then she wrapped the arm and magazine with the bandage. "How does it feel?" she asked.

"It hurts like a mother, my head, too."

"I think you're out of action for a while. I guess that makes me the captain now," Linda said. Haley thought she detected a note of triumph in her voice. "And my first official captain's order is for you go below and lie down. The girls and I can handle the boat."

"We're not going to go back?" Taylor asked.

"No, we'd have to motor all the way through the Horse Latitudes. Bill was right when he said we should pick up the southeast trades soon. The position is logged into the GPS. We shouldn't have any problems." She moved behind the wheel and hit the start button. The engine came to life and Linda shifted into forward as Haley brought up the swim ladder.

An hour later the trades Bill predicted were pushing them from behind. Linda and Taylor went forward to raise the main as Haley guided *Dark Witch* around into the wind. Once they had the great sail up, Haley turned till the wind was at their backs. *Dark Witch* seemed to be scooting over the sea, keeping pace with the swells from behind. They came back to the cockpit and Linda shut off the engine and engaged the autopilot. Then they unfurled the big jib and the smaller staysail and in no time they were doing twelve knots with a following sea.

"How's Bill doing?" Haley asked when Linda came up from checking on him later. She'd been going down about every twenty minutes, making sure he was okay. The wind was brisk, chilling her from behind.

"He has a slight fever. I don't know what that means, but I think he should stay down, at least till morning."

"That's too bad. Does it still hurt?"

"He says it does, but he has a low threshold for pain."

"I'll bet it hurts plenty," Taylor said. "I broke my arm a couple of years ago. It wasn't a picnic."

"Wind's picking up," Linda said.

"Should we reef up?" Haley asked.

"I don't think so. She's been out in a lot stronger than this with everything out."

"Did I hear someone say we should bring in some sail?" Bill said, coming through the companionway.

"You're supposed to stay in bed," Linda said.

"I'm a lot better." He turned his face into the wind, then he studied the sails. "You're right, Linda. She's going fine. I wouldn't do a thing." He took a seat in the cockpit, shielded his eyes with his good hand and looked out at the pink sky around the setting sun. "I'm betting this wind will hold us the rest of the way."

"I think you're right," Linda said.

"I think we should open a bottle of that champagne," Bill said. Haley glanced at Taylor and smirked. She was glad they'd brought it back. There were only five bottles on board. The two would have been missed.

"I don't know," Linda said.

"Come on!" Bill said. "It'll help dull the pain. Besides, no one's going to get drunk or anything."

"I wouldn't mind some," Taylor said.

"See, babe, we gotta keep the paying guests happy."

"Do you know where it is, Taylor?" Linda asked.

"Yeah, I do." She winked at Haley, then scooted down the companionway. She was back in a flash with four plastic wine glasses, the champagne and a bowl of ice. "In case anyone wants it cold," she said. They all did. Linda popped the cork while Taylor dropped a couple of cubes in each glass.

"To a successful journey," Bill said, raising his glass.

"To a successful journey," they all said, clinking plastic.

"It goes perfect with all the stars," Taylor said.

"Sweet and wonderful," Haley said. They were gliding along as if they were on a magic carpet. The sails were full, the stars were bright. There was no moon, but that only made the stars appear even brighter. Haley loved it. "I feel like I'm at home," she said.

"Me too." Taylor leaned back. She poured herself the last half glass from the bottle and sipped at it. "Want me to get another?" she asked.

"Sure," Bill said. "It's a nice night. I can't think of a better way to spend it." Haley noticed that Bill squeezed Linda's hand when he said it. She also noticed that Linda was still on her first glass and barely sipping at the champagne. She smiled at her and Linda smiled back. It was a good thing that one of them wasn't drinking, just in case something were to happen. They were out at sea, after all.

"Okay," Taylor said, back on deck with another bottle. "Ready or not, I'm ready to pour." She giggled.

"Just a little for me," Bill said. "You girls can finish it." He allowed her to pour only the tiniest amount. It was as if he was receiving a secret signal from Linda to go easy.

"I think you girls should get some sack time," Linda said, when they'd finished the bottle. Haley nodded. She was sleepy. "We'll let you sleep through till midnight. That's five hours. Then we'll do hour on, hour off till morning. That okay with you guys?"

"Sure," Taylor said.

Below and alone in her cabin, Haley sat on the edge of

her bed, listening to all of the boat sounds. It was like she was in a giant bell and a huge hunchback was clanging it. She should have passed on that last glass, she thought. She took deep breaths. She didn't think she was drunk, but she didn't think she was quite sober either. The cabin seemed stuffy. She was afraid to open the overhead hatch at sea. She didn't know what do to and she was afraid that she might throw up.

"Haley." It was Taylor calling her.

She pushed herself off the bed and poked her head into Taylor's cabin. She was on her back staring up through her open hatch. In typical Taylor fashion, she wasn't worried about water gushing down. If it got wet, then she'd worry about it.

"It's beautiful," she said. "Come look." Haley lay down next to her friend and stared up at the starlit sky. "Can you ever imagine living anywhere else after we've seen this?" Her hand found Haley's and their fingers intertwined. "It's not so bad, really," Taylor said, and she kissed her. This time it was Haley's tongue that did the snaking as she wrapped her arms around her friend.

Then a loud blast ricocheted throughout the boat. Dynamite was Haley's first thought.

CHAPTER THIRTEEN

SANDY WOKE WITH THE SUN as it reflected through the glass windows, covering the ceiling in color bars, like light reflected through a prism. He'd slept through the night, even though the heat was on high. He was finally getting used to it. He turned toward Gayle, sleeping under the covers despite how hot it was. Ten days now and it still amazed him how she could do that.

He tossed the covers aside and sat up without taking his eyes off of her. The bruises that had covered her face were gone now. There was a red scar under her eye where the stitches were fading away, but the shiner was history.

He stretched, then reached behind himself and

scratched an itch on his back. She was starting to look human again. And it seemed that she was getting used to moving around the hotel room on her crutches. He scratched another itch, this time behind his neck. Maybe it was time he started sleeping in his own room. He shrugged the thought aside. He hated to admit it, but he'd miss her and the way they talked each other to sleep every night.

"Time to wake up," he said.

She didn't stir.

"Come on, Gayle. I'm famished." He picked up one of her crutches from the floor and gently poked her with it. She came awake laughing. It was the same every morning.

"What time is it?" she said.

"Time for breakfast. I'm going to order ham and eggs."

"I weighed myself on that scale in the bathroom last night," she said. "First time I've done that. At first I wasn't too upset, because the scale's in kilos, but I know how to multiply by two-point-two and I didn't like the answer I got, so I think I'll be skipping breakfast for a while. Would it bother you so much eating downstairs? I don't have the greatest will power in the world. I couldn't diet and watch you eat at the same time."

"No problem, but other than the fact that you're turning into a walrus, how do you feel?" He laughed and ducked as she threw one of her pillows at him.

"I feel great," she said, laughing too. "My foot tingles so I know it's there, but it's not throbbing."

"That's a good sign. You're healing."

"I hope so. I'm getting so sick of this room. Sometimes I feel like the walls are closing in on me."

"It'll be over soon. The cast comes off in three weeks.

You'll be walking up a storm after that."

"I'm counting the days," she said.

"I'm going next door to shower and dress," he said, as she picked up the remote. He knew that she was hoping to get the latest news about Stacy's campaign on CNN.

In his own room he showered and shaved. He was pulling his sweatshirt over his head when he thought about Dylan's PowerBook in the closet. He'd been so caught up with his feelings for Gayle during the last week and a half that he'd forgotten about Dylan's journal. Well, not quite forgotten. He'd put it out of his mind. But he couldn't put it off any longer. As badly as he didn't want to know, he was going to have to read the rest of her journal.

"I'm gonna eat at this little coffee shop I found a while back," he told her, back in her room.

"You're not upset about me not eating with you?"

"No, it's fine. I don't see the kilos that scale's talking about, but if you want to start a diet, don't expect me to go along with it. If I don't get my morning eggs, I'm a bear all day."

"You know, we've changed, you and me, since we've been here," Gayle said.

"How so?"

"For me, things that used to be important aren't so important anymore."

"Like what?"

"Like whether or not I become first lady, for one. Also I'm beginning to doubt God."

"You've never been too religious," he said.

"But I've always believed."

"You've been through a tragedy. What you're going through is normal."

"Maybe."

"How've I changed?"

"Look at what you're wearing, old Levi's and a sweatshirt."

"These are my running clothes."

"Yeah, but you wear them all the time now. I don't think you've ever left your house without a tie, unless you were going running. You used to care so much what people thought about you. Now you don't appear to give a damn."

"I guess you're right." Being the younger half brother, and black, he'd always felt like he had to try harder. He always dressed to impress. Now he didn't care. He was finally at peace with himself and who he was.

"What happened to that man who wouldn't be caught dead without a tie?"

"I think that guy died out on that balcony," Sandy said.

Thirty minutes later he was back in that same coffee shop, facing the same Maori waitress. He asked for a menu, meeting her scowl with a smile. He set the computer case at his feet.

"Been awhile," she said.

"Not that long." He wondered if she ever smiled.

"Almost two weeks. I didn't mean to chase you away. Sometimes I scare the customers, especially the foreign ones."

"No, I just don't eat out much," Sandy said.

"But you're here now. You want coffee?"

"Sounds good."

"How do you take it?" Her dark hair was pulled back and tied in a bun, making her look even older than she was. But Sandy guessed she was long past trying to hide her age.

"Make it hot and black. And I'd like three eggs over easy, toast, bacon and ham. Milk, cold. Orange juice, also cold. And whatever kind of potatoes you're serving. I guess I don't need this after all." He handed her back the menu.

"A little hungry this morning?" she said. He thought he saw the beginning of a smile. Maybe he was winning her over.

"If the food doesn't come hot and fast I'm going to start on the table," he said. She laughed as she scribbled his order on a pad.

"I can have coffee and Danish in front of you before you can spit," she said.

"Add the Danish to my order and do it," he said.

"It's done." In seconds she was dropping the Danish in front of him and pouring the coffee.

The food came almost as fast and Sandy tucked into it with a passion. And it wasn't because he'd been so long without eating. Since that night he'd kissed Gayle in her sleep, he'd felt a new energy. He hadn't lied when he told her that his old self had died out on that balcony. He was a new man on a new road. True, he didn't know the direction of the highway, but he was on it nevertheless, speeding to whatever destination the devil desired.

He finished the meal, signaled for the check, and paid. "Keep the change," he said.

"We don't tip in New Zealand."

"Americans tip. Besides, I'd like to stay through lunch and I'd like you to keep the coffee coming."

"You don't have to tip me, this is my place. All you have to do to win my heart is eat up my food the way you just did."

"Burgers here any good?"

"Sun come up this morning? I make the best burgers on the planet."

"Then I'll work till you bring me a couple of those burgers and a coke for lunch. If that's okay?"

"Just set up your computer. I know you want to. I'll keep your coffee topped off and see that no one bothers you." She didn't smile, but Sandy heard one in her voice.

He would have enjoyed talking with her longer but that PowerBook beckoned. It had been a long time since he'd looked at it and he didn't want to do it now, but he had to know. He started the computer and double clicked on *21 July* in the *Seventeen* folder and read:

> *Today was a better than average day at the Castle. We went sailing right after breakfast. Even Taylor and Haley, the horsewomen, came. Mom and Dad smooched and drank wine. Uncle Sandy told funny stories that had Haley laughing like crazy. She's so obvious. Someday Uncle Sandy is gonna be in real trouble. Gran and Simon took turns behind the wheel and I watched them like a hawk.*
>
> *Did I see anything? Yes I did. But was it unusual or out of the ordinary? Hard to tell. They seemed to touch a lot. More than you'd expect, but not so much that you'd notice if you weren't looking. And they seemed to smile at each other a lot. If you looked at them differently than mother and son, the way I was, you'd swear you were seeing young lovers. It*

was creepy. God knows, I'm in no position to call what they're doing wrong. If they are doing anything. It's still not proved. But if they are, well Simon's not her natural son. Still, it's weird to think about. I mean, Simon's old, but she's way old.

I'm back. Tonight instead of sneaking into Taylor's room, I snuck into the paperback library. I left the door open a crack and sat on the floor, with my back against a bookcase. It was dark and I could see out the crack as good as any spy peeking in a keyhole. I was worried about being discovered, because I didn't have any logical reason for being where I was. Still I chanced it.

Time really is relative. It moves so slow when you're waiting in the dark. Two hours seems like two days, especially when you're worried someone might decide to come in for a book and catch you spying, but it didn't happen.

What did happen was Gran. She wasn't even sneaking. She just went into Uncle Simon's room like it was the most ordinary thing in the world. I waited a few minutes that seemed like an hour, then I left the library and took a real chance. I listened at the door. But I shouldn't have worried about being caught, because they were going at it hot and heavy. Oh, not so loud as to raise the dead, but I got an earful at that door.

Shame on you, Gran.

Sandy sat back and sighed. Part of him wanted to just delete the journal from the hard drive and forget about it, but that would be like Dylan dying all over again. He couldn't do it. Besides, most of the stuff on there was harmless. Maybe it would be better just to clean up what Dylan had written, then give Gayle the computer without saying anything about the journal. She might never find it, but when or if she did, at least there wouldn't be anything on there that would cause anybody any anguish.

He sighed again. He had a lot of work to do.

* * *

"Hey, Nick," Connie Jakome said, "there's a guy at Tattle Tale you might want to talk to." She was only one of the many unpaid interns at the station, but she was determined to turn her position into a paying job. She wanted to work in a newsroom more than anything. Ever since she'd first seen the old Mary Tyler Moore show as a little girl, it had been her dream.

Nick Nesbitt looked up from his magazine. He was at the station early to do voice-overs for the evening news.

"Why would we want anything to do with them?" Like most professional news people she knew he loathed the popularity of tabloid journalism, especially the television kind.

"Because Dylan Sterling kept a journal."

"Really?" he said. "How do you know this?"

"An old boyfriend works over there. He says she wrote a lot of steamy stuff, but they don't want it."

"Why not?" he said. If Tattle wasn't interested, he probably assumed there was nothing there.

"It's on a CD. They think it's a fake. And even if it isn't, there's no way to prove it's authentic."

"They've never had any scruples before." He picked his magazine back up.

"You don't take on someone as powerful as Senator Sterling unless you have all of your ducks in a row," she said. "But I think this is the real thing. Maybe you couldn't use the journal, but you'd find out a lot of interesting stuff about the Sterlings. Something you could use to your advantage, I'll bet."

"What makes you think it's the real deal?" He turned a page.

"Because the kid who found it works at a computer store in Wellington. That's in New Zealand."

"I know where it is." He put down the magazine. She smiled. He was interested now.

Nick held her by the arm as they made for the boarding gate. Connie was beaming as she strode next to him. She was only twenty-one and had never been out of California, except for a two day vacation in Vegas and that didn't really count, so she was excited about going to New Zealand. She had the Lonely Planet Travel Guide in her purse and she intended to read it all on the long plane ride. She was determined to be worthy of his confidence in her.

It took her a day to track down Christopher Davis, the kid with the disc, and another for her to convince Nick that she was indispensable. After all, she'd explained, he could hardly have his name connected with anything involving the Sterlings. They'd just say he made it all up, because he was after Gayle's job and because he had such an obvious reason to be mad at Dr. Sterling.

Then they had to wait another day for the station to decide who'd fill in for Nick. Even though he had vacation time coming, they didn't want to let him go with Gayle out sick. But he'd pleaded that he needed the time to relax and get his head together and they'd relented. The hard part was her three or four calls a day to Davis in Wellington. He was nervous about selling the journal and he thought that she was stalling him. He seemed to be rethinking what he was doing. Well, soon it would all be over. He'd have his money. Nick would have the journal. And she'd have a paying job at the station as Nick Nesbitt's assistant.

She was so proud, she was bursting. She was going to be working with Nick Nesbitt, anchor on the nightly news. And who knows, if she performed well, he might help her get on camera herself. It was her dream. And she'd found the perfect dream maker in Nick. He wasn't like any of the others. He didn't offer to help her just so he could get her into bed. No more of that for her. No more fucking old and degenerate men just so she could stay at the station. Nick wasn't like them. He hadn't even made an advance, because he was happily married. Everybody at the station knew he didn't fool around. She was so lucky and she was going to do her best to prove to him that she deserved this opportunity. There was nothing she wouldn't do for him and she was finally on her way. A cloak and dagger kind of adventure awaited her in New Zealand and a new future was holding its arms out for her.

"Let's check out the back of the plane" Nick said. She was sitting by the window, he had the aisle. He stood and offered his hand. "Come on," he said.

"What?"

"It's a surprise." Her heart swelled as she stood. If he wasn't married, she thought, she could go for him, even though he wasn't really her type. He led her back to the restrooms, then glanced around the plane, shifting his eyes back and forth as he opened one of the doors and stepped inside, pulling her in after him.

"What?" she giggled, but she shut up when he unfastened his belt and dropped his slacks. Then his hands were on her shoulders and he was pushing her down. She dropped to her knees with his hands entwined in her hair, guiding her mouth to his erect penis. He wasn't any different after all, she thought, gagging as he pushed himself deep into her throat.

* * *

Gayle sighed, then turned off the television. She was getting cabin fever. Danny's DVD system had made a tremendous difference. She watched movies while Sandy was out during the day.

At first she didn't know why he had to leave every day. He could take care of her as well as Danny. But when she examined her feelings she knew he was pretty smart, playing the tourist all day long. They were getting entirely too close as it was. Maybe it was time he started sleeping in his own room. She resolved to talk to him about it as soon as he got back. She didn't need him there at night anymore. She thought about the late night movies they watched. Would he still stay up and watch them with her if he was sleeping next door?

She looked at the clock, 5:45. He should be back any minute and they'd order dinner from the hotel menu. Dull. At first she'd reveled in the meals, but now after so many of them, she was ready for a change.

She thought about the girls. Their big adventure had ground to a halt in Whangarei and they'd called every night, which helped, because Stacy hardly called at all. But now they were off on the sea again and she wouldn't hear from them till they docked in Noumea. She missed their calls.

"Hey, Cinderella." Sandy poked his head through the connecting door. He was wearing a suit. She hadn't seen him in one since the day of Dylan's funeral. "These are for you," he said.

"Yellow roses. You shouldn't have."

"But I did. It's because of the special occasion."

"What do you mean?"

"We're going out tonight."

"You're kidding?"

"No, he's not." It was Katy, the physiotherapist from the hospital.

"She's going to help you dress and you'd better hurry, reservations are for 7:00." Katy came into the room as Sandy retreated and closed the door.

"I know Danny's a good nurse," Katy said. "But there's some things you really need a woman for."

"I guess," Gayle said.

"Okay, up on those crutches, we're going to wash you. Then make you up like a princess. Then we'll gown you and send you to the ball. I'd like to see Danny do that."

"Yeah, but isn't this above and beyond a nurse's duty?" Gayle said, sitting up.

"No, this is the best part. Now off with that robe." Gayle shrugged it off.

An hour later she was sitting across from Sandy in the Seaview Restaurant. They had a window booth that overlooked the marina, the sea and the stars. It was sheer agony, crutching her way to the elevator and then to the restaurant, but sitting here, sipping wine, with this view, it was worth it.

Even the menu she was so tired of earlier looked fresh. And when the food came she attacked it with relish. She'd ordered Steak Diane, the same thing she'd had on her first day in the hotel, and it was every bit as delicious now as it had been then.

Sandy was his usual self, sometimes shy, sometimes not. Mysterious, but forthcoming. He was an enigma, constantly puzzling her.

"You know, I feel like I've been living with you all of my life," she said. "It's sort of like we're an old married couple. You leave in the morning for work and come back in the evening. Then we go to sleep in separate beds. Where do you go?"

"All over," he said. "Just walking and looking. I thought you needed the space." He paused. "I thought you'd get tired of me."

"What a stupid thing to think. If you're leaving on my account, don't. I enjoy having you around." It wasn't what she'd planned on saying, but it was what she felt.

"Good." He laughed. "Because I'm getting tired of trying to think of things to do. I'd much rather hang around and wait on you, but then Danny would be out of work."

"I think he's getting tired of the job anyway," Gayle said. "He likes the study time, but I don't think I'm the kind of a challenge he needs. He misses the hospital, I can tell."

"Oh, by the way, the police called me right after I got out of the shower. They had Dylan's computer. It was in the car. So while I was wandering around today I went by and picked it up."

"Her journal," Gayle said. "She kept a journal on it. Heaven help you if you ever called it a diary. I'd forgotten all about it."

* * *

"So tell me about the journal," Nick Nesbitt said. They were standing in the lobby of the Apple Centre. The long-haired nerd was fidgeting. Nick appeared more relaxed than Connie had ever seen him at the station.

"This black guy, Dr. Sterling, brings this PowerBook in with a crashed hard drive. I recognized him right away, cuz I saw him on CNN when he saved that girl. He says the computer was in an accident. I knew right away that I should copy everything on it, cuz famous people got secrets too, only they might pay to keep 'em quiet, know what I mean?"

"Yeah, I know." Nick seemed revolted by the kid. Connie certainly was. But then what Nick made her do on the plane had revolted her, and now she looked forward to doing it every night. Go figure.

"So you wanna know what's on it or what?"

"Five hundred dollars. Your money. My first and final offer," Nick said. Connie gasped. He was going to blow it. That was only two hundred-and-fifty US, the kid would never go for that.

"Man, it's worth hundreds more," he said.

"Then why haven't you sold it?"

"No one believes me. They say I got no proof. That I coulda made the whole thing up. But I didn't."

"And why should I believe you?"

"You're here, that's gotta count for something."

"I'm here as a friend of the family. I'm not out to destroy anyone." He reached into an inside coat pocket and came out with a wallet. He pulled out a roll of bills and counted off five New Zealand hundreds.

"I'll take it." The kid snatched the money from Nick's hand. Connie closed her eyes. Nick kept surprising her. They'd been in New Zealand for almost a week. They'd taken their time driving down from Auckland, stopping at the small cities, staying at tiny motels, making love for hours. At first, after he'd forced himself into her mouth on the plane, she'd hated him. But in retrospect, she couldn't blame him. She'd fucked and sucked most of the other men at the station. Shit, all they had to do was crook a finger and she'd head to the men's room and drop to her knees. But Nick did more than just fuck her. He treated her like an equal. He talked to her, shared with her. He was alright.

"Do I have to tell you how upset I'd be if I were to see any of this come out anywhere else?" he told the kid.

"Hey, I never said it was an exclusive."

"Do you know anything about the Sterlings?" Nick said.

"No, just what I read in that journal." The kid was smug.

"Then maybe I better tell you a little something."

"I'm all ears." The kid was smirking now. Connie wanted to slap him.

"When people fuck with the Sterlings, they fuck back, harder. They squash anything that gets in their way. You fuck with one and the whole clan comes down on you. But you won't have to worry about them, because I'll get to you first."

"Are you threatening me?"

"You fuck with me and I'll come back and slit your throat. I won't send someone from America and I won't call some local hood. I'll do it myself." He smiled, but he didn't look too friendly. "I wanna be real clear here. You call anyone else about this journal and I'll be back and do you personally." Nick was whispering, but his words whipped through the room.

"I got it." The kid had gone white. "I won't tell no one, honest." He handed Nick a disc.

"Then you'll never hear from me again." He turned and left. Connie followed him out.

"Well, kiddo," Nick said, once they were outside the store. "You've earned yourself a paying job at the station, that's for sure. And not because we're getting it on." He held up the disc. "This was good work." He put it in the inside pocket with his wallet.

"Thanks," she said. Then, "What are you going to do with it?"

"I'll have to read it. Then I'll decide. I've heard stories about Stacy Sterling. If there's anything on here that proves them, I'll have to talk to Gayle."

"What?"

"Hard as it is to believe, we're friends. I wouldn't do anything to hurt her."

"Not even for a story?"

"Not even."

"But what if you could get her job? What if you could go to the network?"

"I don't want the network, and I don't want her job bad enough to hurt her to get it. She's been good to me. She lets me be on camera as much as possible."

"Everybody knows you're after her job."

"Wrong. Everybody knows I want it. There's a difference. I won't walk over her to get it and I would never use what might be on this disc to blackmail her out of it. I have to look at myself in the mirror every morning and right now I like the man I see. I want to keep it that way."

"I didn't know." No wonder she was falling in love with him.

"Cynthia and I are divorced." He stopped walking and turned to look at her.

"What?" She felt her heart stop.

"Have been for two months now." He put his hands on her shoulders and met her eyes.

"How come you didn't tell anyone?"

"It's no one's business. I've been living in this cramped bachelor's place. I don't like it. I need something bigger. But I want my own office. A place where I can work undisturbed. I'm working on a book about Edward R. Murrow and I need at least two hours of privacy a night."

"What are you saying, Nick?" She could hardly breathe. Her heart was pounding now. There was a slight breeze. She tasted it. It was heavenly.

"You wanna get a place together?"

"Oh, my God!" She threw her arms around him and hugged him.

Chapter

Fourteen

A CONTINUOUS BLASTING SOUND followed the explosion. Like a terrified circus trainer cracking his whips at a crazed lion.

"What's going on?" Taylor said, breaking the kiss.

"We gotta find out." Haley jumped off the bed, dashed through the boat with Taylor breathing down her neck. They scurried up the companionway, expecting the worst.

"What happened?"

"We blew the clew out of the jib," Bill said.

"What's that mean exactly?" Haley looked forward. The big sail was snapping like a dragon's tongue, lashing out at the night, daring anyone to come close. Linda slapped a winch handle into the furling winch and started grinding away. The fury gradually went out of the sail as it wrapped around the headstay, until it was gone altogether when she snugged the line into the self-tailing jaws.

"Aw fuck, we're gonna lose speed now," Bill said, ignoring Haley. He was shaking. He wasn't wearing anything but a T-shirt and shorts. It was a cold night and Haley thought he should have more on, but sweat ringed his brow and he had a glazed look in his eyes, so maybe it wasn't the cold that was making him shake.

"Are you alright?" Haley said. The champagne glow was gone now, she was completely sober.

"No, I'm not. I'm burning up." He turned to her and met her eyes. Her question seemed to calm him for a moment.

"You're shaking, too. You'll get pneumonia if you don't put something on."

"I've been telling him that, but he won't listen," Linda said. It was quiet again and *Dark Witch* was sailing flat over the water. "Our speed's down to seven knots," Linda said, looking at the speed log. "It's going to take longer to get there than we'd originally thought."

"How much longer?" Taylor said.

"A couple of days," Linda said. "That could be a long time for Bill with his broken arm."

"I'll be okay," Bill said as the sky lit up in the distance. "Lightning, but it's nothing to worry about, it's miles away." The boat slid to port and the boom started to come around. "Now what?" he said. Then, "Haley get the wheel! Turn to the right! Right! Right! Right!"

Haley jumped behind the wheel and started spinning

it to starboard as Linda jumped to the mainsheet winch. She ripped the line from its jaws and started pulling on it, stopping the boom from slamming across. Then as Haley brought the boat back to port, she started easing out the sheet, till once again they were back on course.

Bill moved behind the wheel with Haley and started pushing buttons on the autopilot. "It's not responding," he said.

"Great," Linda said. "So now we have to drive the boat the whole way." She didn't sound happy.

"It's not my fault," Bill said.

"Nothing's ever your fault," she said.

"Come on, you guys," Taylor said. "You've had something bothering you ever since we left. Maybe if you'd spent a little more time worrying about the boat and a little less worrying about each other, things wouldn't keep breaking."

"Things aren't breaking!" Bill shouted.

"Don't take it out on her," Linda said.

"Yeah," Haley said. "We're all in this together and if you two can't see that, then we're in big trouble, because Taylor and I are new at this. We need you guys calm and collected. Not down below fighting or trying to avoid each other. Just give it a rest till we're safe at harbor."

"She's right," Linda said. "Sorry." Then to Bill, "Truce?"

"Truce," Bill said, but Haley didn't think he sounded too sincere.

"Why don't you guys go down and get some rest. We'll stand the first watch."

"That's okay, Haley," he said. "We said we'd do it and we'll do it."

"Bullshit, Bill," Taylor said. "You look like shit."

"I can handle it," he said.

"Death always has room for one more," Haley said. "And right now it looks like he's waiting on you." Then to Linda, "Make him go below. Get him warm, because if you don't, only three of us are gonna get to New Caledonia."

"Okay," Linda said. "Bill's got the position programmed into the GPS, so all you have to do is follow the course. If anything happens, shout down and I'll come right up."

"Okay, babe, let's go below and put me to bed," Bill said. He smiled at Haley. Now he looked sincere, but there was something else there, too. He grimaced. He was in pain.

"Thanks, guys," Linda said, softly so he couldn't hear. "He's so stubborn, but I'll try and get him to sleep some. We have morphine on board. I'm going to give him a shot."

"You can do that?" Haley said.

"We live on a boat. You have to be prepared for anything." She started for the companionway. "I might be awhile, but don't worry. No catnaps tonight. I'll be back as soon as he's down."

"She makes it sound like he's a big baby," Haley said, once Linda was below and out of earshot.

"He's a man," Taylor said. "They never grow up." Lightning lit up the sky off the starboard side.

"Did that look any closer?" Haley said.

"I don't think so. No thunder. It must be miles and miles away. Look, there it goes again." The distant lightning was a light show rippling through the thunderclouds. Taylor looked to the sky behind them. "I never get tired of looking at the Southern Cross. Just the sound of it reeks with adventure."

"Well we're having that adventure Sandy wanted us to have, that's for sure." More lightning filled the far away sky. "I could watch that for hours."

"Me too," Taylor said. And they did.

Linda came up with some sandwiches and coffee for them around ten. "I didn't want you to think I'd forgotten you, but you seemed to be having such fun up here. I didn't feel like intruding."

"We were having fun?" Haley said.

"Yeah, I think we were," Taylor said.

"How's Bill doing?" Haley asked.

"He's sleeping like the big baby he is. Out like a light and down for the count. Now it's just us girls and the big, dark ocean."

"Yeah," Haley said. She felt like she was beyond the edge of the earth. Lightning lit up the distant sky again. A few seconds later thunder rolled from the northwest. "Uh oh, it's getting closer."

"It's still a long way away. We should be okay." Lightning flashed again. It was far away, but this time it was in front of them.

"Did you see that?" Taylor said.

"It'll probably blow past by the time we get there," Linda said, but Haley didn't think she sounded very sure.

An hour later the wind shifted around, coming out of the northwest. And it picked up speed, howling through the sails. The boat heeled over and Haley was fighting the wheel, struggling to keep her on course.

"This is shit scary," Taylor said, as a ten foot swell rolled under them and something crashed down below.

"You're not turning into the swells quickly enough," Linda said. "Let me show you." Haley gave up the wheel to her and watched as Linda turned into an approaching swell, then away, riding it down. "You have to get in the groove," she said. "It's hard because it's so dark and you can't see them, but you'll get the feel of it. Just remember up, then down. Try it." She moved aside and Haley took the wheel again, imitating what she'd just seen Linda do. "That's great. Bill was right, you're a natural. See if you can keep it steady while I go below and see what that was."

"What was it?" Taylor asked when she came back up.

"Dishes. Galley cabinet came open. Glass everywhere and I can't wake Bill. It's the heroin. It's happened before. I'm going to have to tie him down. I'll be a few minutes."

"Did you hear that?" Taylor said, when she was gone. "She said heroin."

"Yeah," Haley said. "Now we know why they don't seem to get cold and why they sweat so much."

"He seems pretty cold now," Taylor said.

"I think he took too much."

"Look over there." Taylor pointed off their starboard side, into the wind. "No stars." Lightning cracked, illuminating the thunderclouds on their right. Thunder roared, telling them they weren't so far away any more. "This sucks, Hale."

"Big time." Haley kept working the wheel, gauging the swells. "Darn, missed that one," she said. Water foamed over the bow, churning and bubbling.

"It's getting worse." Taylor spoke loudly to be heard over the sound of the sea.

"What's going on?" Linda said, coming back up.

"I'm having a hard time keeping her under control," Haley said.

"We're going to have to reef."

"In this?" Taylor yelled.

"We don't have any choice. We could lose the rig if it gets much worse." Haley missed another roller and more water foamed over the side, some of it spilling back into the cockpit.

"What's that mean, exactly?" Taylor said.

"The mast falls down and we die," Linda said.

"Let's reef."

"Okay, Taylor you're going to have to come up to the mast with me." She lifted up the cockpit cushions and pulled out a couple of harnesses from the locker below. "These are inflatable life vests." She put one on. "If you go overboard, pull on this," she said, holding a plastic ring attached to a wire. "It inflates the vest." She handed one to Taylor.

"What about Haley?"

"We only have two." She clipped a jack line to her vest.

"That's pretty stupid!" Taylor yelled.

"I agree. Bill's cheap. It's one of the things we were fighting about." Lightning lit up the sky in front of them. Three seconds and the thunder blast followed.

"You guys better hurry," Haley said. "It's getting closer."

"Right." Linda clipped a jack line to Taylor's vest. "When we get up there we clip on to the mast. And remember, one hand for you and one hand for the boat. Be holding on at all times. Got it?"

"Let's do it," Taylor said. Haley had to admire her friend. She had more guts than brains. There was no way she'd go up there.

"Okay, Haley, turn her into the wind. Now." The wind fell out of the main even before she'd completed the turn and it started whip snapping, as did the staysail. Stereo whip cracks that jolted fear through Haley with each snap.

"I changed my mind. We're gonna drop it all the way and tie it off. It'll be quicker and safer," Linda yelled.

"I'm ready," Taylor said.

Linda scrambled on all fours up to the mast with Taylor on her heels. Haley watched as they wrapped their jack lines around the mast and clipped on. Then Linda took the main halyard out of the self-tailing jaws and dropped the sail. The lazy jacks held the main to the boom as the girls struggled to their feet. Linda grabbed the sail ties out of the cloth basket under the boom and handed some to Taylor and they tied the sail down. In less than five minutes they were back in the cockpit.

"Bring her back on course," Linda said. Haley obeyed. The staysail filled as *Dark Witch* came around and Haley saw that she quickly reached five knots, but no more. The windspeed indicator put the wind at thirty-knots, gusting to thirty-five. "That's good for now," Linda said. Then, "I'm going to go back down and check on Bill."

"It's a lot easier to control now," Haley said as Taylor scooted back behind the wheel with her.

"Heroin? Life vests for them, but not for us? What kind of deal did Sandy get us into?"

"I think we get off this boat ASAP," Haley said.

"But not right now," Taylor said.

Linda came back up. She had her vest in her hand. "Here, Haley, put this on. And both of you clip on to something."

"What about you?" Haley said.

"I'm going to have to stay below. Bill's delirious. I'm afraid he might hurt himself. If it gets worse, bring in some of the staysail to slow her down even more. And remember, up and down. I'll come up and check on you every chance I get." Linda was speed talking and it wasn't lost on the girls.

"Fuck," Taylor said, holding the wheel as Haley put on the vest.

"He's a junky," Haley said.

"Fucking junkies," Taylor said.

"I hate junkies," Haley said.

"I just want off this boat."

"Think she gave herself a hit when she did him?" Haley said.

"She seems like she's speeding to me, but at least she's not out," Taylor said. Water broke over the deck and the boiling foam rolled down to the cockpit, drenching them.

"I'm soaked," Taylor said.

"Go below and get their foul weather gear. They're not gonna need it."

"On my way," Taylor said.

Haley concentrated on staying in the groove. Working the swells reminded her of dodging in and out of traffic in her new Porsche. She loved that car. Red and sleek. Fast and powerful. It had been all she'd ever wanted. Then Dylan died and she'd come to New Zealand and everything changed. Now she didn't know what she wanted.

Taylor came back up with the foul weather gear. "Linda's speeding like a jackrabbit and getting worse every second. That's why they've been so irritable the whole trip. But at least she's coherent." She pulled off her sweatshirt, then dropped her wet Levi's. She's picture perfect, Haley thought. Taylor pulled on the yellow pants, breasts jiggling as she bent and straightened. They were the perfect size. Large enough to be attractive, but not so big that she had to wear a bra. Taylor wiggled into the top of the rain gear, covering her breasts. "Now you," she said.

Taylor moved behind the wheel as Haley pulled off her wet clothes and put on the fowl weather gear. When she was finished, Taylor said, "Okay, captain, I give the ship back to you," and Haley took the wheel again.

"This isn't so bad," Haley said. Then lightning struck in front of them, the thunder coming less than a second later.

"Oh, shit!" Taylor said. "I'm going to get Linda." She went below. She was quickly back. "Bill's zonked, Linda's zoned. She's crying. She thinks he's dead."

"Is he?"

"No way. I checked. But she ain't gonna help us, girl."

Within minutes they were in it. The sea turned choppy. They took water over the deck with every swell. Clouds rolled in, stealing the stars. The night turned black as the plague. The wind picked up, taking their speed up to eight knots under the staysail alone.

"Too fast!" Taylor yelled. "I'm going to crank some in." She picked up a winch handle and furled half the sail, slowing them to a safer three knots.

Lightning cracked directly overhead. It was one with the thunder, lighting up the night sky like a million flash cameras going off at once. Gone was their night vision. Haley was steering by instinct alone. Lightning cracked again, thunder boomed. It was all around them. Haley felt like they were dancing at death's door.

And it went on like that, without let up, till just before the dawn when Taylor shouted, "I see stars ahead!"

They were both behind the wheel and clipped on. They'd been taking turns, one sitting, one steering.

"Yesss," Haley said, "yes, yes, yes."

"Light at the end of the tunnel."

As quickly as it had started, it was over. The swells turned into gentle rollers and dawn found the wind and sea behind them again. Taylor unclipped, took off her life vest and tossed it on a cockpit seat. Then she helped Haley out of hers, throwing her vest with its companion.

"We did it," Haley said.

"Yeah," Taylor said. Then, "Hey, think we can bring that main up by ourselves?"

"Of course we can!" Haley started turning the boat into the wind as Taylor started for the mast. She smiled as her best friend raised the sail and she was spinning them back on course before Taylor was back in the cockpit.

"Look at that," Taylor said. "Eight knots."

An hour later, Linda poked her head out. "I see you've got it under control."

"Yeah," Taylor said. "No thanks to you guys."

"We've got some problems," Linda said.

"You've got one big one and if I thought it'd do any good, I'd go down there and search till I found it and throw it overboard, 'cept then you guys would probably go into withdrawal or something and be even worse."

"We're handling it," Bill said, coming up the hatch.

"The fuck you are," Taylor said. "What if the storm had been a lot worse? We coulda been in deep shit."

"But it wasn't a lot worse," he said.

Haley wanted to kick that smug look off of his face, but instead she said, "If you guys are up to it, I think we'll go below and get some rest. We haven't had any sleep in over twenty-four hours."

Without waiting for an answer, she went below with Taylor following. They flopped on the opposite settees. Haley lay on her back, eyes closed, waiting for sleep. Just as she started to drift off she found herself thinking about Kevin Kirk and *Ghost Dancer*.

"Haley," Taylor said from across the salon.

"Yeah."

"I wanna chase the Tangerine Dream."

"What?"

"I want us to buy *Ghost Dancer*."

Haley felt a bolt of pure joy shoot through her. Was this what it had been like for Taylor and Dylan? Thinking the same thoughts?

"I know it's a giant step," Taylor continued, "but we have the insurance money. I could sell those diamond earrings and that pendant Gran gave me for my birthday. Plus I've got fifteen thousand in the bank. And we could sell Dylan's boat. She'd want that. I really want to do this. I don't want to go to college. I don't want a normal job. I don't want to be a wife and settle down and raise a bunch of kids. I don't want the malls and the traffic and the newspapers and the computers. I don't want any of that. I just wanna follow the Tangerine Dream. I want us to do it together."

"You can stop," Haley said. "You had me convinced with 'I want us to buy *Ghost Dancer*.' I was thinking the same thing."

"Oh, Hale. Do you think they'll just let us run away?"

"We're not running away from anything," Haley said. "We're just running to something different."

"Think we'll have enough?" Taylor said.

"I'll sell my car," Haley murmured, then she drifted off to sleep and dreams of sunshine and sailing ships.

At noon Linda woke them for sandwiches and coke. The girls were young and second wind came easily, so when Linda suggested hour on, hour off turns behind the wheel for the rest of the trip, they agreed.

Three days later, Haley was behind the wheel with the rising sun when Taylor yelled out, "I see it. Land." They wound their way through the reef as the sun was going down among streaky pink clouds in the western sky, barely setting anchor by nightfall.

They pulled up to the customs dock in the morning and cleared in. Haley and Taylor were not on the boat when she left the dock after the paperwork had been completed.

They spent an hour walking around the small French town of Noumea, before stopping at a small brasserie and ordering croissants and café au lait.

"Let's stay a while," Taylor said. "It's nice here."

"I'd like that." Haley said.

They found a hotel in the center of town and booked a room for a week. The first thing Taylor did after they closed the door was to pick up the phone. It took her less than five minutes to get Gayle on the phone at the Sterling Hotel. She assured her that they were fine and that they would be back in New Zealand in a couple of weeks at the latest.

"Let me talk," Haley said. Taylor handed over the phone.

"Hey, it's me," Haley said. "I just wanted to let you know that I loved the experience. I can hardly wait till you're better and we can all go sailing together. You are going to be so impressed with us." Haley thought it better not to mention the storm, the drugs, the damaged jib, the broken autopilot or the crumbled exhaust elbow.

"I'm looking forward to it," Gayle said. They said their goodbyes, then Haley called her parents to tell them where she was and that she was okay.

"One more call." Taylor took the phone and in no time was connected to New Zealand information and then to Kevin Kirk. "It's ringing," she said. Then, "Sure about this?"

"Yeah," Haley said.

"Mr. Kirk, is that you?" Taylor said. Haley listened with her ear to the phone. She inhaled Taylor's scent and found herself getting aroused as Kirk answered.

"It's me."

"This is Taylor Sterling. My friend Haley is listening. "We were the girls on *Dark Witch*. Do you remember us?"

"I do."

"I'm calling from New Caledonia. I'm going to make you an offer. It's not negotiable. There's a boat here we're interested in, but frankly, we like yours better."

"Make your offer," he said.

"We'll pay you one hundred thirty thousand in U.S. dollars. Cash. But you throw in a new generator, fix that fridge, and put on a new anchor winch so that we can move aboard as soon as we get back to New Zealand. That's three of the four conditions. The fourth is that we take delivery in Wellington. If that's satisfactory, I'll call my bank in California and ask them to wire you a ten thousand dollar deposit today, and the balance in a couple of weeks. Deal?

"Not quite. A hundred and forty thousand and I'll install a new generator and fix the refrigerator compressor. You buy and install the windlass, and that's my non negotiable counter."

"Deal," she said. "Give me an account number to wire

the money to."

And that was all there was to it. They'd bought a boat. They were committed. There was no going back. Did she want to? There was only one way to find out. She reached a tentative hand to Taylor's cheek and stroked it. Taylor smiled and Haley kissed her.

Taylor raised her hands and Haley pulled off her sweatshirt, exposing her breasts with those perfect pink nipples. She took one in her mouth and gently sucked on it, the way she would like hers to be sucked.

"I want to see you," Taylor moaned. Haley pulled away from the breast and pulled off her own sweatshirt. She reached behind herself and unhooked her bra. Her large breasts sprang into view. "So beautiful," Taylor said. She took one in her mouth and sucked on it the way Haley had done hers. Then they were working at each other's Levi's and in seconds they were both nude on the bed and in each other's arms.

Haley quivered with anticipation and found herself moaning and arching her back when Taylor's hand found the center of her. "Oh, sweet Lord," she cried as Taylor worked her to a climax that burst upon her in hardly any time at all. She sighed. It had finally happened. They'd finally done it.

"It wasn't so bad, was it?" Taylor said.

"Oh, you," Haley said. She rolled on top and shivered with the feeling of her naked breasts against Taylor's. She kissed her friend, sliding her tongue into her mouth. Taylor moaned and arched her back under her. Haley felt the moisture of her as their pubic hair intertwined. Another spasm of pleasure raced through her as she broke the kiss and lowered her mouth to Taylor's nipples, sucking on first one, then the other.

Taylor squirmed below her, as if she were having an orgasm herself and Haley had yet to touch her down there. She sucked a little harder on a nipple, running her tongue around it. She was working up her courage.

Finally she put her hands to Taylor's breasts and lowered herself further. She ran her tongue in her navel. "Haley?" Taylor whispered. "You don't have to."

"I want to," Haley said. Then she lowered her mouth to that soft mound. Taylor squirmed beneath her, arching up to meet Haley's tongue. And Haley lapped at her sex until Taylor screamed in delight.

CHAPTER
FIFTEEN

GAYLE WOKE IN A COLD SWEAT to a gray morning. Her foot was screaming, as if a thousand bees were stinging it at once. She'd had the cast on for five weeks and five days. Two more days. Then it came off and the pins came out. She thought of them as spikes, driven in by a hooded torturer. She'd never make it.

She struggled to a sitting position and looked out at the new day. Sandy stirred on the other bed. She smiled. He'd become part of her. Always there, always ready to help, never complaining. The perfect husband. But he wasn't her husband. Stacy was, and he was off in America, running around the country, doing what he loved. He'd promised to call every day, she was lucky if he called one in three. And then he only talked for a few minutes.

A boat under sail caught her eye. It was blowing out there. The boat was heeled with everything out, slicing through the waves like an Olympic skater gliding over the ice. No reefing for that sailor. He was a man who knew how to ride the wind. At first she thought he was going to sail by and continue on through Cook Strait. Only the most skillful sailor would attempt that in the weather she was seeing. She wished she was out there with him, face in the wind as they sailed close hauled against the current.

Someday, she told herself as the boat tacked through the wind. He wasn't going through the strait after all. He was coming into the harbor. She was intrigued now. He was heading in under full sail, the wind driving him relentlessly landward, as if he were going to beach his great sailboat in front of the hotel.

She wished she had binoculars so she could see the crew scurrying around the deck as the helmsman shouted orders. What a thrill. She watched, entranced, as the boat sailed closer. A bird of prey sliding on a wind stream, low over the cresting swells. No crew. The revelation shocked her. The helmsman was sailing alone. It was a Phoenix 60, painted white, and the man at the helm was a sailor, still she feared for him as his boat came dangerously close to the moored yachts.

She clutched her hands to her breasts and gasped as he spun the boat to port and into the wind. He dashed from the helm and released the jib sheet. The great sail started flapping as the boat immediately stalled. She smiled with the appreciation only one sailor can have for another as he cranked the jib in with a demon fury, then he was moving forward to drop the main as the boat rocked with the swells. In seconds he was at the bow dropping the anchor.

"Neat," she said.

"What?" Sandy mumbled from the other bed.

"Nothing," she said. She wondered what Stacy would think if he knew his brother had been spending every night in the bed next to hers. Then she smiled. He wouldn't think anything at all. He'd know Sandy would never even sneak a peak. And he knew her. Theirs was a relationship based on trust. Then why hadn't she told him? Because it was nothing. It was just more convenient, that was all. Not worth mentioning.

"How you doing this morning?" He yawned, sat up and stretched, hands reaching for the ceiling. He smiled. She saw a new wrinkle on his forehead. A vertical line between his eyes. It intersected with a short wrinkle between his eyebrows, making a crucifix. Worry lines. She started to mention it, when a new shot of pain rippled up her leg.

"My foot hurts. A lot. I should have listened to you and Dave and at least bought the bloody pills. Then I'd have some to take."

"You want an aspirin?" he asked, getting out of bed.

"Yeah, four or five," she said. "Could you call Dave and see about some pain pills? It really hurts."

"Alright." He looked at his watch. "He could be there by now. I'll call in a few minutes." He went into the bathroom. She heard him urinating into the bowl. The toilet flushed. In such a short time they'd become very familiar. The faucet came on. He was brushing his teeth. He came back out with a glass of water in one hand, four aspirins in the other.

"Thanks." She gobbled the aspirins all at once, chasing them with the water. They tasted like chalk in her mouth and the water only seemed to swirl the unpleasant taste around.

"So, did you finish the journal?"

"No, I'm taking it slowly," she said. The PowerBook was on the nightstand. She'd been reading from it a little at a time.

"Maybe it's not too good to linger over it," he said. He was wearing his usual sweat pants with an old T-shirt. He looked athletic. But then he was a runner, like the girls. And a weekend basketball player. He'd always been in shape.

"Not healthy, you mean?"

"Something like that."

"I'll do it tonight," she said, and she meant it, because he was right. But it had been so good to read Dylan's words, to relive the last couple of years with her. The silly little memories that all of a sudden didn't seem so silly anymore. She grimaced. It really hurt.

His brown eyes held a look of concern, as if he felt her pain. He'd visibly aged in the last six weeks. Or maybe he'd been aging all along and she'd never noticed. They'd all been getting older, but when your life's sailing along on an even keel, you tend to see the brighter side of things.

"Do I look older to you?" she asked, interrupting his reach for the phone. He sat back and met her eyes. "I mean, of course, I'm older than when we first met. And I know I look it. I'm talking about since the accident. Do I look like I've aged since then?"

"Nobody could look their best after what you've been through," he said. "No, that's not what I meant. You look tired, not older. No, that's not it either." He laughed, then she did, too.

"You're not exactly flattering me," she said.

"Sorry. I'll just call room service and have them send up a hammer so I can nail my tongue to the wall."

"I noticed that you've got some gray starting to come in. I'm three years older than you. If I think of you aging, then I have to admit that I am, too."

"I saw them for the first time the other day." He put his hand to his forehead, running his fingers through his curly hair. "Think it'll all turn white?"

"Maybe. You'd look good like that. But gray hair never looks good on a woman under sixty. It makes them look a lot older than they are. My mother told me that."

"You don't have any gray hair."

"But I feel so old. And my blasted foot hurts. Make that phone call."

He called the hospital. Dr. Collins was there and to her surprise Dave told him to bring her in to the fracture clinic straightaway.

"What should I wear?" Gayle shivered at the thought of having to get dressed. Until now she hadn't thought much about it. She couldn't squeeze her swollen foot into her tight jeans and for sure it was too cold out to wear a dress.

"Your pajamas and robe, I guess," Sandy said.

"No way. I'm not going out like that."

"Why not? You're going from the hotel to a cab to the hospital. Nobody's going to see you."

"I don't care if I'm just going down the hall. I'm not going out dressed like an invalid."

"You are an invalid, kind of."

"I don't care."

"How about you wear a pair of my sweatpants? You'll look like you're going jogging,"

"Very funny," she said, but that's what she wore. His sweatpants fit fine and she had no trouble getting them on over the foot and the cast. She donned one of Dylan's sweatshirts instead of the fancier sweaters of hers, but she decided against a jacket. She wasn't going to be outside any longer than it took to get from the hotel to a cab anyway.

He helped her as she crutched her way out of the room and down the hall. She exited the elevator feeling as if she'd run a marathon. She thought she was going to die, smothered in her own sweat, but a cold wind off the bay chilled her when she got outside and somehow she found the strength to take the few steps to the cab.

She tried to fold her body into the front seat, because it looked the easiest at first, but it was impossible. She couldn't bend her leg enough. She wanted to cry.

"Come on," Sandy soothed. "You can stretch your leg across the back." He helped her in and she scooted to the other side of the car with her back against the door, her broken leg on the seat, her good leg on the floor. They were barely able to get the door closed. And every bump the small Japanese car took sent bullets of pain shooting up her leg. "Oh, boy," she said, gripping the seat as the cab shot through the traffic.

The cabbie took them right into the ambulance bay, where Sandy and a hospital orderly helped her struggle out of the car and into a wheelchair. It was so cold in the huge garage. Her foot felt like it had been rubbed raw with hot charcoals and then dunked into a bucket of ice.

They wheeled her upstairs, where they took x-rays.

"But I only came for some pain pills," she protested.

"Doctor's orders," the technician said.

"What doctor?" she said.

"Me," Dave Collins said, coming into the x-ray room. He was wearing a Hawaiian shirt that reminded her more of a holiday than a hospital. "We're going to take the pins out in a few minutes, so I need a good picture. I wouldn't want to forget any." She gave his joke a weak laugh. She was flat on her back on a gurney. She felt so helpless.

"Hey, Mrs. S. I'm your taxi driver again."

"What a coincidence, Danny." She smiled. She'd missed him. He was an up person and his sense of humor had been infectious.

"Not really. Dr. Collins told me you were coming in. I'm the nurse who's going to cut that cast off." He helped her from the x-ray table onto a gurney.

"I'm glad," she said. "Glad that you're here for me and glad that the cast is coming off." She was sitting on the gurney with her feet up. Her right foot was only throbbing now, as if a car had just run over it.

"I'm just off duty, but I wanted to be the one to take it off. I thought maybe you'd be more comfortable if I did it." He smiled and gave her hand a gentle squeeze. He was a good and true friend.

"Thanks, Danny. I appreciate that. I really do." She lay down and he slid a pillow under her head. Once again she was staring at acoustic tiles. They'd replaced some of them in the six weeks since she'd been here last.

"What'd you watch last night?" He asked as he slid the gurney out of the x-ray room.

"*Pretty Woman* with Richard Gere and Julia Roberts." Danny had left his expensive video system hooked up for her and he'd been supplying her with movies, telling her to call when she'd seen them all and he'd exchange them for more.

"Hey, I love that movie." He wheeled her into a large

ward and pulled a curtain around the gurney.

"Everything looks fine," Dave said as he pulled the curtain aside and approached her. He was holding a set of x-rays, which he stuck up on the wall in front of a bright light. "One, two, three, four, five," he counted. He crossed the room and opened a red tool box. It looked just like the kind her auto mechanic back in California might have. He took out a pair of pliers and she gasped.

"Pretty scary," she said.

"Not really," he said. "It won't hurt. Well, not much. You might experience a slippery sensation as the pins slide out."

"Sandy!" she called out.

"I'm here," he pushed the curtain aside and came in.

"I don't think I'm ready to have the pins out," she said. "Besides, they're not supposed to come out till the day after tomorrow."

"You're healed." Dave lifted her leg.

She watched, shaking, as he clamped the pliers onto one of the pins in her foot. One of the two between the big toe and its neighbor. "I don't know about this."

"Relax," he said. Then he pulled the pin out.

"Jesus Fucking Christ!" Her scream was heard throughout the ward and she broke into an instant sweat, almost fainting when she saw the thick red blood ooze out of the wound.

Quick as a flash he pulled on the second pin, but it didn't come. Flesh and bone had grown around it. He held the foot down with a hand firmly on the cast and gave the pin a second hard jerk.

"You said this wouldn't hurt, Dave!" She hated it that she couldn't hold it in. That she was screaming like she'd been scalded. She was embarrassed.

"Maybe a little." He tried to calm her with his smile. His green eyes twinkled. He was going for the third pin.

"Fuuuuuuuck!" she howled, not embarrassed anymore, and not caring that she'd drawn an audience of nurses, orderlies, other patients and a doctor or two. Dave reached for the fourth pin. "Stop," she wailed. She was breathing hard, hyperventilating. She was drenched in sweat, and shaking. This wasn't right. It wasn't how it was supposed to be done.

"What?" He stopped

"I want a local."

"We're almost done." He pulled out the pin. Her leg was filled with indescribable pain, but she was deliriously happy when that fifth pin came out. She didn't realize till it was over, but Sandy had been holding one of her hands. Danny had been holding the other.

"My two knights," she said.

"How do you feel now?" Dave asked.

"Like Mel Gibson in that Braveheart movie. You know the part at the end where he's tortured to death in front of the whole cast. That's how I feel, Dave. You should have used a local."

"It's usually not necessary," he said. "But it's all over now. You'll be right in no time."

"Okay, Mrs. S." Danny said. "Now we go and get that cast off. I know that's something you've been looking forward to."

He wheeled her down a hall to a large room she recognized as the place where she'd had the cast put on six weeks earlier. It vaguely reminded her of her first art class in junior high school. The same high ceiling windows. The same long pole with a hook on the end to open them. The smell of the plaster cast as Danny cut it off with a small battery operated circular saw was like plaster of Paris.

"And off she comes." Danny shut off the saw and gently pried the cast off. "Is that a sight for those pretty eyes of yours?" Danny said.

"Misty eyes," Gayle said.

"Right, misty eyes." He was beaming.

"I want you off the crutches as soon as possible," Dave Collins said, coming into the room. "Get a cane, but don't use it till you're tired and absolutely have to."

"How long before I can walk?"

"Three or four days. Maybe a week. Get that cane." Even the constant throbbing of her foot couldn't dull her elation. The pins were out. The cast was off. She was going to walk again. Soon.

"I want to sit up," Gayle said.

"I'll help you," Mrs. S." Danny said. She felt his strength as he helped her up. She dangled her legs over the side. The right leg barely bent. Blood rushed to her foot. Pain shot up the leg. It was as if the spikes were still there.

"Hurts." She stared at her swollen foot. Red dots between her toes told her where the spikes had been. One of them had a drop of wet blood dripping from it.

"It'll stop hurting after a few days," Dave said.

She wiggled her foot. New bolts of pain seared up her leg, but the foot moved. She moved her leg, raising it till it was sticking straight out.

"Doesn't hurt as much when I hold it up." She lowered it again, slowly moving it through the pain. "It's stuck," she said.

"What?" Dave asked.

"I can't move it any more than this." She was sitting

erect on the gurney, her left leg perpendicular to the floor. Her right was barely bent. "I'm sending the message down the leg to move, but it's not going. I can't bend it any more than this and it hurts like a hurricane."

"That's natural," Dave said. "You haven't used it in six weeks."

"No, it's more than that," she said, fighting a rising panic. "I can't move it."

"It'll come back, you'll see. Quicker than you think." He picked up a pencil and wrote something in her chart.

* * *

Sandy felt her rapid heartbeat through her trembling hand. Perspiration covered her brow and beaded above her lip. She was worried and scared. She'd thought she was going to be magically better when the cast came off. It wasn't going to be that way at all. He knew it. Dave knew it. Why wasn't he telling her?

"I've scheduled your first physio session with Katy Surrey for the day after tomorrow. You should spend as much time as you can on the crutches," Dave said.

"I thought you said you wanted me off these sticks as soon a possible," Gayle said.

"It won't be possible in two days," he said.

"How about a week? Will it be possible then?"

"Maybe. We'll see," he said.

Sandy ached for her when he saw her frown. She reminded him of a little girl who'd just been told her pet cat had died. For a second he thought she was going to cry. But she bit her lip, stiffened her shoulders and said, "Can I have the pain pills now?"

Dave laughed, then said, "No."

"Dave, it hurts," she said, petulant.

"Alright, but just enough for today and tomorrow. Then you're on your own."

"That's fair enough," she said. Then, "Now, I want one now."

"You're serious?" Dave said.

"It's why I'm here. It was your idea to take the bloody spikes out. I think I've been real good. Six weeks and nothing stronger than aspirin. A day without my foot feeling like it's in a meat grinder isn't too much to ask, is it?"

"I'll be right back," he said. And a minute later he was, with a glass of water and two blue pills. Sandy didn't know what they were and he didn't ask. "These will ease the pain for the rest of the day. Take two more when you go to bed. That's all you get. When you wake most of the pain should be gone. After what you've been through for the last six weeks you'll hardly notice it."

"Thanks, Dave." She swallowed the pills. "When does the pain stop?" she kidded as she handed him back the glass.

"You'll be feeling pretty good by the time you get back to the hotel. A little drowsy, maybe. You might even feel like a nap."

"He was right, Sandy," she said, once they were back in her room. "I do feel like a nap. I think I'll just lie back and close my eyes."

"And the pain?" he asked.

"Gone for now."

"Then I'll leave you for a bit."

"I'll miss you," she said.

"I'll be next door watching television," he said.

"You've been so good to me," she murmured. Then she closed her eyes. He picked up the PowerBook and left her alone with her dreams

Back in his room he booted up the computer. He'd sanitized Dylan's journal so that now it was nothing more than a typical teenage diary. No rotting bones in secret closets anymore. Not on Dylan's computer. Gayle could read it and remember happier times.

He put the CD copy he'd made of the original journal in the computer. There was something he wanted to read again, before he destroyed it.

He doubled clicked on *Seventeen,* and opened the second entry.

> *I saw them quite by mistake when I went to replace the broken VHF radio on Wind Song. They were eating at one of those outdoor restaurants in that shopping center by the marina. Dad and Jennifer. At first it looked innocent and I almost called and waved, but he reached over the table and brushed her cheek with the back of his hand.*
>
> *That was more than a friendly caress, it was more like a fondle and it spoke a thousand words. There was something going on between Dad and Jennifer that wasn't kosher.*
>
> *How could he? It'll kill Mom if she finds out. Dad and Jennifer. Is it because she's so young? Is he trying to recapture his lost youth?*
>
> *I went to the boat and dropped off the radio, then I got in my car and parked outside the restaurant. I got a spot where I could watch. Nothing else funny happened during their lunch, and if I hadn't seen him touch her like that I'd have thought nothing of it. Just lunch*

with one of his staff. But she works in SF so what was she doing down here? Good question. And I had seen him touch her that way, so for sure I had an idea something was going on.

When they finished they got in separate cars and went separate ways. I followed Dad. I don't know why. I guess I'm just too curious for my own good. I shouldn't have done it. Sometimes not knowing is better than knowing. But I'm like Haley that way, I have to know everything there is to know.

He went to the Surf Motel. He didn't have to check in. He already had a room. I parked as far away from it as I could get and still see. Any minute I expected Jennifer to show up, but I was wrong. The girl that came was young. Maybe younger than me. She was tall with hair longer than mine and she wore a slinky evening dress at two o'clock in the afternoon. She walked like a hooker. She was a hooker. No doubt about it.

Part of me felt like crying. But I didn't. I can only hope Mom doesn't find out. I'll never tell. This is something I won't even tell Taylor or Haley. This is one secret I have to keep absolutely to myself.

I went back to Wind Song and changed out that radio. Then I went by Comp USA and bought a computer game. I need some mindless entertainment in my life.

Sandy closed his eyes. For a year and a half she'd lived with that. If it was true. Could she have been mistaken?

Was this why she'd been so much closer to her mother? Why everyone called Dylan Gayle's child and Taylor, Stacy's? He ejected the disc, dropped it on the floor and stomped on it. It's over. It never happened. She'd made it all up. He'd done the right thing.

CHAPTER SIXTEEN

HALEY AND TAYLOR SAT ACROSS from the banker. He was squinting against the late afternoon sun streaking in the tall windows. They'd been back in the States for only a few hours and had come straight to the bank from the airport.

"I'm Taylor Sterling." She offered her hand. The banker shook it. He was older and it seemed he appreciated the formality. Haley imagined him trapped in a bow tie life with no way out. It was silly, but she couldn't think of any sane reason a man would wear a tie like that unless he was forced to.

"You're here about the money, I suppose," he said.

Typical banker, right to business.

"Yes," Taylor said.

"Your father opened an account in each of your names. It's amazing how quickly a life insurance company pays when there's a United States Senator in the family."

"My father can be intimidating," she said.

"I understand that you bank at our branch by the beach, Taylor," he said, ignoring her remark. "Does this mean you'll be banking with us now?"

"No, sorry. Actually we're here to kind of take the money out. I'll be closing my beach account as well."

"I'm listening," he said. Haley didn't think he was anywhere near as pleased to be doing business with them now. But then that's the way of bankers. They're friendly when you're putting money in and not friendly when you're taking it back out.

"We'd like you to wire it to the account of a Kevin Kirk at the Bank of New Zealand in Auckland. I have the routing directions here."

"All of it?" He arched an eyebrow. "The whole hundred thousand?"

"The whole enchilada. My fifty thousand and hers."

"Is that what you want, too?" He turned his gaze to Haley.

"What she said, the whole enchilada," Haley said.

"It's a business deal," Taylor said. Then, "Do you mind if I make a quick phone call?" She was reaching for the phone even before he nodded that it was okay. "How do you get an outside line?"

"Dial nine," he said and Taylor started punching numbers.

"Mr. Kirk," she said into the phone. "I am making arrangement to wire you one hundred thousand as we speak. Would it be okay to pay you the remaining thirty thousand in cash when we meet in Wellington?" After a short pause, she said. "Thank you, we're looking forward to it."

"You called New Zealand. That's long distance."

"The bank can afford it," Taylor said.

"That's not the point."

"Look, sir. If it was my father sitting here, would you ask him for time and charges? If so, call the operator and get the cost for the call and I'll pay you. If not, I'll tell my dad how helpful you've been and we'll be on our way."

"It's nothing." The banker's face was a mask, but Haley just bet he was seething.

"Okay," Haley said, when they were out of the bank. "Your parents or mine, which do you want to do first?"

"First, I want a long lunch. Then a shot of courage," Taylor said.

"You can't buy that."

"Don't I know it."

"That's the stupidest thing I ever heard," Taylor's dad said. They were in the living room of the Sterlings' Newport Beach home. Stacy was standing in front of the big bay window, backlit by the evening sun. Cast in shadow like that, Haley thought he looked like an angry bear the way he waved his arms when he talked.

"Yeah, it's not very bright," Taylor agreed, "but we're doing it anyway." Haley wondered what he'd do if he knew that they'd already sent the money. That plus the ten thousand Taylor had had wired from her personal bank account. He'd really blow his top.

"Do your parents know about this?" He said to Haley. He was fuming, but he was holding it in. He was a good politician. And like a politician he was trying to spread the blame for the bad news. They weren't going to do this. Not if he could help it.

"They think it's just as dumb as you do, Stacy," Haley said. "My dad had a cow and I thought Julia was going to faint."

"Can you blame them? They care about you. They can't just let you go sailing off the edge of the earth. What kind of parents would they be if they allowed that?"

"Actually it's not a question of allowing," Taylor said. "We're eighteen, we can do what we want."

"Nobody can do what they want," Stacy said, calming now.

"What a sad thing to say," Haley said.

"That's not it at all." he sat in an overstuffed chair opposite the sofa the girls were sitting on. "People have responsibilities, obligations. You can't just walk away from them." The sun was still behind him and Haley got the impression that he'd set the room up that way on purpose. As if he were some kind of old west gunslinger who wanted the sun at his back.

"What about Dylan? You were going to let her go sailing off around the world all by herself," Taylor said.

"That's different," he said. "It was something she'd worked at for years. She'd paid her dues. No one died so she could have the money to live her adventures."

"That's not fair," Taylor said, fighting tears.

"No, it's not," Stacy said. "But it's the truth. And if Dylan were here she'd agree with me." At this moment Haley hated him.

"She wouldn't. That's why she had the insurance. So that if anything happened we could live her dream."

"Well you don't have the money. It's a good thing I

took care of it. Otherwise you'd be off and there'd be nothing I could do to stop you."

"What are you talking about?" Taylor said.

"I banked the money for you. Two accounts. Joint. My name and yours. You get it when you graduate from college or turn twenty-one, whichever comes first. It's what Dylan wanted." He was lying.

"But—" Haley started to say something, but Taylor squeezed her hand and she shut up. The phone rang. It was closest to Haley, so she picked it up. She'd been answering the Sterling family phone as if it were hers all of her life.

"Hello," she said.

"Is Senator Sterling there?" The voice had a husky quality to it. Kind of like the way a sexy movie star would talk.

"Who's calling please?" The girls had all been trained since childhood. Official calls came on the official phone. If anybody asked for somebody named Mister or Senator on the family phone, find out who it was if you could, then hang up. The number was unlisted. It was for friends and family only.

"Just put him on."

"A little edgy, aren't we?" Haley said.

"Who is this?" the caller asked.

"I think you have it wrong," Haley said. "I'm the one that's supposed to be asking that." Haley heard the click as the caller slammed the phone down.

"Who was that?" Stacy said.

"I don't know. She hung up."

Another phone rang. The official one in Stacy's office off of the dining room.

"I'll be right back," he said as he pushed himself out of

the chair. There was a bounce in his step as he left the room. It's the same woman, Haley thought. She'd called the family phone by mistake.

The girls remained seated and silent. Haley stared out the window at her Porsche parked at the curb in front. It was a warm summer evening. All she wanted to do right now was to take a drive and forget about parents. Just her, Taylor, the Porsche and the San Diego Freeway.

"That was a girl from the office. I've got to go. Papers to sign before I go back to Washington." Haley noticed that he didn't say what girl, what office, or what papers. That was very unlike him. A zillion times she heard him say something like, 'Janis from the Frisco office wants me to go over the talking notes before I meet Jim Gordon from Pepsi. Gotta go.' He'd always been specific, including his family in everything.

"He lied," Taylor said, as Haley drove away from the curb.

"Yeah. That's not like him." Haley wondered for a second if Taylor was referring to the money or the excuse he made as he'd brushed them off.

"He must think I'm awful stupid."

"Maybe he's just not thinking at all," Haley said. But she was thinking and what she was thinking about was that women on the phone. Haley didn't want to say anything, though, because it would hurt Taylor. Besides, she didn't know anything. Not for sure.

"We've always been so close. He knows I know where he banks. It would only be natural for me to go there if I wanted the money. And any party on a joint account can take the money out. He should know I know that. Heck, for all he knows we could be on our way to the bank right now," Taylor said.

"But they weren't joint accounts. If they were, the man at the bank would have said." Haley sighed. Taylor hadn't picked up on Stacy's lie about the girl from the office, but then she hadn't heard her on the phone either.

"Maybe not," Taylor said. "Not if he didn't have any reason to think we were doing anything wrong."

"Think he'll call your father?"

"Why should he?"

"It's a lot of money," Haley said.

"To us," Taylor said, "but not to the bank. Besides, it's already gone. It's a done deal."

"I almost told him we'd already sent the money," Haley said. "If you hadn't stopped me, you and that woman on the phone, I'd have blurted it all out."

"That would have been bad," Taylor said.

They exited the freeway as the sun was going down and after a few minutes Haley shut the engine off at the sprawling Hacienda Stables.

"You wanna say goodbye or just do it?" Haley said.

"I have to see her one last time," Taylor said.

"Yeah, me too," Haley said.

The orange sky was turning dark as they approached the stalls where their horses were stabled.

"Hey, Suzy Q, it's me." The animal came to the gate on command and Haley held a hand out to be nuzzled. "Looking for sugar, aren't you, girl? Sorry, I'm a little short today." But the horse didn't seem to mind. In fact, she seemed glad to see her.

She looked down the aisle. Taylor was stroking the shock of white on her horse's head that had given her her name. She was crying. She left her own horse and went to her friend.

"We can't keep them."

"I know. Let's go do it," Taylor said.

"Taylor, Haley, I heard about Dylan. I'm so sorry."

"We were just going over to the office to talk to you, Jimmy," Taylor said.

"I'm here now. How can I be of service?" He was short and as thin as he was back when he was a jockey thirty years ago.

"We're leaving the country shortly and we probably won't be back," Taylor said as she wiped a tear from her eye with the back of a hand. Haley was content to let Taylor handle anything that had to do with business.

"I'm sorry to hear that. We'll miss you." He looked out at the darkening sky as he brushed a fly away with his hand, then asked, "What about the horses?"

"We want you to find them good owners. Girls like us who will treat them right. We'll come back tomorrow and sign the papers."

"I could sell them pretty quick if I wasn't too picky," he said. "Get you a good price, too."

"Jimmy, we love those animals and we know what they're worth. We'll take a lot less if you find them a good home. Not just anybody. And certainly not some riding stable that will work them to death. And we'll give you a real good commission. A hundred percent."

"Wait a minute. You're giving them to me?"

"Only if you find them each a girl who will love them like we did," Taylor said.

"Jeez, I love you girls," he said and Haley knew he wasn't just saying it because they'd given him the horses to sell. He'd taught them both how to ride. They'd known him since grade school. He was a dear friend and Haley knew they could trust him.

They spent the night at Taylor's. Haley's parents

were going to a concert at the Santa Monica Civic and wouldn't be home till late, and Stacy had to go up to San Francisco and wouldn't be home at all. So even though they'd traveled thousands of miles to come home, it seemed like no one cared. In fact, Haley got the impression that her parents were pretty eager to bundle her off to Stanford. They hadn't missed her at all, but she wasn't really surprised.

Stacy, on the other hand, was a different story. She would have expected him to roll out the red carpet for them. Dinner at a fancy restaurant. Some wine, even though they weren't old enough. The usual Stacy charm as he regaled them with stories of capitol hill. Who was in. Who was out. It wasn't like him to take off the way he'd done.

In the morning they went by the stables and signed their horses away. Then they drove to Balboa Island to see Keith Thorstein, the Sterling family lawyer. Keith was an old family friend and it was Saturday, so if he wasn't on the golf course, he'd be at home.

His wife, Stella, answered the door. She was short, slender, and looked as if she'd just come from a total makeover at the beauty shop. "Taylor, Haley, what a pleasant surprise." Then, "We were so sorry to hear about Dylan."

"Yeah, it was tough," Taylor said. Haley wondered if everybody was going to say that, and if so, for how long. "This isn't really a social call, Stella," Taylor said. "We came to see Keith about Dylan's boat."

"Did I hear my name taken in vain?" He was a big man with a shock of gray hair that stood out like a beacon over his deep tan.

"Hi, Keith," Taylor said.

"Why do you need this old lawyer? You girls aren't in any trouble, are you?"

"No, no trouble," Taylor said. "We just wanted to know how to go about selling Dylan's boat."

"Just have your father sign a couple of papers and find a buyer," he said.

"Why do we need him to sign anything?" Taylor asked.

"Well it's complicated. She didn't have a will, not one on file anyway."

"My dad told me she left the boat to us."

"Yes and no. She told me if anything happened to her, she wanted you two to have everything she had left. That would include the boat. But she thought if anything did happen, it would be at sea and the boat would be lost with her. So she was only talking about personal effects, nothing of any real value, except to you guys. We were going to draw up a will someday before she left on her great adventure, but we never got around to it. I told your father what we'd talked about and he must have told you that she wanted you to have the boat."

"So it's really Dad's boat now?"

"In a way, but I'm sure he'll sign it over to you."

Taylor reached into her purse and took out a dollar. "Here, Keith, for legal services rendered," she said.

"I see." He took the dollar and put it in his shirt pocket.

"We gotta go. Sorry to pick your brains and run, but we have a lot to do and not much time to do it in."

"What was that all about, the bit with the dollar bill?" Haley asked as she started the car.

"He took money for legal services. That makes everything we said privileged. He could lose his license if he tells Dad that we were here trying to sell the boat."

"But he didn't have to take the money."

"No, he didn't. It was just my way of saying I didn't want Dad to know. And by taking the dollar, it was his way of saying he wouldn't tell." Then after a few seconds, she added, "I hope I didn't make one huge mistake sending the money like that."

"It was a joint thing," Haley said. "If it was a mistake, it was our mistake."

"Thanks," Taylor said. "But it was my idea. I just hope it wasn't a dumb one."

"I'm sure we can trust Mr. Kirk," Haley said.

"Yeah, if things go okay, but what if we don't get the rest of the money? Think he'll give us back what we've already sent?"

"I'd be afraid to ask," Haley said.

"It's a lot of money," Taylor said.

"We're not licked yet. We still have my car. It's got to be worth a bunch."

"Yeah, I guess that's our last hope."

Thirty minutes later they left Newport Imports, dealer of expensive European sports cars, with the disturbing news that although the Porsche was Haley's, it wasn't. She was the registered owner. The Bank of America was the legal owner. Her father was making payments. There was no equity in the car.

"We're thwarted at every turn," Haley said. She was driving north on Pacific Coast Highway. The dashboard clock said it was 3:15. She glanced out to her left. Several surfers were paddling before a breaking wave. Only one caught it. She slowed down and pulled over to the curb.

"What?" Taylor said.

"Him," Haley said.

"Oh, yeah," Taylor said. "He's getting a great ride." The lone surfer rode the wave almost to the beach, then he started paddling back to catch another.

"We don't have enough money," Haley said. "You've got five left in the bank. I've got a little over two. That leaves us twenty-three short. And we still have to buy an anchor winch and have some cash left over for provisions and fuel."

"I could sell my jewelry. I'll bet I could get five or six thousand."

"You're way too young to have to start selling jewelry," Haley said. "If it comes to that, I'd rather eat humble pie and call Kirk and tell him we can't do it." She sighed as another surfer caught another wave. "I know I'm a dreamer, but I thought we had everything under control. It all seemed so possible when we were in New Caledonia. But back here it's like no way, Jose. The dream killers come out in force to stomp on your hope. They want to bend you and fold you and put you in a bow tie world. It's not fair."

"We could get a partner," Taylor said.

"A partner?" Haley turned her gaze away from the surfers and faced Taylor. "How do we do that?"

"We find someone who wants to buy a third of *Ghost Dancer*. Someone we could live with. Someone who has the same dream."

"We could look forever and not find anyone like that. People advertise in the back of sailing magazines for someone like that."

"We could maybe live with Gina Sealy," Taylor said.

"The girl on the ledge?"

"That's the one."

Two hours later Haley parked in front of a steak

house made out of fake logs, with fake snow on the roof. Snow at a Southern California beach. At any other beach in the world it would be out of place, but nothing is out of place in Southern California. Haley put a quarter in the parking meter. They were on Second Street in Long Beach's Belmont Shore section. Second Street was the fashionable place to shop in The Shore with all the latest trendy shops. The restaurant-bars turned into clubs at dusk, places for the upper middle class, the young rich and the college students from nearby Long Beach State to come together. The restaurants served that ice tea that tasted like peaches. Second Street was both upscale and collegiate. A fun place to shop and a fun place to party.

"That's the video store," Haley said. It was on the other side of the street. They stopped halfway across as a couple of Harleys came toward them. The riders were wearing Hell's Angels colors and they had the amazing ability to whistle loud enough to be heard above the roar of their machines.

"Boys with their toys." Taylor waved as they went by. They were still laughing when they entered the store.

"Can I help you?" She was as slender as she'd seemed on television. Her long hair was in a ponytail that swished as she moved her head. Her high cheekbones, firm chin, wide set blue eyes, and lips that looked like they were stolen from a French starlet, all combined to give her a sensual but lost kind of appearance. Haley thought she belonged on a model's runway, not behind the counter in a video store.

"Maybe we can help each other," Taylor said.

"You're the sister," Gina said. Her voice was like a whisper, but she wasn't whispering and she looked straight at you when she talked.

"Yeah, I'm her sister." Taylor linked a hand with Haley and Haley gave her a squeeze. "We thought, no we were hoping actually, that you might like to come cruising with us."

"What?"

"You're our last hope. We bought a boat for a hundred and forty thousand dollars. We've already paid a hundred and ten of it, but we can't raise more than seven or eight more. We like messed up big time." Taylor's voice was cracking, but Haley didn't think she was going to cry.

"You paid that kind of money without a broker and before taking possession?"

"Kinda," Taylor said. "But we trust the man we're buying the boat from, that's not the problem."

"Kinda, what's kinda? Either you paid out over a hundred thousand dollars and have nothing to show for it, or you didn't."

"We did," Taylor blurted. "Pretty dumb, huh?"

"Where did you think you were going to get the rest of the money?"

"We were going to sell my sister's boat, but my dad stopped that. Then we tried to sell Haley's car, but it turns out it's not free and clear."

"You guys must want to go cruising awful bad," Gina said.

"Don't you?" Taylor said.

"Yeah," Gina said. "I do."

"Look, we need a third partner. We have a boat. We have most of the cash, but we need more. You need a boat and you have the insurance money your parents left you. We need each other."

"How do you know about that?" She leaned into the

counter and bore into Taylor with those eyes and somehow Haley knew that she could spot a lie as easily as an eagle spots prey. If she ever faced the Virgin Mary, she'd have eyes like that.

"Sandy told us," Taylor said.

"Isn't everything I told him supposed to be a secret?"

"Supposed to be," Taylor said. She paused as a woman with a small boy rented a movie. When the woman was finished and was headed for the door with the child in tow, Taylor said, "So, you wanna come or what?"

"Tell me about the boat."

"She's a Phoenix 60. She's sitting in New Zealand right now, waiting for us. She just needs a few more things, a little work and she'll be ready to go."

"Go where?" Gina said.

"Away," Haley spoke for the first time since they'd entered the store.

"I don't know if it'd work. I'm not gay."

"We're not gay," Taylor said.

"Yes we are," Haley said.

"Yeah," Taylor said, pausing. "I guess maybe we are. How'd you tell?"

"It's obvious, the way you look at each other. The way you touch. That's the way my folks were with each other. And I've never met anyone in my life that was more in love than them."

"Does it bother you?" Haley said.

"Not unless it bothers you that I'm not," Gina said. Then, "I think maybe you guys should go cruising, because looking like you do and coming from the kind of families you do, there's no way anyone's gonna accept it. And feeling the way you obviously do about each other, there's no way you're gonna keep it secret very long. Does

Sandy know?"

"No," Haley said.

"He's sharp," Gina said. "He'll figure it out pretty quick."

"So, maybe we'll tell them, then we won't have to worry about any secrets," Haley said.

"Really?" Taylor said. "You'd go through that for me?"

"Yeah, I would."

"Why?"

"I guess because I love you. I just figured it out, because of what she said. I love you. I don't want to be with anyone else. Not now. Not ever." She shivered with the words. She was laying it all out. "I don't care who knows."

"I love you, too," Taylor said. She squeezed Haley's hand and a warm glow shot up her arm. No matter what happened now, it was going to be okay.

"So you wanna tell me what I get for my money?" Gina said, smiling.

"Your own cabin," Haley said.

"I'm in," Gina said.

"Really?" Taylor said.

"Look at you guys, all sappy with your feelings for each other. You can't think straight with your goo goo eyes and touchy touchy. You need a keeper. Someone to keep you out of trouble and make sure your boat stays afloat. How could I not be in?"

CHAPTER SEVENTEEN

"**WHAT ARE YOU DOING** in the wheelchair?"

Gayle was shocked by the tone of voice, she looked up, met Katy Surrey's glare. The frown Katy wore added years to her age. No longer was she the helpful young physiotherapist with the Christmas green eyes. She was all business now.

"When the taxi brought me into the ambulance garage, they said I had to ride," Gayle said.

They were in the waiting area across from the nurse's station. Sandy was reading a Dick Francis paperback. Two nurses were drinking coffee. It smelled delicious. Gayle hadn't had any since the accident.

"Don't do it anymore. Use your crutches." Katy said, steel in her voice.

Gayle had at least fifteen years on Katy, but the younger woman was ordering her around like a child.

"The ambulance bay is halfway across the hospital from here. No way can I go that far on them." She wasn't going to be pushed around. There had to be some ground rules laid out right from the start. "Besides, how I get here is my business. So let's get started."

"No."

"What do you mean, no?"

"Just what I said. No. My job is to get you walking as quickly as possible. We can do it my way and you can be walking without aids in a month. It'll hurt. You'll limp. But it's possible. Or you can take it easy. A little at a time and with luck you'll be throwing away those crutches in six or seven months. If that's the way you want it. But if you go that way, you'll go without me, because there's a lot of people that need my help that actually want to get better." She paused, fire in her emerald eyes. "There, that's my speech. What's it going to be? My way or the highway? You decide."

"Do you come on like this with all your patients?" Gayle said. Sandy was curiously silent.

"They don't call me Katy the Terrible for nothing. Danny must have warned you."

"So where do we go from here?" Gayle said.

"We get down to work. You'll be coming here every day at ten o'clock, except weekends. The sessions will last till lunch. In two weeks I'll have you off the crutches and on canes. Then we'll start the pool and we'll see how it goes from there. Okay?"

"Okay," Gayle said, humbled.

"Follow me," Katy said. Gayle started to wheel the chair after her. Katy turned. "On your crutches."

Gayle backed up to were Sandy was pretending to be engrossed in his book. He was acting like he was oblivious to her discomfort, but Gayle knew better. In his own way he was trying to make her feel less embarrassed, but it wasn't working. Blood rushed to her head as she put the brake on the chair. She grabbed the crutches and forced herself up.

"Could I have a cup of coffee first?"

"Say again," Katy said.

"I haven't had any coffee since the accident. I really love coffee."

"You quit?"

"Only because when I drink it I go to the bathroom more. It hurts to get out of bed, so I cut down on my liquids. Coffee was the first to go. I used to drink it all day long."

"Jenny, can I have that coffee?" Katy said to the nurse.

"Sure," the nurse said. She'd heard. "I can't go a day without it. I feel for you, Mrs. Sterling."

"Gayle, please," Gayle said. The nurse held out the cup.

"Sit back down and have your coffee," Katy said. Gayle obeyed and the nurse handed her the coffee. Gayle held the cup to her nose and inhaled. It smelled divine.

"Go on," Katy said. "Taste it. It's part of the therapy."

"Really?" Gayle said.

"You are to drink as much coffee as you like, the more the better." She was smiling. One minute she was Katy the Terrible, the next she was kind and considerate.

Gayle took a sip. "Heaven," she said.

"Drink up, there's more where that came from," Katy said.

"Why?"

"I want your bladder full. The more trips you make to the toilet the more exercise that leg is going to get."

"You're joking, right?"

"In a way, yes. In a way, no. You've had an injury. You've been badly hurt. But you can't give in to it. Giving up coffee, giving up anything you don't absolutely have to, is like giving in. We don't give in here. We don't give up. We struggle and fight and we get better. That's why I do what I do. I get off when my patients get well."

Gayle took another sip of the coffee, then she gave the cup back to the nurse. "Thank you."

"It was my pleasure. Don't take everything Katy tells you too seriously."

"Okay, time for work. Gayle, get out of that chair and follow me."

Gayle pushed herself up again and followed her through a door labeled Physiotherapy, but to her the room was very similar to a high school gymnastics room. She crutched past parallel bars and made her way to a row of tables, the kind you'd expect to see in a doctor's office or a massage parlor.

"Hop up." Katy patted a table. Obviously she wasn't going to help her.

Gayle stood the crutches by the side of the table, turned around with her buttocks against it and put her hands, palms down, on the mattress and stiff armed her way up onto the table.

"Very good. You're not so helpless after all."

Gayle tried to take in the rest of the room without taking her eyes off of Katy. High windows let in the sunlight. She saw exercise equipment throughout the large room. There were two whirlpools off in a corner and a large clock, the kind found in most schools, was mounted on the wall near another set of parallel bars. A faint odor of sweat and a real threat of pain permeated the room. There were ballet bars on two of the walls and one wall had bars running up it halfway to the ceiling. The table Gayle was sitting on was pushed up against the wall bars.

"Okay." Katy took the crutches. "Stretch out, then roll over on your stomach, head against the wall." She lay the crutches against the next table as Gayle attempted to roll over. Her foot, her leg and the fresh scar on her hip where they'd inserted the rod were all screaming. She couldn't go over onto her right side. And moving her right leg up over the left, so she could go over on the other, was out of the question as well.

"I can't."

"I know it's hard, you've been on your back for so long. Try to raise your leg."

"I'm trying, it just won't come up. Not a bit."

"You haven't used the muscles in so long, but it'll come. I'll lift your leg and help you over." She did and Gayle rolled and pushed herself up onto her left side, then she was over and on her stomach. "I want you to practice lifting your leg and getting up on your side like that. Next time you should be able to go over by yourself."

"Okay," Gayle said.

"Now, let's see you bend your leg."

She concentrated, harder then she'd ever tried to do anything, but all she managed to do was send pain sparking from her foot to her thigh, shooting back and forth like trapped lightning.

"Grab onto the bars," Katy said, "because this might hurt." Gayle looked forward and grabbed onto the wall climbing bars as Katy raised her leg.

"Yeouch!" Gayle screamed.

"Okay, too far, I'm lowering it."

"Big hurt," Gayle said through gritted teeth, "Big big."

"No more screaming," Katy said.

"No more." Gayle's fists were white as she hung onto the wooden bar. For the next hour she suffered short periods of excruciating pain, interspersed with longer periods of intense relief as Katy massaged her leg.

"How was it?" Sandy asked when they were in the cab on the way back to the hotel.

"It hurt like heck. I have a long way to go."

For the rest of the day she tried sitting up and bending her leg, despite the stabbing hurt that knifed up it, but as she got used to the pain, she was able to bend it more and more. At the hospital Katy continued to push her limits, and after every session she found that she could bend it even further.

"How was your weekend?" Katy asked a week later as Gayle was pushing herself up onto the table. They'd completed five sessions and Gayle was getting used to the torture of the therapy.

"Fine, everything considered." She hadn't heard from Stacy since she'd started physio and it bothered her. She'd wanted to tell him about her progress and several times she'd thought about picking up the phone and calling him, but she didn't know where he was, not even what state he'd be in. She could have called Freddy Carson, but she didn't want to admit, even to him, that Stacy hadn't been calling her. He must really be busy.

"Did you do your exercises?"

"I did," she said proudly. "Watch." She rolled over by herself and raised her leg till the knee was bent at a ninety degree angle and the flat of her foot was pointed toward the high ceiling. It hurt plenty and she was only able to hold it for a second or so before lowering it.

"Very good. We're moving along better than I expected."

"And I came by myself today."

"No Dr. Sterling?" Katy asked.

"No Dr. Sterling. He wasn't too happy about it. But I can't really be independent if there's always someone around looking after me."

"Good girl."

"So what do we do today?"

"We're going to bend your leg and hold it in position for about ten or fifteen minutes. It'll be painful, but nothing like what you've experienced." Gayle felt her snap some kind of harness around her lower leg, between the foot and the knee. "Okay, your leg's hooked up. Now I'm running a line to the bars behind you." Gayle looked up and saw her run the rope around one of the bars above her head. "Brace yourself."

"I can do it," Gayle said. "You don't have to pull it up."

"Okay, raise it," she said. Gayle did and Katy pulled the rope tight and tied it off. "Now your leg is locked in place. How does it feel?"

"It hurts." The pressure was enormous. It felt like her leg was being pushed beyond its breaking point. "Okay, that's enough. You can unhook me now," Gayle said.

"I've got a couple of phone calls to make. I'll be back in ten or fifteen minutes."

"You're not going to leave me alone?"

"You'll be fine."

"Katy, you can untie the leg."

"Bye." Then she was gone.

"Damn, it hurts," she whispered. She glanced up at the wall clock. The minute hand was on the twelve.

"I'll bet it does." The voice was male and it was coming from behind her, but locked in place as she was she unable to turn.

"What are you doing here, Nick?" she said. Four words, but his imitation Kennedy was written all over them.

"I feel for you." Nick Nesbitt came around to the side of the table so she could see him. "I wish it was me rigged up there instead of you."

"So do I, Nick," she said.

He laughed. Then she laughed a little. "No, I wouldn't wish this on anyone in the world. I feel like I'm on the rack. Any second a hooded man is going to start asking me questions that I don't know the answers to. Then he's going to stick hot needles under my fingernails."

"You always did have a wild imagination," Nick said.

"I asked you before. What are you doing here? It's not like you to give up the prime spot. And how'd you find me?"

"Finding you was the easy part," he said. "I went to the Sterling and asked for you. They told me you were here. As to why, I guess I came to help."

"I don't understand."

"Dylan kept a journal. Some sleazeball down here was trying to sell it to one of the tabloid shows. I owe you, so I came down and bought it to keep it from getting out.

Besides, we're supposed to report the news, not be the news."

"I'm reading it now," she said. "So far it's just typical girl stuff. Damn, this hurts. It feels like there's this giant slowly prying my leg off."

"Call me when you finish it," he said. Something about the way his accent slipped told her that she wasn't going to like what she was going to read. "I'm staying at the Sterling too. Room three-thirteen."

"Why don't you just tell me what I'll find," she said.

"Call me," he repeated. Then he was gone, leaving Gayle to suffer with the physical pain of her bound leg and the mental anguish about what she might find in the journal. She would finish it as soon as she got back to the hotel.

She looked up at the clock again. The big hand had moved to the one. Five minutes. How long did Katy say? Ten or fifteen minutes. Damn her, why couldn't she have been more specific? Five minutes was forever when your leg was roasting in a fire pit.

"Mom!" Two voices burst into the room. She smiled despite her leg.

"Taylor, Haley, the sailors return from the sea. How did you know where I was?"

"We called the hotel from the airport. They said you'd just left for the hospital. We thought it would be fun to surprise you," Taylor said.

"Ah, the hotel, my service." She laughed. "I'm glad you did. Come over here where I can see you. And tell me stories about tropical islands that will take my mind off my damned leg."

"You look lots better," Haley said.

"I sure don't feel it. Can you untie that rope?"

"Sure." Haley reached for the line.

"No. She's got five more minutes, minimum." Katy was back.

"Busted," Gayle said.

"We bought a boat," Taylor said. She was bubbling. "It's beautiful, long and sleek. Hale and me are gonna be sailors."

"You bought a boat?" Gayle said. "Not Dylan's boat?"

"Not Dylan's," Taylor said.

"I don't understand." She's happy, Gayle thought, really happy. Haley seemed happy, too. That sailing adventure Sandy set up for them must have worked wonders.

"We'll talk about it when we get back to the hotel," Taylor said, "'cuz they say a picture is worth a thousand words."

"I just saw the Asshole Nesbitt." A new voice. She couldn't see the speaker, but she sounded young. "I had to duck behind the nurses' station. If he's any kind of reporter at all, he would have been all over me."

"He's a good reporter," Gayle said. "Who are you?"

"I'm Gina." The girl came around the table and stood next to Taylor.

"Mom, this is our new friend, Gina Sealy."

"I know that name. Sandy's mentioned it. You're—"

"The girl on the balcony," Gina said.

"Yeah, Nick would have been all over you. You'd be a good story. Why are you here?"

"Alright, everyone out. We have some more work to do," Katy said.

"Let them stay," Gayle said.

"Only if they don't get in the way." Katy untied the

rope and gently lowered the leg. Relief flooded through her, then joy as Katy's magic fingers started massaging it.

"So, Gina, where did you meet my girls?"

"In a video store," Gina said.

"Why do I get the impression that you're deliberately being vague?"

"Because I am."

"And why is that?"

"Because they don't want me to tell till we get to the hotel and I promised I wouldn't."

"Okay, Gayle, I can see your heart's not really in this today," Katy said. "So just a quick exercise on the parallel bars and then you can go."

"Out of jail early." Gayle laughed.

"Okay, up." Katy helped Gayle over onto her back, then up into a sitting position. She handed her the crutches and Gayle got off the table by herself.

"You're getting better every minute," Katy said as Gayle followed her to the parallel bars. They were lowered to just below waist level, so she was able to stand between them and support herself with her arms stiff at her sides.

"So you want me to walk through them?"

"Nope, hand me the crutches, then turn around and face me." Gayle gave over the crutches. "Now," Katy said when Gayle was in place, holding a bar with each hand, "try and raise that foot."

Gayle tried. Nothing happened except hot pain. "Feels like my foot is in a meat grinder."

"Come on, lift it," Katy said.

"I'm trying, nothing but hurt."

"Come on, Gayle, don't wimp out on me. Raise the leg."

"I can't!"

"Come on, Mom," Haley said. "You can do it."

"Yeah, you can do it," Taylor echoed.

"Nothing, nothing," Gayle said. Sweat dripped from her forehead into an eye. She tried to blink it away. Her arms were shaking. She felt like she was going to fall.

"Get mad and raise that fucking leg!" Gina yelled. She was so close that her mouth was right next to Gayle's ear. "Raise it!" The sound blasted through her head. She felt Gina's hot breath on her cheek.

"You can't talk to me like that."

"Shut the fuck up and raise that leg!"

Anger zapped her, killing the pain. She wanted to hit the girl, but instead she let out a wild yell. And she raised the leg a foot off the ground.

"Way to go, Gayle," Gina said.

"Very well done," Katy said. "You get a gold star today, Gayle." Quick as it had come, her anger was gone, replaced with a kind of pride of accomplishment. "Very interesting method," Katy mumbled. "I might use it sometime." She took the crutches from where she'd set them against the wall and put them into a closet.

"What are you doing?" Gayle said.

"You've graduated to canes." Katy pulled a pair of gray canes with elbow braces out of the closet.

"I was just getting used to the crutches," Gayle said.

"I know. You were doing so well. That's why you get the canes a week ahead of schedule." She offered them to Gayle. "Try them." Gayle let a hand go from the bar and took one of the canes. "Put your arm through the elbow support and hold on to the handle. Gayle did it and Katy handed her the other one. "Now let's see you walk." Gayle took a step. Then another. It was much harder than the crutches. Each step was torture.

"I think I'd like the crutches back," she said.

"I know it's harder and it'll take some getting used to. So I have a treat for you."

"What?"

"You can ride down to the ambulance bay today. But I want you walking through the hospital on Monday, not riding."

"Aye, aye, captain," Gayle said. Then, "Who wants to push? Taylor, Haley or the drill sergeant?"

"It would be my pleasure," Gina said. "You get yourself to the chair and I'll do the pushing."

Gayle was standing in the middle of the physio room. It wasn't that far to the chair. Thirty feet or so across the room, another fifteen or twenty to the chair. But the way she felt, it might as well be blocks away.

"What are you talking about?" Gayle said. "She said I could ride." She looked at Katy and the girls. They were all quiet. Taylor and Haley looked embarrassed, Katy, amused.

"It's like going to the store, Gayle," Gina said. "You gotta go to the car. It doesn't come into the house to pick you up."

"I don't even know you. Why are you doing this?"

"Three years ago my dad had too much to drink and drove a rental car into a tree in Vanuatu. He broke both legs and several toes. He was on his back for four months and it looked like it was going to be forever. Then the government told him that when his visa expired in six weeks he was outta there. Fly, sail, swim, they didn't care, it was time to go. Besides, cyclone season was fast approaching. What dad didn't know was that no way would those kind people have kicked out an invalid. Dad was a popular guy anyway. They all loved him."

"So why?" Gayle asked, intrigued in spite of herself. They were all looking at Gina, curious. Gayle's arms were getting tired, her foot was screaming. But she wasn't going to give in, at least not yet.

"Mom and I went to the prime minister and asked him to do it. It was the only way we were ever gonna get Dad back on his feet. But he was one stubborn son of a bitch. He needed lots of encouragement and I was it, because my mom was just too gentle to be a nag. I don't do nag very well either, but we learned that I can do drill instructor great, if I have to. I got that old pirate walking and we sailed out of there before that six weeks was up. If I can shout him to walking, stubborn sod that he was, I can sure do it to you."

"I like this woman," Katy said.

"I do too, I think," Gayle said. She bit her lip and slowly caned her way to the chair. She sat in it and sighed as she handed the canes up to Haley. "Okay, I did it. Now what?"

"Now we can go." Gina moved around behind the chair.

Gayle closed her eyes and said, "It was bad enough that I had to put up with Katy the Terrible. Now I have to deal with Gina the Horrific as well."

"I'll take that as a compliment," Gina said. Then she wheeled Gayle to the elevator and on to the ambulance bay, where they called a cab.

"I don't think we can all fit in," Gayle said.

"Nonsense," Gina said.

"No, seriously. I take up the whole back seat."

"Why?"

"I can't bend my leg."

"Sure you can. I saw."

"My God, it was tied up."

"You can sit in front," Gina said. "You'll be fine. Come on, I'll help you."

Gayle noticed that Taylor and Haley hadn't said a word since Gina had shouted at her when she was trying to lift her leg. Gina offered her a hand and then helped her into the front seat. She was gentle but firm when she helped her bend the leg.

"Hurts like hell," Gayle said.

"How do you go to the toilet?" Gina asked.

"I keep it stretched out. It's not easy."

"You'll be better real quick, I promise," Gina said. Then to the driver. "The Sterling."

"You know Wellington?" Gayle asked.

"Sure, she's been cruising in the South Seas her whole life," Taylor said, finally speaking.

"Really? All your life?" Gayle said.

"I was born on a boat."

"You don't look old enough to be out on your own. So where are your parents?" Gayle asked as the cab left the ambulance bay and pulled out into traffic.

"They died on it."

"Oh, my God. I'm so sorry." Gayle shivered with sympathy and pain. Her leg felt just like it did when Katy had it tied up. The ten minute cab ride seemed like forever and when Gina opened her door after they pulled up in front of the Sterling, she felt like getting out and kissing the ground.

"Okay, Gayle, here are the canes. You can do it." Gina said.

"Yeah, I can," Gayle said and she followed Haley and Taylor into the hotel. Gina stayed by her side.

"Look, there's Sandy." Haley pointed toward the restaurant. It looked like he'd just finished breakfast. Haley waved and Sandy waved back. Then he saw Gina and it looked like his heart skipped a beat. He stood and came toward them. He came straight to Gina, like the others weren't there.

"Hi, Sandy." Gina offered her hand.

"What are you doing here?" He shook it.

"It's a surprise, Uncle Sandy," Taylor said. "We'll tell you once we're upstairs."

"I don't like surprises, not even on Christmas or my birthday."

"You'll like this one," Haley said. Then they were at the elevator and Taylor pushed the call button.

"How long are you here for?" Sandy asked when they were in Gayle's room.

"For a while," Haley said.

"Then I should call downstairs and get you a room," he said.

"That won't be necessary," Gina said. "I can bunk with Gayle for a while and the girls won't be needing a room." Gayle felt his confusion. This was where he slept, but they both held their tongues. Innocent as it was, it wouldn't look right if anyone found out they were sleeping in the same room.

"What do you mean the girls won't need a room?" Gayle asked.

"We won't be staying in the hotel," Haley said.

"Then where?" Sandy asked.

"Out there." Haley, pointed out the window.

"I don't get it." Sandy said.

"You get it, don't you, Gayle?" Gina said. "If you could live anywhere out there you wanted, where would you live?" She was pointing to the boats in the harbor.

"The Phoenix. The white Phoenix," Gayle said.

CHAPTER
EIGHTEEN

"WE'RE GOING TO GO OUT TO THE BOAT and pay off the owner and get the girls situated," Gina said. "Then I'll dinghy back." She looked at her Rolex. "Give me about two hours." Gayle thought it strange the way Gina seemed to be taking charge.

"Nice watch," Sandy said, "I haven't seen it before."

"My father gave it to me. I was wearing it when the boat went down. I couldn't wear it till lately. Too many bad memories, but I can deal with them now."

"I'm glad to hear that," Sandy said, but Gayle thought she heard a note of doubt in his voice. "You've come a long way."

"And she's gonna go a lot farther," Taylor said. "We all are." She was smiling, brimming with happiness.

"How were you able to afford it?" Gayle asked.

"With the money Dylan left in that insurance policy," Taylor said.

"That can't be enough," Sandy said.

"It wasn't. We tried to sell Dylan's boat but Dad wouldn't let us. He doesn't want us going, obviously. He thinks we should go to Stanford. Then we tried to sell Haley's car, but we couldn't do that either, her dad's making payments. Then we remembered what Sandy said about Gina and the money she had from her parent's estate and we looked her up and asked her to buy in with us. So in the end, even though Dad and Haley's parents were against us, it worked out great."

"I should have let Gina give that money away, but me and my big mouth convinced her to hang on to it," Sandy said after the girls were gone.

"So you don't think it's a good idea either?" Gayle said.

"They're only eighteen," he said.

"Well then that makes it unanimous, but I think maybe we better be a little smarter about it than the folks back home were. Remember what Taylor said, they think Stacy and Haley's parents are against them. If we fight them on this, they'll just dig in their heels. We have to appear to be on their side. We have to act supportive."

"You're right," he said. "Gentle persuasion, that's the way. Gina seems reasonable enough. Give it a little time and she'll see that they should go to college. I wouldn't worry about it."

But she saw that he was worried. Worried just like they were his kids.

Gina was back a half hour earlier than she'd promised. "The girls are as excited as a Mexican kid chasing a piñata."

"How long before you plan on leaving?" Sandy asked.

"We were going to take off just as soon as I changed out that worn out windlass, but we've changed our minds."

"Why?"

"We're staying till Gayle's walking."

"What?" Gayle said, surprised.

"This is a critical time for you. Between me and that girl at the hospital, we can cut your recovery time down considerably. I'm going to be like your own personal trainer. By this time tomorrow you're going to wish I was dead." She smiled, a little girl kind of smile. She was so small. She reminded Gayle of those paintings of the slender kids with the big eyes she used to see all over the place when she was a little girl.

"That's great," Gayle said. "God knows I need all the help I can get." She didn't really want Gina's help, but if she refused it, there wouldn't be anything holding the girls back. They could be gone in just a couple days if she didn't watch it. Besides, she was becoming too attached to Sandy. Attached in ways that she was afraid to think about. She needed a little space.

"I think it's good that you're staying," Sandy said.

"But you're not, Sandy. Not right now. Because Gayle's getting a bath."

"Actually I've been washing myself. Sandy just brings me a bowl with water in it, soap and a washcloth and I go to town."

"That's not the kind of bath I was talking about," Gina said.

"You mean like in the tub? With hot water?"

"With hot water," Gina said.

"Get lost, Sandy," Gayle kidded.

He laughed, threw his hands up in the air and left the room, closing the connecting door after himself.

She turned to Gina, once he was gone. "So why are you really here? And why are you so eager to help me walk?"

"I'm here because the girls had nowhere else to turn," Gina said, without any irritation in her voice. "And I want you to walk because I don't want them worrying about you when we're out at sea. I'll need one hundred percent of their concentration. It's a big boat and it'll be hard enough for the three of us to handle without them feeling guilty about leaving you as an invalid. But I suppose if you played your cards right, you could stay so sick that they'd never leave. Or maybe just long enough so that they'd change their minds. It's possible."

"Would that be so bad?" Gayle whispered. "If they didn't go? If they went to college and got an education?"

"Yes, Gayle. It would be very bad." Gina was whispering now, too.

"I don't understand."

"I wish I could make you, but I can't. Not right now."

"When?" Gayle asked.

"When you're better. I promise I'll tell you everything."

"They're my girls. You're scaring me."

"They're fine, Gayle. They're about as lucky as two humans can be. And they're happy. You must have seen that. Don't rain on their parade. Support them. Now let's get you out of those sloppy clothes and into that tub."

Gayle pulled the sweatshirt over her head and Gina

helped her off with the sweatpants. Then she dumped them in the wastebasket.

"You're kidding? What am I going to wear?"

"Something that makes you feel good. Besides, you don't need those ugly things anymore."

"My foot's the size of a bowling ball."

"We'll figure something out. Here's your canes. Meet me in the bathroom." Gina went to the bathroom and had the water running by the time Gayle came through the door. The steam rising from the tub looked glorious.

"Okay, here's the deal," Gina said. "You're gonna lean on me and step in with your left leg. I'll take your weight, and once you're in, I'll help you get the right leg over." Seconds later Gayle was sitting in the tub.

"Can you possibly know how good this feels?"

"Oh, yeah," Gina said. "I'm from a cruising family, remember? I've gone months without a hot bath." She soaped a washcloth and started scrubbing Gayle's back. When she was finished she said, "If you want me to leave you alone for a few minutes, I'll go and check out the television."

"It's surround sound. You have to turn more than one thing on to make it all work. Danny, the nurse I had, loaned it to me."

"You mean you had a male nurse, then Dr. Sandy to take care of you? No feminine help? No wonder you look like such a slob."

"I don't look like a slob."

"No, not for a guy. When's the last time you shaved your legs? Or under your arms? Or combed out your hair?"

"Not that long."

"Yesterday or the day before?" Gina said.

"Well maybe a little farther back than that."

"See. You sit here and soak. Then shave. From now on you're gonna look good, and I mean good. I'll be back in ten or fifteen."

Gayle sank back in the water and let it soothe her. It felt so good, a pleasure. She sighed, a slight moan. Her thoughts drifted to Sandy. She was falling in love with him. She could hide it from others, but she couldn't hide it from herself any longer. She closed her eyes and moaned again and pictured his face in her mind's eye, but it was quickly pushed away, replaced with pictures of Taylor and Haley. What was it that Gina wouldn't tell her? Then she thought about Dylan's journal. What had Nick seen in it? She certainly hadn't seen anything that could hurt anyone. And how did he get it anyway? And why would he want it?

For a story, she answered herself. He saw a story there. Shit, she was a reporter. She should have asked him more questions at the hospital. She should have found out what he was up to. But her leg had hurt so damned much she wasn't thinking clearly.

"Okay, Gina. I'm ready to get out," she said.

Gina came in right away. "What about shaving?"

"I've got something I have to do. Can you help me back to bed?"

Once Gayle was on it, with her robe around herself, she turned on the computer. She read through Dylan's journal while Gina watched television.

"Could you do me a favor?" Gayle said when she was finished.

"Sure. What?"

"I've been reading my daughter's journal on the laptop. I've been told there's some harmful stuff here, but

I sure as hell can't find it. Could you read it?"

"I don't think I'd feel comfortable reading Taylor's journal."

"Not hers. Dylan's. I don't know why, but I think it's important."

Gina turned off the set. Two hours later she closed the computer, got up and set in on the bureau next to the television. Then she sat on the bed opposite Gayle.

"Did you see anything there I should be worried about?" Gayle asked.

"No, and that would worry me if I was you."

"Why's that?" Gayle asked.

"People underestimate me because I look so young and because I'm so tiny. They think I'm a kid, but I'm not. And I'm not stupid."

"I don't think you're a kid and I don't think you're stupid. Say what's on your mind. That's why I asked you to read it."

"I saw Nick Nesbitt at the hospital. For sure he didn't come all the way down here to wish you well."

"For sure," Gayle said.

"So, I guess that somehow he must have got a copy of the journal and read it. He told you about it and you're concerned. You read that," she pointed at the computer, "and you didn't find anything to worry about. But the Asshole Nesbitt is down here waving it in your face. So you read it again, with a closer eye and some of the passages don't quite ring true. Like it doesn't sound like a teenage girl wrote them. You can't be sure. You can't put your finger on it. It just doesn't feel right." She paused. "How'd I do?"

"You did fine." Gayle picked up the phone.

"So, now you're going to call the asshole and see what

he has?"

"Yeah, and what he wants." But when she asked for Nick's room the operator told her that he'd left for the States on the afternoon flight. However, he'd left a message that if anyone called for him to tell them he'd be back in a few days and not to worry.

"That makes me worry all the more," Gayle said.

"It would scare the shit out of me," Gina said.

* * *

Sandy woke with a yawn and a stiff neck. He rubbed it. The room was dark. He looked at the clock radio. Six-thirty. Too early to face the dawn. A week had gone by since Gina had moved in next door and he still wasn't used to sleeping alone in the large suite. Until she'd showed up to take over their lives, he'd been happy, after a fashion.

But he had to admit that he hadn't been helping Gayle with her exercises. In fact he hadn't helped or encouraged her at all in that regard. And when he examined his conscience, he had to admit that maybe he didn't want her to get better. Maybe he liked her being dependent on him. He'd lost that now. And if things kept progressing the way they were under Gina, she wouldn't be dependent on anyone.

Now Gina and Gayle ate breakfast in the coffee shop downstairs. Gina wouldn't allow her to dine in the room any more. She'd gone out and found a pair of extra large sheepskin slippers that Gayle could get over her swollen foot. And she'd found some good looking jeans with baggy legs that fit over the slippers, so it wasn't obvious she was wearing them.

After breakfast Gina would motor out to *Ghost Dancer*,

in the dinghy, but she was always back by the time Gayle returned from the hospital. Then they walked the hotel hallway. Back and forth for hours. And every time Gayle showed any sign of tiring, there was Gina, verbally kicking her in the rear to keep her going.

The phone rang. It was Gayle. "Their windlass came in today, Gina's going to help the girls install it. So I need a breakfast date in about half an hour or so. What do you say?"

"I'll knock when I'm ready." He jumped out of bed and headed for the shower. He'd missed eating with her.

In the café they ordered bacon and eggs over easy, hash browns and coffee. He looked around the restaurant. It was about half full. A man in a business suit was reading the paper and eating alone at the table next to them. The other occupied tables all appeared to have businessmen at them.

"This is nice," Gayle said. "It seems so long since we've eaten together."

"Gina seems to have completely taken you over," Sandy said. "Not that that's a bad thing. I see how she kicks your ass all day. If it goes on much longer, you'll be jogging before the end of the month."

"From your mouth to God's ears," she said. "But really, I'm progressing at a super pace. Katy says she's never seen anything like it."

"Speaking of seeing things. When do we get to see the boat?"

"Day after tomorrow. The girls want to take us sailing on their maiden voyage."

"It's about time. We haven't seen them since they've been back. They never leave the boat. Gina ferries out food and supplies. They could be dead out there for all we know."

"They're not dead," Gayle said.

"I know. So, how's it coming with Gina? Have you convinced her that the girls should go to college and not to some South Seas isle? Stacy's getting worried."

"You've talked to Stacy?"

"I called him yesterday. You didn't tell him about the boat. He's upset about it."

"Yeah, well if he called me a little more often, maybe he'd be a little more up to date on things."

"He said he'd talked to you the other day."

"He calls me once in two weeks and I'm supposed to fill him in on every little detail? Sorry, Sandy that's not how it works."

"I'd say spending over a hundred thousand dollars for a sailboat isn't a little detail."

"And I'd say that was between me and him." She was speaking calmly and he could see she was fighting tears. It was time to back off.

"I'm sorry. I just assumed he knew."

"Well, it must not be that important to him, because he didn't call me back to ask about it."

"I didn't know you two were having problems."

"We're not. You have to communicate to have problems. We're not doing that and I don't know why." Her eyes were tearing up. "I'm sorry Sandy, all of a sudden I don't feel very hungry." She pushed her chair away from the table, took up her canes and started for the exit.

"Stupid," he mumbled, sinking his head into his hands. "Stupid, stupid, stupid."

* * *

Gayle was crying as she made her way across the hotel lobby. She pushed the elevator call button with a shaking finger. She hated the way the Sterling men stuck together. Why did he have to call Stacy? And how come he knew where Stacy was and she didn't? Sterling men. She'd fallen out of love with one and in love with another. What was wrong with her?

The elevator doors opened. She entered and pushed the button for her floor. The doors were closing when she saw Nick Nesbitt come into the hotel. Connie Jakome, one of the interns from the station was with him. Her first thought was that she didn't want Nick to see her crying. Her second thought was about the journal.

She heard the phone ringing as she fumbled the key into the door. By the time she got it open, it had stopped. But she wasn't worried. He'd call back. And he did fifteen minutes later.

"Hello, Nick," she said when she picked up the phone.

"How'd you know it was me?"

"Lucky guess."

"Did you finish the journal?"

"I did, but I'm beginning to suspect your copy may be different than mine. Why don't you bring it on up?"

"Five minutes," he said and hung up. He made it in two.

Gayle answered his knock and invited him in. "You didn't tell me you were going back to the States," she said.

"I was following up a story," He was shaking slightly. "Look, can we get right to this?"

"Sure."

"When I first heard you might not be coming back to

the station, I was saddened. Then I started to think maybe I could be your replacement. It's my life's ambition, to anchor the news in Los Angeles. It's all I want. I could get it with this story, but it would mean destroying your family and I won't do that, not for any job and not for any amount of money."

"That's very decent of you, Nick. But I don't know what you're talking about." She'd planned on going back to work just as soon as she was able. But something told her to hold her tongue and find out what Nick meant. He never did or said anything without a purpose.

"This journal," he said, holding up a spiral bound notebook, "has to be kept in confidence. And that's not all. After I read it, I remembered a call I got from a young prostitute four or five years ago. She'd told me that your husband was a client of hers. I didn't believe it, of course, and even if it were true, so what. But after reading what your daughter wrote about him, I decided to follow it up. The girl is twenty now. She was sixteen when Stacy was paying for sex with her. She knows others. At least three, there's probably more. He lies about his name, but he's got a famous face. I've written their names and phone numbers on the last page. I'm sure the senator can work out an arrangement with them to keep them quiet, if you get my drift."

"What do you want from me, Nick?" She was sick. Nick was a lot of things, but he was a good reporter. If he said he had the names of four teenage prostitutes that Stacy had been with, then he did.

"Nothing. It wouldn't hurt if you recommended me as your replacement, if you're really not coming back. I've been craving the job for years and it would have been mine if your brother-in-law hadn't stuck me with that

Asshole Nesbitt thing."

"That was unfair of him," she said. "They're just such high-born, sanctimonious shits." She didn't know why she said it, but it was the way she felt.

"I'm sorry about all this." He sighed. The shaking stopped.

"Look, I have to go to the hospital. I'll start reading this on the way. Could we have dinner tonight and talk after I read it?"

"Name the spot," he said.

"No, you better name it. All I know is this hotel and I don't think it would be a good idea if Sandy saw me with you."

"Right," he said. And he told her of a place downtown where he was sure they wouldn't be seen.

As soon as he'd left, Gayle called the hospital and cancelled her regular appointment with Katy. Then she sat down to read. When she finished she lay back and closed her eyes. It was all too much. Mind shock. She shut down and fell asleep.

"Hey, wake up."

Gayle opened her eyes. Bright sun was streaming in the window. "What time is it?"

"One-thirty and the anchor winch is in."

"I missed my session with Katy today." Gayle reached under her pillow and brought out the journal. "Here's why. I'd like you to read it. It might take a while. But first there's something I want to tell you." She told her about her meeting with Nick, everything, including the stuff about Stacy and the teenage prostitutes.

An hour later Gina put it down. Gayle had been sitting silently the whole while, looking out the window at the boats in the anchorage, especially *Ghost Dancer*. She kind of wished that she was going away on her with the girls, because now there was no doubt in her mind that the girls were going.

"So tell me about Taylor and Haley. Are they like Taylor and Dylan were?"

"They're in love."

"What are you talking about? That's not possible."

"It is. They're really in love. Romeo and Juliet kind of love. They may grow out of it, they may not. But sure as the sun sets in Kansas, you break them up and they'll die."

"How do you know?"

"My parents were in love like that. Even after twenty years of marriage they were miserable if they were parted longer than an hour. You could see the joy in my dad's eyes every time he laid eyes on my mother and you could see it reflected in hers. That's the way Haley and Taylor are."

"And that's why they're staying on the boat. So they can make love all day long?"

"Actually I don't think they do that very much at all. They just need to be together. To touch each other. That's why I won't let them off the boat."

"You?"

"I'm sort of their unofficial keeper until they get these emotions under control. They can't hide their feelings from others. You wouldn't want them holding hands and all that in front of Sandy, or anybody at the hotel, or Nick Nesbitt. It's just better if they're out of sight for awhile."

"So what should I do about that?" Gayle pointed at the journal.

"You're asking me?"

"You're my friend."

"Yeah, we are friends, aren't we?"

"Yes. So give me some friendly advice."

"To me it looks like the Asshole Nesbitt knows you don't want to quit, but he doesn't have the guts to come right out and blackmail you. So he pretends he knows you're quitting and he does you this great favor, knowing you'll quit for real and help him get the job he wants to keep the journal hush hush. That way he can tell himself he took the high road. And who knows, if your husband did become president, he'd still have his teenage sex story and look how many more miles he'd get out of it then."

"So what would you do? Don't feel like I'm putting pressure on you. I've already made up my mind."

"Well, what Taylor and Dylan did is nobody's business. And there's no reason in the world why what Simon and his stepmother are doing should be in the newspapers. If it makes them happy, then I'm all for it. Again, it's nobody's business."

"I agree," Gayle said. "Go on."

"If it was my husband, I'd wanna stick it to him."

"I wanna burn the bastard," Gayle said, "but I won't. I have a daughter who looks up to him and I can't take that away from her."

"What are you going to do?"

"I'm meeting Nick for dinner downtown. I'd like you to come along."

"You don't need me. You can get around by yourself now," Gina said.

"I know that. I want you to come because you're my friend and I need your support."

"I'd be glad to go."

Nick was there ahead of them. Sitting at a table in a far corner, as if he really believed someone might recognize him here, so far from home.

"What's the deal with you and Connie?" Gayle said as they pulled up chairs.

"We're getting a place together." He looked Gina over, but if he recognized her he didn't say.

"I thought you were married."

"The divorce has been final for over two months."

"Oh jeez, I'm sorry. You should have told me."

"You know me. I don't like to trot my problems out in front of my friends."

"Yeah, keep your private life out of your business, but I thought we were closer than that," Gayle said.

"I'm sorry, It was a hard time for me."

"I certainly know about hard times."

"Yeah, you got 'em now, that's for sure."

"I have a deal for you. I have a lot of clout at the station, they owe me. I got you a six month trial run. If you get the numbers, then the job is yours for keeps. If you don't, then you're out."

"That's fair. I couldn't ask for anything more."

"There's a condition."

"Anything." His palms were sweating. His smile was broad.

"I was going to ask you to forget about the journal."

"Of course."

"And everything in it."

"Forgotten. When I get back to the hotel, I'll destroy the disc. It's the only copy. You have my word."

"Are you sure you can trust him?" Gina said. Nick sat back, doing his best, Gayle thought, to look offended, but she knew he'd heard the question a thousand times before. So had she. All reporters had.

"Gina, I've known Nick a long time. He can be an

arrogant, self-righteous, jerk-off. But he has two endearing qualities."

"And those are?" Gina asked.

"He'd go to jail before giving up a source and he'd die before breaking his word."

"Thank you, Gayle. I think that was a compliment. And coming from you, it means a lot. You really can count on me, you know."

"I know I can, Nick."

"I'll always owe you." He held out his hand.

She took it. "I said, I was going to ask you to destroy the journal." She didn't release his hand.

"Yeah?" he said.

"But I've changed my mind."

"What?" Both Nick and Gina spoke at once.

"Burn the bastard."

"Gayle?" Gina said.

"But leave my daughters out of it. And Simon and Adele too. You can cream him good enough with that child genius of his and the kiddy hookers. Do it live. It'll be a great story."

"Are you sure?

"Just make sure you cover your ass." She squeezed his hand, then released it .

CHAPTER NINETEEN

SANDY WAS SITTING in front of the television watching the afternoon news. The sound was off and he barely noticed the changes in the flickering pictures. Soon he'd be out on the water with the girls. He pushed himself from the chair and went to the window to look out at *Ghost Dancer*. The sun was directly overhead reflecting off her white paint job. She was the prettiest thing in the harbor. What he wouldn't give to be able to hang it all up and just go sailing off into the South Pacific. It wasn't as if he couldn't afford it. He even had a boat—sturdy, fast and ready to go. But he had responsibilities. His brother was running for president.

Stacy had asked for his help, a request that couldn't be denied, because family came first. He wanted the girls back home by the end of next week at the latest. He needed photographs for the new campaign literature, family shots. An adoring wife and a heartbroken daughter. Gayle's crutches would remind the voters about his recent tragedy without him having to bring it up. And Taylor's wistful eyes would drive it home. He needed his family by his side if he was going to get elected. Sandy thought it cold and calculating, but then Stacy was the one running for president. It was the family's duty to rally around him. Case closed.

There was a knock at the connecting door. "Ready?" Gayle said from the other side. She opened it and stuck her head in. "Time to go and see our girls' big mystery." Ordinarily he would have been looking forward to today. He should be happy for the girls. They were young and all they wanted was a little adventure in their lives before they had to knuckle down and get about the business of being adults. But Stacy needed them, Taylor at least. Would she forgive him for bringing her the news that she had to go back?

"I'm ready." He flicked off the television with the remote. Then turned to her and gasped. Not so long ago she was so helpless. Not now. Her eyes were sparkling, without a hint of pain, and she was standing without the canes.

"Can I come in?"

"Yes, of course," he said. She looked ravishing. He hoped his eyes didn't betray his feelings.

"I can do this." She took a tentative step. Another. Then three more to the sofa.

"I am so impressed." He clapped and saw her blush.

"My first steps without the canes. I was going to wait till I got to the hospital to try, but I wanted you to be there when I did it."

"I'm glad I saw it. Where's Gina?"

"Right here." Gina came through the door carrying the canes. "What do you think of our patient?"

"I'm speechless."

"I talked to Katy. One more week and no more torture sessions. You and the hospital will be quits," Gina said. Wonderful news, Sandy thought. It made his task so much easier. Now they only had to convince Taylor that it was time to go home.

"I wish I could say that I'll miss her, but I won't." Gayle laughed.

"Okay, here's your walking sticks, let's go down and meet the girls," Gina said.

"I'm ready," Gayle said. She sounded excited. Sandy was too.

"Look." Gina pointed out the window. "Here they come." Sandy saw the Zodiac as it pulled away from *Ghost Dancer* and was easily able to make out Taylor at the throttle and Haley up front, even from this distance. "It's time to go."

They made it to the dinghy dock just as the girls were approaching.

"Hey, Mom," Taylor yelled. They were waving. Taylor cut the power and the Zodiac coasted to the dock with Haley standing in front. She tossed the painter to Gina, who wrapped it around a dock cleat.

"How are we going to do this?" Sandy asked.

"Gayle can sit on the end of the dock and you and I can lower her down. The girls can help her from the dinghy." Gayle handed her canes to Haley and sat with her feet dangling over the dock. They were hanging about a foot from the Zodiac's rubber tube. Sandy took one side, Gina the other, and they helped her down. Haley offered a shoulder from below and Gayle managed, with her help, to sit on the tube. "See, no problem," Gina said as Sandy climbed down.

Haley hopped out of the dinghy as Gina took Taylor's place by the throttle-tiller. "Come on, Taylor," Haley held a hand out. Taylor took it and Haley pulled her up to the dock. "See you in about an hour," she said to them. Then she took the painter off the cleat and tossed it to Sandy as Gina pulled the starter cord and the engine sprang to life.

"They're not coming?" Gayle said.

"They've been cooped up for a week," Gina said. "They were getting cabin fever, so they're having lunch ashore."

"You're kidding?" Gayle said.

"You're right, I'm lying. The real reason they're not going out with us is because they're nervous about how you're handling the situation. So we decided that maybe it would be better if you saw the boat and checked it out for yourselves, without us hanging on your every word. You're both sailors. You know boats. They think that once you see how well *Ghost Dancer's* been cared for and how sound she is, that most of your reservations will melt away."

"Most of mine have already melted away," Gayle said.

"But they don't know that," Gina said. They'd been sitting with the engine in neutral and Gina let the Zodiac gently drift away from the dock. She seemed content to let the current turn the dinghy around.

"You mean you're actually thinking about letting

them go?" Sandy said.

"Let's look the boat over. Then we'll talk about it," Gayle said.

Gina added full power and the twenty-five horse Evinrude roared. The Zodiac jumped up onto a plane, skimming over the waves. Conversation wasn't possible and that was a good thing, Sandy thought, because he needed some time to figure out what had changed Gayle's mind and to marshal his arguments. Surely though, once they saw how important it was to Stacy, they'd put all of this on hold and rush back to California.

"Isn't she gorgeous!" Gina shouted as they approached.

"She's even more beautiful close up," Gayle shouted back.

Gina cut the power and the Zodiac coasted into place under the boarding ladder. Sandy marveled at the way she handled the dinghy. She'd obviously been born to it.

"Now how are we going to get me up?" Gayle said.

"Piece of cake," Gina said. "Sandy first. I'll help you from below."

Sandy climbed up, turned and offered his hand to Gayle. There were only two steps on the ladder hanging over the side. Gina helped her get her left foot into the bottom step as Sandy grabbed one of her hands in a Viking grip. He hoisted her up and helped her over the lifelines.

"It's only four steps down into the companionway. It shouldn't be a problem for you, Gayle. Just remember that you're not an invalid anymore. You're just a cripple now." She pulled on the starter cord and the roaring engine drowned out her laughter.

* * *

"Stay tuned for Senator Stacy Sterling's Town Forum on ABC, coming up live in thirty minutes," the announcer said. "Senator Sterling will be asked the tough questions by four of L.A.'s leading newsmen, the studio audience and the viewers at home. Find out why he wants to be president and how he plans to change the direction of our nation if he's elected."

"Are you sure this is the way you want to do it?" Connie Jakome turned down the set. "You can still back off." It was 5:30 in Los Angeles. Nick was staring in the mirror, eyes kind of glazed, almost like he was staring through himself. "Are you listening?" They were in Nick's dressing room. He was one of the four newsmen about to question Senator Sterling.

"Yeah." He turned away from his reflection.

"So, you're gonna do it?"

"I've come this far."

"I still don't think it's a good idea. The station's gonna hate it that you didn't do it over there, on your own program."

"I want to do it face to face. I want to see his lying eyes dance when I ask him the questions. Besides, there's a certain poetic justice to this. Sterling money bought two hours of primetime US air. Then he gets four local stations to cough up a newsman each so it'll look fresh and homespun, but I know what he's really thinking."

"What?"

"He figures we'll be so puffed up because of the national exposure that we'll just lob softballs. I can hardly wait, because I plan on leading off with a hundred mile an hour pitch."

There was a knock at the door. Connie got up and answered it.

"Hey, Nick. How's it going?" It was Brad Jenson from the CBS affiliate. His shock of white hair seemed especially bright this evening and his blue eyes were shining. He was pretty excited about the national exposure, Connie thought, but she couldn't understand why. He was fifty-eight and lazy. No way would CBS ever tap him for the network.

"Okay, Brad. Yourself?" Nick said.

"Fine, fine. There's been a last minute change."

"What?"

"Instead of having all four of us out there at once, we're gonna moderate in rotation. The senator was afraid it would look like we were ganging up on him."

"So how we gonna do it?" Nick said.

"The show's two hours, so the senator wants thirty minute shifts. Me first, then Phil, Bob and you're last."

"So let me guess, you and Phil question the senator, Bob fields the questions from the audience and I take the phone calls?"

"Phil and I will be dealing with some questions from the audience, too. But yeah, basically that's it."

"Swell."

"Hey, it's not my fault. It's the way the senator wants it." He stepped back and closed the door.

And what the senator wants the senator gets, Connie thought, because he was paying, but more importantly because it looked like he was going to be the next president. He had charisma, a good looking family and the sympathy vote because of his daughter's death. And he was a bastard, but nobody knew it. Not yet.

"What do you think of that?" Nick said.

"I changed my mind. I think you should get him tonight. Fuck the suits back at the station."

"That's my girl," Nick said. Then he kissed her.

"So you gonna take any phone calls during your segment or what?"

"I don't think so," he said.

* * *

"Gina's a hard taskmaster," Sandy said after he'd helped Gayle into the cockpit, where they took seats across from each other.

"She is, but look at the results."

"It's hard to argue with success. Look, before we check out the boat, there's something we need to talk about."

"I've got something to say, too," Gayle said.

"Me, first." He didn't relish the role that had been cast for him and he wanted to get it over with as soon as possible. "I talked to Stacy again. He needs you and Taylor back by next weekend."

"We're not going."

"This is important. He needs you. It could mean the election."

"If he gets elected it'll be without us."

"What are you talking about?" he said.

"How did you get Dylan's computer?" Her words were a warning shot sizzling up his spine.

"Say again?"

"It's important to me."

"I told you, the police called and I went by and picked it up." He lied and it was like he was pointing a knife to his own heart. But to tell her the truth was to push it in.

"So anyone who works at the police station could

have played with it? Maybe taken it home for a few days?"

"I suppose. Why are you asking?"

"Someone copied Dylan's journal, then they changed the one on the computer so we wouldn't know."

"Why would they do that?" He wanted to tell her the truth, but he was afraid to. He felt like a wimp and there wasn't a thing he could do about it.

"For money I guess," she said. "It's already cost me my job."

"I don't understand." Now he felt as if he was sinking in quicksand.

"Somebody tried to sell it to the tabloid press, but Nick intercepted it. He brought me the real journal. There's things on there nobody should ever know about. Things about the family. Stuff Dylan never should have written down."

"What are you talking about?" He was sick.

"She wrote personal stuff about the Sterlings. Things I would have killed to keep quiet. Fortunately all I had to do was let Nick have my job. But there's more."

"I can't believe it." Sandy looked into her misting eyes. He wanted to reach out to her. To take her in his arms.

"Somehow Dylan found out Stacy was having an affair with that child genius in his San Francisco office. Nick already had a source on Stacy and another teenager. A prostitute. But he wasn't going to use it till he saw the journal. After he read that, he went out and found three other prostitutes that he'd been with. All teenagers."

"Oh, Christ. I had no idea. I'm so sorry."

"The person who let that journal out of the box did me a big favor."

"What are you talking about?"

"Can you imagine the hell my life would have been if Stacy were elected and his proclivity for little girls came out? And it would. One of those young women would say something. If not them, then someone else. There have to be others. I mean, can you see me standing behind him with those Nancy Reagan eyes while he lies about it? I'd be on the cover of all the news magazines, along with pictures of his whores. Christ, Bill Clinton was a saint by comparison. People would pity me. I'd rather be dead."

"You could work this out."

"Sandy, I don't want to. It's over. I guess it's been over for a long time. I just didn't know it."

"I'm sorry to hear that."

"Are you?"

"What do you mean?"

"I think you're in love with me," she said. "And I know I'm in love with you." Water lapped against the ship. A gentle breeze played through her hair. A fist gripped his heart. She was his brother's wife and, God help him, he loved her. "I'm serious," she said after a long silence. "You don't have to say anything. Just nod your head if you love me."

He nodded.

"So what are we going to do about it?" she said.

"I don't know. I have to think. I never expected you'd ever love me back. I didn't think you knew. I never would have said anything."

"I know. That's why I had to."

"What about Stacy?"

"I think he loves me, but not as much as he loves his job or the idea of being president. I've settled for second best from him for so long. I just don't want to do it any more. I think I would have left him even if I didn't know about the little girls." The way she said it, *the little girls*, made it seem so dirty.

"It would never work, you and me," he said. The wind picked up and he shivered. He wanted her, but there was no way. Just no way.

"It can work if we want it bad enough." She held out her hand and he took it. Then she pulled him to her side of the cockpit. She put a hand behind his head and pulled him into a kiss. She kept her hand firmly in place, in case he wanted to break it off, but she needn't have worried.

"Wow," he said when she released him.

"We don't have to go back. Gina's moving onto the boat tonight. It'll be just you and me back in the hotel again. After the girls leave in a few days, we can get a place here and live happily ever after."

"But the family?"

"Hush, don't think about that now." She pulled him into another kiss and a kind of fire rippled through him. Never had he known such happiness.

"Let's go below," he said a few minutes later.

"I don't think that's such a good idea," she said and he felt his heart plummet. "Tonight will be soon enough. I don't want it to be a quickie. I want you all night long, forever." And his heart rose from the depths and shot toward the heavens. Such was the effect she had on him.

He sat back and she nuzzled up into the crook of his arm as they stared over the harbor, looking toward the land and the tall Sterling Hotel in the background. He loved her so much. But he loved Stacy, too. And Stacy's quest for the presidency was a lifelong Sterling ambition. He'd wanted it for Stacy every bit as badly as Stacy wanted it for himself. Without Gayle at his side Stacy had virtually no chance of getting the nomination.

He was supposed to be helping Gayle recover so she could return home as soon as possible. He wasn't supposed to fall in love with her. And she wasn't supposed to fall in love with him. She'd never go back to Stacy now. Not as long as she had him to cling to.

"It's cold," she said and he pulled her in closer. She felt so good next to him, so natural.

"Sometimes life just isn't fair," he said.

"Yeah, but if we really want it, we can have a life. Other people get through this kind of stuff."

"It would haunt us forever," he said. Maybe Stacy could find a way to keep Nesbitt quiet, he seemed like the kind of guy that could be bought. And maybe his candidacy could survive a divorce, but never on God's green earth could it survive his wife leaving him for his brother. Stacy would be laughed out of politics.

He couldn't do it. He couldn't ruin his brother's career, even if his deplorable behavior was true. He couldn't leave Gayle either, not after they'd declared themselves to each other. There had to be a way. He was smart. He'd come up with something. Maybe if they kept a low profile till after the election. But win or lose, they'd still have the same problem. Once it became known that they were together, Stacy would be a laughing stock. If he did somehow get elected, it would overshadow his presidency. It was a classic no win situation.

And it was his fault. His fault the journal had come to light. If he had just left that damn computer alone and minded his own business all of that stuff Dylan had written about would have stayed buried. It had to be that kid in the computer store. How had he contacted Nick? Would Nick tell Gayle it was him? What would she think of him once she found out? Could she ever forgive him for deceiving her? Would she still love him?

And what if Stacy couldn't buy off Nesbitt? What if he went public with the journal? It would destroy Taylor when her relationship with her dead sister came out. The tabloid press would have a field day with her and it would never stop. Her life would be over before it started.

A chill ran through him when he thought about his mother. He loved her with a passion. Simon too. The kind of life they led together was wrong, but it was theirs and theirs alone. It would kill his mother if it was made public and Sandy couldn't live with that.

It was all too much. He wanted to cry. Instead he turned into the wind, took a deep breath and sighed.

* * *

"Ladies and gentlemen, Senator Stacy Sterling," Brad Jenson said. Applause followed the introduction as Stacy took the stage. "I'm sure you all know the senator is running for president. Tonight he's going to tell you why. Then he's going to answer the tough questions put to him by the newsmen who know him best, the anchors from the local Los Angeles television stations. And after that he'll be fielding questions from the studio audience and then from you at home."

Connie thought Brad was laying it on a bit thick. Nick was right, there'd be no tough questions from him.

"Thank you Brad." Stacy was looking to the right of the camera. Connie followed his gaze. It was Jennifer Updike and she was staring at him with adoring eyes. "I hope that after tonight you'll all understand why I want the top job."

"Senator," Brad said in his deep voice. "I hate to get personal right off the bat, but you're running for president. You've just suffered a tragedy and as much as I know how you'd like to keep it private, America has a right to know how you're dealing with it. After all, if elected, you'll have the fate of the world in your hands."

"We had a private funeral for my daughter, Dylan, in New Zealand, because we didn't want to parade our grief in front of the nation," Stacy said. "But that's not what you want to know. Is it?"

"Not really," Brad said. Jesus, Connie thought. Jenson was letting Sterling lead him by the nose. He probably told him what questions to ask. She could hardly wait till Nick was up on that stage with him.

"When Dylan died I almost pulled out of the race. It was a horrible blow. But she wouldn't have wanted that. We're a close family. We've worked together for this. It was a family effort and if she were here, she'd tell me to keep on. Besides, Sterlings don't quit."

The audience erupted in applause. Connie felt like puking.

The rest of Brad's interview went like that. Softball after softball. By the time Phil Nelson took the stage, America had seen a good man fighting to overcome his grief. A man who wanted only the best for his family, his country, the world. And Phil's questions were as soft as Brad's. What was wrong with them? Sterling had always been popular with the press, especially the local media, and his wife was one of their own, but this was ridiculous.

Bob Braxton from KYQR took the stage and fielded questions from a sympathetic studio audience. And of course they'd be sympathetic after the way they'd been manipulated. Thirty minutes and not one question out of Braxton's mouth. "And now," Braxton said, when he was finished, "Nick Nesbitt from KYTV to take questions from our at home audience."

There was a smattering of applause as Nick took the stage.

"A question first, Senator, if I may?" Nick said.

CHAPTER TWENTY

HALEY STOOD IN THE FRONT of the Zodiac. She was holding onto the painter and leaning back. She felt like a water skier as Gina drove it flat out. They skimmed over the waves, water spraying from their sides, a slick wake trailing behind. She was breathing the sea air, feeling the wind on her face, reveling in happiness. Nothing could steal it away. It was hers forever.

She turned and looked over her shoulder. Taylor was sitting on the tube opposite Gina. Haley flashed her a smile and Taylor gave her the thumbs up sign back. She shivered with delight and the chilly breeze. Her hair was whipping in the wind. Her heart was beating fast. The sun was high in the sky, but she was as cold as when she went skiing at Aspen.

A dolphin broke water alongside the dinghy. Gina immediately cut the power, taking the speed as slow as she could and still be on a plane. "They're beautiful," Haley said. Another one broke the surface, swimming alongside. So close she could almost reach out and touch them.

They swam in front of the Zodiac, then magically one of them ducked below the surface and came up, shooting several feet above the water. Then it traded places with the other one. They swam along with them for a bit, then broke off and headed out to their left.

"Hale look," Taylor said. "There's zillions of them."

Gina stopped the dinghy and killed the engine. They watched as the dolphin pod swam by. Hundreds of them, curving in and out of the water.

"I've never seen anything like it." Haley smiled with delight.

"People that live in houses never see anything like this," Gina said.

"So many," Taylor said.

Haley saw a young couple watching the dolphins from a boat anchored close by. She waved and they waved back. It was a magic moment and it went on for about five more minutes, then the pod was out of sight.

"They're the most beautiful animals," Gina said, then she started the engine, added power and again they were shooting over the gentle swells.

Haley saw Sandy and Gayle in the cockpit as they closed on *Ghost Dancer*. Gayle waved and Sandy went forward to the boarding ladder to accept the painter as Gina maneuvered the Zodiac alongside.

"What do you think, Sandy?" she shouted up. "Is she beautiful or what?"

"She's beautiful," he said. Haley handed him the painter. How her life had changed in such a short time. She used to be so in love with him. Now he was just a dear friend. The girls boarded, then Sandy led the painter to the stern and cleated it off so that the Zodiac would trail behind as they sailed the afternoon away.

"Okay," Gina said. "We're going to sail off the hook." She started the engine as Taylor went forward to the windlass. "We're going to go off on the staysail. I only started the engine because we're in a crowded anchorage. If we screw up, I want to be able to get us out of trouble quickly."

Taylor had her foot on the windlass button and she signaled back when they'd broken loose from the bottom. Haley went to the sheet winch, took the line out of the self-tailing jaws, then released the furling line from its winch and unfurled the sail. Gina was turning to starboard as the sail filled. Taylor was still bringing up chain as the boat settled on a port tack. After she signaled that the anchor was up, Haley furled in the staysail. Then eased out about a third of the jib. She saw that Sandy and Gayle were impressed. It was important to her that they respected their ability.

"I'm shutting off the engine," Gina said. Then, "Now I'm releasing the runners. As we're going to put her through her paces today, we won't be using the staysail. After we get well out of the harbor, I'll bring her into the wind so we can raise the main."

"Pretty impressive," Gayle said. Haley thought that Sandy was being curiously silent.

"I'm going to work the wheel today," Gina said.

"Haley's going to work the sheets and Taylor will be forward to pull the jib through when we tack. Unfortunately, because of the roller furled staysail, the jib won't come through by itself. We either have to roll half of it in every time we tack or have someone go forward to help it across. On a cruising boat, where you go for days on one tack, the staysail is a godsend, plus it makes a great storm sail, but for just having fun, tacking and jibing, it's a bloody nuisance."

"Isn't that kind of dangerous, her up there like that?" Gayle said.

"Oh, Mom. I've done it before on *Dark Witch*. Besides, I'll be clipped on. I won't fall off."

"I still think it's dangerous," Gayle said.

"Living is dangerous, Mom."

"I won't argue that." Gayle laughed. Haley was impressed. Gayle hadn't insisted that Taylor not do it. She was treating her like an equal, not like a kid.

"Okay, I'm bringing her into the wind," Gina said. Taylor scooted up to the mast and raised the main. Then Gina turned back to starboard and they heeled over on a port tack, slicing through the waves as Gina had her pointed out into the open ocean.

"Let out the jib," Gina ordered and Haley released the line from the furling winch and eased it all the way out. *Ghost Dancer* heeled over more and Haley took some spray in the face as she tightened up on the sheet.

"We're cooking," Sandy said. The windspeed indicator read twelve knots.

"She'd do more if we tightened up on the sail, but I think we'll hold it here for a bit," Gina said.

"I'd like to try a tack," Taylor said.

"Okay, get up there," Gina said.

"Be careful," Gayle said.

"I'm ready," Taylor yelled back. She was holding on to the furled staysail.

"I'm ready," Haley said. She'd released the starboard sheet from the tailing jaws, taking a wrap off the winch, and was holding the line in her right hand. She had the port sheet in her left with two wraps around the winch.

"Okay, I'm going through the wind. Now!" Gina cranked the wheel to port. The jib started to luff as the boat crossed the wind. Haley released the starboard sheet and started pulling in on the port. Up front, Taylor grabbed the great sail by the bottom and pulled it forward of the staysail till enough of it was through so that the wind could finish the job. She ducked as it billowed above her head, then she scooted back to the cockpit as Gina finished the turn and they were on a starboard tack.

"How about it, Mom, are you impressed or what?"

"I am amazed," Gayle said.

"I think that's enough showing off for now," Gina said. Then, "We have cold beer in the fridge if either of you want one."

"I wouldn't mind one," Gayle said.

"Me either," Sandy said. "I'll get 'em." And he went below, returning shortly with two cold ones.

Gayle popped the tab and took a long swallow. "It's great," she said. She seemed happy to Haley as she drank her beer and enjoyed the afternoon. Sandy, on the other hand, seemed troubled. The others might not notice, but she'd been studying him all her life. She knew his moods.

* * *

Connie thought Nick looked different without his traditional blue blazer with the station logo on the pocket. Tonight he was wearing a simple long sleeved brown sweater with a white shirt underneath, open at the collar. He looked younger, less professional, but more human. The senator with his gray, three piece suit was dashing by comparison. He'd been under the lights for the last hour and a half and wasn't sweating a bit. He was one cool customer.

"Hello, Nick, you don't have to be formal with me. We've been friends a long time." Stacy smiled. Connie felt a tingle at the back of her neck. The senator was shit handsome and in complete control of the audience.

"No!" Nick said. "We've known each other a long time, but we've never been friends." Connie gasped, as did several people in the studio audience. "Your wife and I are friends. I know and like Taylor and believe me when I tell you that I miss Dylan as if she were my own daughter, but I have to ask you the tough questions that my colleagues wouldn't or couldn't."

Connie held her breath. So did everyone else. Connie didn't know it could be so quiet in a studio with such a large audience. Nobody was talking. Nick had stolen the show and from the smug expression on Senator Sterling's face, Connie could tell these men were at war and that the Senator planned on coming out the victor.

"It sounds like you don't like me very much."

"No, Senator, I don't. I don't like you very much at all." Nick waved the papers he was holding in his hand. "I wish I could say that my opinion of you wasn't going to cloud the way I treat you here tonight, but I can't. It's not very professional, I know, but like I said, my colleagues didn't ask the tough questions, so I have to."

"Isn't this the segment for the call in questions? Or maybe you think the voters aren't gonna ask the tough questions either."

Nick turned toward the camera showing the green light. "Not long ago the senator's wife and daughter were in an accident with a drunk driver in New Zealand. You all know that Dylan lost her life and that Gayle Sterling is recovering from her injuries. And as many of you know, Gayle is the anchor on the KYTV Nightly News. I've been filling in for her till she gets back.

"Recently a story came to my attention that involves you." He turned toward the senator. "Anyone else would've run with it, but because your wife is my friend, I flew down to New Zealand to confer with her."

"Really, Nick—"

"I know Senator, an attack of ethics, a fatal disease in either of our professions. But Gayle is a friend. I'd rather pass on a story than run with one that would hurt her. She knows and approves of what I'm doing here tonight."

"Then get on with it," Stacy said. Connie saw the anger sparking from his eyes. He was a powerful man. Maybe Nick was going too far.

"I have here a sworn affidavit from Christopher Davis."

"Never heard of him," Stacy said.

"He's sworn that your brother, Dr. Sanford Sterling, brought a computer in for repair in Wellington, New Zealand."

"So?" The senator took a step toward Nick. For a second Connie thought he was going to strike him.

"Davis repaired the computer, but not before copying Dylan's journal."

"You dare to make my dead daughter's diary public." Stacy was in Nick's face now.

"Not without her mother's permission," Nick said.

He sounded sad, as if he didn't want to go on. "Dylan wrote about the affair you're having with your young assistant, Jennifer Updike."

"You really are a piece of work, Nick." The senator stepped back, clutching a hand to his breast in mock disbelief. "Someone puts something on a computer and you go before a television audience and treat it as gospel. What's wrong with you? Anybody can put anything into a computer, for all I know, you wrote it yourself to discredit me. Everybody knows you're after my wife's job, now apparently you're after mine, too. You should be ashamed."

"No, Senator. You should be. I don't like this aspect of my business. I've always believed people like you and me should be allowed private lives. And if she had been twenty-one when the affair started, I wouldn't bring it up. If she had been eighteen, I would've remained silent. But the affair started right after she started working for you, when she was seventeen."

"Dylan couldn't have known that," Stacy stammered.

"Neither could I. I took a shot," Nick said.

"You dare!" Stacy's face went red and he started shaking. He wasn't pretending now and Connie thought he didn't look so handsome any more.

"Does the name Donna Lucus mean anything to you?" Nick said. He was a sea of calm compared to Stacy's raging anger.

"What are you talking about?" Stacy spat the words.

"She's twenty-one now, but she was seventeen when you paid for sex with her."

"A prostitute?"

"Who's on the record." Nick held up an affidavit. "As is Jessica Savarino, sixteen when you paid for sex with her, although she lied and said she was seventeen." He held up another sheet of paper. "And Mary Lou Tucker, seventeen when you took her to bed in San Francisco." He waved another sheet of paper in the air. "And Laurie Tanaka, sixteen." Another paper in his hand.

"It's all lies," Stacy said. "It's slander, left wing garbage to keep me out of the White House."

"No, it's four teenage prostitutes on the record and your daughter's diary accusing you of having an affair with Jennifer Updike. I'm not so foolish as to believe I've uncovered them all, Senator. So here's the *Tough Question*. How many underage girls have you taken to bed in the last year?"

"You bastard."

"I wish I could say I'm sorry, Senator, but I saw the tears in your wife's eyes." He turned toward the camera. "There you have it, ladies and gentlemen. The so called, *Tough Question*. How many, Senator?"

Stacy stormed from the stage. "You'll hear from my lawyers."

"Lawyers," Nick said. "That's no answer, Senator."

There was a thud as Stacy slammed a hand into the bar on an emergency exit door, then an alarm went off.

* * *

Sandy took a long swallow from his beer. Sweat ringed his brow and for a second Haley thought about Bill and Linda, their drug habit and how they sweated in the cold, but surely Sandy didn't have a drug problem. He rubbed the back of his neck, then put a hand up to shield his eyes against the sun as he looked out over the stern.

"You have a couple of tanks lashed down there." He pointed to two diving tanks lashed to the lifelines on the port side aft. "Did any more diving gear come with the boat?" At last, Haley thought. He was showing an interest.

"Are you a diver?" Gina asked from behind the wheel.

"Sure am."

"Look under the cockpit seat."

Sandy and Gayle stood up and he raised the cushion, then the locker cover. He brought up two buoyancy control vests. He laid the BCs on the other cockpit seat between Taylor and Haley and brought out two regulators. "Good stuff," he said as he brought out the weight belts.

"Yeah, the last owner was into diving," Taylor said. "Gina's gonna teach us."

"Where's the masks and fins?"

"Other side, under Haley and Taylor," Gina said.

"Wind's picking up," he said.

"Yeah," Gina said.

"It might turn into a blustery day."

"We're used to it," Haley said as Gina turned a little off the wind, keeping the ride as flat as possible.

"You girls have really turned out to be quite the sailors," Gayle said. "I'll have to admit I won't worry nearly as much about you as I thought I was going to."

"I don't know," Sandy said. "It takes a lot longer than a few weeks at sea to train for an around the world sail. I'd be worried plenty."

"Oh, I'll worry," Gayle said. "What mother wouldn't. But I'd worry if they were off at college, too. I guess it goes with the mom job."

Haley laughed. "Yeah, the mom job. You did that for me ever since I was a little girl and I really appreciate it. I think I belong more to you than my own parents."

"Then you'll listen to me when I tell you that you've made some hard life choices at an awfully young age. Just a few weeks ago you were looking forward to college, now you're not. I'll support the both of you, no matter what you decide to do, because I love you and because you're adults now. That means you're supposed to be able to make up your own minds. But I just want you to think things through before you go jumping in."

"You know," Sandy said, "college can be the best time of your life. You can't imagine what it's like, living in the dorms, learning new things every day, finding yourself. Sometimes I wish I could go back."

"I've found myself, Sandy," Haley said. "And I'm having the best time of my life right now."

"But it won't last. It never does."

"We'll take the chance," Taylor said.

"But you won't be prepared for the future. How will you earn a living after this is all over?" A pair of gulls flew overhead, coming down to inspect the boat. Looking for scraps maybe, or maybe it was just where the breeze took them.

"I hope it's never gonna be over," Haley said. "But to answer your question honestly, I'd have to say, I don't know."

"You know, I've never been able to say that about my life. I've always known where I was going, until lately anyway." His voice faded with the last.

"I think that's kind of sad," Haley said.

"Me too," Gayle said. She'd been listening with rapt attention, nodding when Haley spoke, head still when Sandy did. *She knows about me and Taylor,* Haley thought. *She knows and she doesn't care.*

"I don't know. I've always believed you had to have

direction, and that certain things in life mattered," Sandy said.

"Like what?" Gayle said. *Ghost Dancer* rode over a swell as Gina turned into it, then back down it.

"Family and loyalty, I guess."

"And you think by living on the sea, we're turning our backs on that?" Taylor had her hands in her lap. Her thumbs were playing with each other.

"Aren't you?" Sandy said.

"I don't think so. I think family loyalty works two ways. If this is how Haley and I want to spend our lives, I think our families ought to support us."

"How about your father? He's running for president. He needs you by his side to get elected." He cast his eyes downward when he said it, away from Gayle's gaze. Gayle shook her head. She was disagreeing with him.

"I love my father, Sandy, but I don't want a life in the public eye. Besides, it's better for him if I stay away."

"No, he wants you with him. You and your mother."

"I'm gay."

"No one has to know," he said. "Besides, that's all over now."

"You don't seem surprised, Sandy," Gayle said. Haley looked at Gayle. What were they talking about?

"It's not over. It's never gonna be over. Hale and I are gonna make a life together."

"Haley?" Sandy's mouth hung open with the question.

"Yeah, me," Haley said.

"Now you are surprised, Sandy," Gayle said. Haley barely heard her above the sounds of the sea. She sounded disappointed. Something was going on between them.

Sandy reached across the cockpit seats and picked up

a weight belt and starting fidgeting with it. It was obvious to Haley that he'd rather be someplace else, anyplace else.

"Let's tack again," Taylor said. She sensed something too. She was trying to lighten the air.

"Baby, I can't ever remember you being this enthusiastic about horseback riding." Gayle turned away from Sandy, toward her daughter.

"I just love it," Taylor said. She turned to Gina. "I'm heading up." She had the harness on with the tether in her hand as she made her way to the staysail where she clipped on. "I'm ready," she yelled back.

Haley went to the winches and got the sheets ready. "Me too," she said.

"Here we go," Gina yelled and this time she cranked the wheel to starboard. Haley worked the sheets, releasing the port sheet and hauling on the starboard and Taylor screamed.

"Help her!" Gina yelled. Haley looked up. Panic filled her. Somehow the sheet had gotten wrapped around Taylor's leg. The wind had caught the huge sail and it was billowing and flapping. Taylor's right leg was jerked high off the ground and she was frantically holding on to the furled staysail while the jib was trying to tear her apart.

Sandy rushed forward as Gina spun the wheel back to port, trying to get *Ghost Dancer* headed into the wind, to take the wind out of the sail.

"My God!" Gayle said. She clutched Haley's hand for support as the drama unfolded in front of them.

Sandy grabbed the flapping sail, pulling down on it with all of his weight, trying to take some of the pressure off the rope wrapped around Taylor's leg. Haley shivered. Fear stabbed her, running through her like cold blood.

Sandy was fighting the sail as it jerked Taylor around. He couldn't do it by himself.

"I'm going!" Haley dashed forward. She jumped into the air, grabbing onto the sail just under where Sandy was gripping it. Their combined weight pulled the sail down enough to loosen the sheet. "Hurry, Taylor!" Haley screamed, but Taylor needed no urging. In seconds she had her leg out of the trap.

"I'm free," she said, and Haley let go of the sail and dropped to the deck, but Sandy didn't. The wind caught the snapping jib and dragged it out, pulling Sandy along with it. Haley caught his expression just before he went over the side. And out of the corner of her eye she saw Gina and Gayle throwing the cockpit cushions into the ocean to mark where Sandy had gone into the water.

Taylor screamed. Haley held onto the furled staysail with one hand while she struggled to unclip Taylor with the other.

"Okay, you're not clipped on, let's get back to the cockpit." Taylor clutched the staysail. Haley jerked on the harness. "Now! We have to go now!" Together they made their way back to the cockpit.

"Roll in the jib," Gina yelled as she started the engine. The diesel rumbled to life as Haley cranked on the furling winch. "Taylor!" Gina shouted. "Drop that main!" Taylor went back to the mast and took the main halyard off a deck cleat and the sail dropped. "Get back here, don't worry about tying it off!" Gina yelled as she was adding power and spinning the boat around to find Sandy.

"I see the cushions." Taylor pointed. Gina drove the boat over to them.

"Do you see him?" Gayle said.

"No," Haley said. She looked at the diving gear

thrown on the cockpit sole in the mad dash to get the cushions overboard, and she knew they'd never find him. Two vests and two regulators, but only one weight belt. And she remembered that look on his face as he went over. At first such anguish. Then the misery was gone and he was no longer troubled.

CHAPTER
TWENTY-ONE

EIGHTEEN MONTHS LATER Haley was up on the bow as Gina guided *Ghost Dancer* through the anchorage in Port Villa, Vanuatu. Taylor was standing at the shrouds, holding the baby. Sandra, Sandy for short, was six months old and she had just spit up. Haley laughed at Taylor's discomfort.

It was a clear summer day. Christmas was two days away. It was still odd for Haley to think of December as summer, she'd given up trying. The days were the same for her now. Sunday or Thursday, it made no difference. She woke to paradise—warm days, tropical seas, Taylor's love, Gina's friendship and the wonder of a child she adored.

Sandy started to cry and Haley thought of a sad day and that other Sandy. His body was found floating among the moored boats in Wellington Harbor the day after he'd gone over the side. He wasn't wearing the weight belt. Had it somehow come off? Had he changed his mind at the last minute? Or did he not have it on at all? Did it fall overboard during all of the activity? They would never know. Haley tried for months after the tragedy to picture him just before he went over, but she couldn't remember whether he had it on or not. All she saw was that last peaceful look. She'd wanted to believe it was an accident, but in her heart she knew better.

They buried him with Dylan and Charlotte back in New Zealand. Another sad day. Stacy had flown in from the States. Adele and Simon were there, too. The family, of course, knew all about Stacy's fall from grace at the hands of Nick Nesbitt, but curiously enough they didn't blame Gayle.

Stacy had gone too far and they all knew it.

And Stacy for his part seemed to know it, too. He cried when they lowered his brother's coffin into the ground. Haley had never seen him cry. Later Gayle said that she hadn't either, and at the funeral, it was Gayle who comforted him.

The brothers had been so close, it was hard to believe that one was gone. Simon went the following month, perforated ulcer. Now he sleeps with Charlotte, too. Adele lasted less than sixty days without Simon. They said it was cancer, but Haley saw her at the two funerals and she knew what it was. A mother should never have to bury her children. She died of a broken heart and now she sleeps with her sons and Dylan. Charlotte has a lot of company.

"Too close to the coral." Haley pointed to the coral reef on the port side. Gina turned a little to starboard. Now they were headed straight for the Iririki Island Resort. Fifteen minutes later she saw the small tourist villas with their thatched roofs. She wished she had time for a night there and a hot bath, but they were smack in the middle of cyclone territory in the middle of cyclone season. They were only staying long enough to check in with customs, pick up their mail via the Poste Restante system at the post office and to buy some provisions. Then they were gonna get out of Dodge and head up north to safer waters.

The water was flat calm and Taylor came up to the bow with Sandy. "I'll put down the anchor, I know you want to hold her."

"Yeah, now that you got baby throw-up all over your shirt." Haley laughed. She loved Gina's baby like it was her own. "Come here, kiddo." She held out her arms and Taylor handed her over. "Look, trees." She pointed to a couple of palm trees on the shore, but the child wasn't interested.

"She'll talk when she's ready," Taylor said.

"I guess you're right," Haley said.

Taylor turned back to Gina and pointed to the right of the yacht quarantine area. Gina turned and in five minutes they had the anchor down. Thirty minutes later a customs officer came aboard and cleared them in. In less than an hour after laying the hook they were in the post office getting their mail. There was no line at the Poste Restante window as most of the cruisers had sailed out of the cyclone area over a month ago.

"Hey guess what?" Gina held a letter in her hand. "Danny's at the top of his class again."

"That's great," Haley said. She was still holding Sandy.

"Coochie coo." An older man tickled Sandy in passing and the baby laughed. "He looks just like you," the man said.

"Thank you," Haley said. The girls had long given up telling strangers that Sandy was Gina's child. Danny's Maori blood combined with Gina's Irish genes to produce a child with Haley's mixed skin coloring. Not only that, but Sandy kind of looked like Haley, too, so it was a natural mistake and people kept making it. Haley didn't mind.

"I sure wish Danny was here now," Gina said. They'd met at the other Sandy's funeral and it was love at first sight.

But it was a different kind of love than Haley and Taylor had. Danny was bound for medical school and Gina was bound for the sea. Haley couldn't imagine a day of her life without Taylor, but Gina and Danny seemed to be doing just fine from afar. True, they had to leave New Zealand before they'd planned, because Gina knew she'd never be able to leave if Danny found out she was pregnant. The guilt and the tears would've been too much.

Sandy was born in Noumea and Danny flew up for the delivery. Gina had a difficult birth and they were forced to stay longer than it was safe, waiting for her recovery. She was better now and they'd be out of the cyclone area in a week. Thank God the weather forecast was good. It was hard for Danny to accept that Gina was going to live on the sea with his child, but he was going to spend two months a year with them till he finished medical school. After that, who knows?

"Hey, I got a guess what, too." Taylor also had an open letter.

"Okay, what?" Haley said.

"Guess where Mom is."

"Russia," Haley said.

"Albania," Gina said.

"Nope, they got their domestic wars, but she's in Iraq."

"And to think she owes it all to that Asshole Nesbitt." Gina laughed. After Nick's story on Stacy hit the airwaves CNN offered him a job. It was the big time, but Nick had been telling the truth all along when he said he didn't want to go any farther than the local news. However he recommended Gayle and she got the job. In no time at all she was a roving foreign correspondent. More like a war correspondent. If there was shooting, Gayle was there.

"She says she had dinner with Dad in Paris last month."

"Wow, two months ago dining and dancing in London, now dinner in one of those fancy French restaurants on the Champs Elysées," Haley said. "I bet they're gonna get back together."

"You're such a dreamer, Hale," Taylor said. "She doesn't say it was on the Champs Elysées and she doesn't say it was romantic."

"But I bet it was. I bet they're gonna get back together and live happily ever after."

"She's a dreamer alright," Gina said and they all laughed, Sandy too.

The Bootleg Press Catalog

RAGGED MAN, by Jack Priest
ISBN: 0974524603

Unknown to Rick Gordon, he brought an ancient aboriginal horror home from the Australian desert. Now his friends are dying and Rick is getting the blame.

DESPERATION MOON, by Ken Douglas
ISBN: 0974524611

Sara Hackett must save two little girls from dangerous kidnappers, but she doesn't have the money to pay the ransom.

SCORPION, by Jack Stewart
ISBN: 097452462X

DEA agent Bill Broxton must protect the Prime Minister of Trinidad from an assassin, but he doesn't know the killer is his fiancée.

DEAD RINGER, by Ken Douglas
ISBN: 0974524638

Maggie Nesbitt steps out of her dull life and into her dead twin's, and now the man that killed her sister is after Maggie.

GECKO, by Jack Priest
ISBN: 0974524646

Jim Monday must rescue his wife from an evil worse than death before the Gecko horror of Maori legend kills them both.

RUNNING SCARED, by Ken Douglas
ISBN: 0974524654

Joey Sapphire's husband blackmailed and now is out to kill the president's daughter and only Joey can save the young woman.

NIGHT WITCH, by Jack Priest

ISBN: 0974524662

A vampire like creature followed Carolina's father back from the Caribbean and now it is terrorizing her. She and her friend Arty are only children, but they must fight this creature themselves or die.

HURRICANE, by Jack Stewart

ISBN: 0974524670

Julie Tanaka flees Trinidad on her sailboat after the death of her husband, but the boat has a drug lord's money aboard and DEA agent Bill Broxton must get to her first or she is dead.

TANGERINE DREAM, by Ken Douglas and Jack Stewart

ISBN: 0974524689

Seagoing writer and gourmet chef Captain Katie Osborne said of this book, "Incest, death, tragedy, betrayal and teenage homosexual love, I don't know how, but somehow it all works. I was up all night reading."

DIAMOND SKY, by Ken Douglas and Jack Stewart

ISBN: 0974524697

The Russian Mafia is after Beth Shannon. Their diamonds have been stolen and they think she knows where they are. She does, only she doesn't know it.

TAHITIAN AFFAIR: A ROMANCE, by Dee Lighton

ISBN: 0976277905

In Tahiti on vacation Angie meets Luke, a single-handed sailor, who is trying to forget Suzi, the love of his life. He is the perfect man, dashing, good looking, caring and kind. She is in love and it looks like her story will have a fairytale ending. Then Suzi shows up and she wants her man back.

BOOKS ARE BETTER THAN T.V.

THE BOOTLEG PRESS STORY

We at Bootleg Press are a small group of writers who were brought together by pen and sea. We have all been members of either the St. Martin or Trinidad Cruising Writer's Groups in the Caribbean.

We share our thoughts, plot ideas, villains and heroes. That's why you'll see some borrowed characters, both minor and major, cross from one author's book to another's.

Also, you'll see a few similar scenes that seem to jump from one author's pages to another's. That's because both authors have collaborated on the scene and—both liking how it worked out—both decided to use it.

At what point does an author's idea truly become his own? That's a good question, but rest assured in the rare occasions where you may discover similar scenes in Bootleg Press Books, that it is not stealing. Writing is a solitary art, but sometimes it is possible to share the load.

Book writing is hard, but book selling is harder. We think our books are as good as any you'll find out there, but breaking into the New York publishing market is tough, especially if you live far away from the Big Apple.

So, we've all either sold or put our boats on the hard, pooled our money and started our own company. We bought cars and loaded our trunks with books. We call on small independent bookstores ourselves, as we are our own distributors. But the few of us cannot possibly reach the whole world, however we are trying, so if you don't see our books in your local bookstore yet, remember you can always order them from the big guys online.

Thank you from everyone at Bootleg Books for reading and please remember, Books are better than T.V.

JACK STEWART & KEN DOUGLAS
PHOTO TAKEN IN TRINIDAD, 2000

317854

Made in the USA